night
squad

night
squad

david goodis

VINTAGE CRIME / **BLACK LIZARD**

vintage books • a division of random house, inc. • new york

First Vintage Crime/Black Lizard Edition, March 1992

Library of Congress Cataloging-in-Publication Data
Goodis, David, 1917–1967.
Night squad / David Goodis. — 1st Vintage Crime/Black Lizard ed.
p.   cm. — (Vintage crime/Black Lizard)
Originally published: Greenwich, Conn. : Fawcett Publications, 1961.
ISBN 0-679-73698-0
I. Title.   II. Series.
PS3513.O499N5   1992
813'.52—dc20   91-50180 CIP

Series design by Iris Weinstein
Manufactured in the United States of America
10 9 8 7 6 5 4 3 2 1

night
squad

1

At 11:20 a fairly well-dressed boozehound came staggering out of a bootleg-whiskey joint on Fourth Street. It was a Friday night in mid-July and the humid heat was like a wave of steaming black syrup confronting the boozehound. He walked into it and bounced off and braced himself to make another try. A moment later something hit him on the head and he sagged slowly and arrived on the pavement flat on his face.

Three local muggers bent over the boozehound. One of them went through his pockets and got the wallet and the loose silver. The others took the wristwatch and the cuff links and the tie clasp. Then the first mugger happened to look up and saw Corey Bradford standing under a lamppost on the other side of the street.

"Hey you," the mugger called to Corey. "You got any plans?"

Corey didn't answer. He stood looking at the three muggers. They'd moved away from the unconscious boozehound and were grouped near the curb, gazing at Corey and waiting for him to say or do something.

He remained silent. He didn't budge. His expression was placid, showing only a mild acceptance of what was happening.

The first mugger called to him, "Well, what's it gonna be? You just gonna stand there?"

Corey shrugged. He didn't say anything.

The three muggers looked at each other. One of them said, "Come on, let's walk. He won't do anything."

"He might," the first mugger said. "He just might."

Then the third mugger spoke up. "Say, what is all this? Who is he?"

"Name's Bradford," the first mugger said. "I know him, he lives around here."

"Is he trouble?"

"He could be. I've seen him work."

"He got a badge?"

"Now now," the first mugger said. "They took it away a month ago."

"Then what the hell are you worried about?" the third mugger said fretfully. "Come on, let's shove—"

"No, wait," the first mugger said. "I wanna be sure about this. I better talk to him."

"Talk about what?" the third mugger said louder. He was getting annoyed. "What's there to talk about?"

"Just wait here," the first mugger said. He walked slowly across the street. He came up to Corey Bradford and said, "All right, first I'll tell you this—you don't worry me. You don't worry nobody now."

Corey shrugged again. He inclined his head slightly and let out a little sigh.

The mugger moved closer and said, "Without that badge you're nothin'. You can't blow no whistle and you can't show any hardware. Ain't a move you can make and you know it."

Corey's eyelids lowered slightly, lazily. And a dim, lazy smile drifted across his lips. He looked at the mugger and didn't say anything.

The mugger frowned. He bit the corner of his mouth, then muttered, "Another thing you can't do. You can't rat. You wouldn't rat. Or maybe you would. You're just hungry enough—"

Corey didn't seem to hear. He'd turned his head and was looking at the unconscious boozehound on the other side of the street. He murmured to the mugger, "You hit him hard?"

"Just tapped him."

"With what?"

"Blackjack," the mugger said. His frown deepened and he took a backward step, carefully, slowly. It was a defensive maneuver and he knew it and it bothered him.

Corey went on looking at the fallen man on the other side of the street. He murmured to the mugger, "You hit him too hard?"

"For Christ's sake, I told ya. Just a light tap. He was ready to pass out anyway. Won't even raise a lump."

Just then the boozehound was starting to regain his senses. He stirred, rolled over, got to his knees and crawled a little. Then he lifted himself to his feet and walked around in a circle, and finally sat down on the pavement. He looked all around him, then looked up at the black sky and said loudly, clearly, "I'll tell you what the trouble is. The trouble is, we just can't get together, that's all."

The mugger said to Corey, "You see how it is? He's all right. He won't need no stitches, he won't need nothin'. I tell ya he's in good shape."

"What did you take from him?" Corey asked.

"Whaddya mean, what did we take? What's that to you?"

Corey showed another lazy smile. He closed his eyes for a moment, as though he was getting somewhat weary. Then his eyes half-opened and the smile faded. He looked directly at the mugger and waited.

The mugger shifted his weight from one foot to the other. "All right," he said. "All right, Corey."

"So what did you take?"

"The wallet," the mugger said. He gestured toward his two associates on the other side of the street. "They got his watch and some other things. The watch is strictly drugstore. The entire haul won't bring us more than—"

"Let's see the wallet," Corey cut in.

The mugger took another backward step.

"Come on," Corey said slowly, wearily. "Come on—"

"You louse," the mugger said. "You louse you." He took the boozehound's wallet from his pocket and handed it to Corey. There was a five and seven ones. Corey took six singles and returned the wallet to the mugger.

The mugger put the wallet back in his pocket. He looked Corey up and down. Then he turned toward the curb. As he stepped off the curb he turned again, faced Corey and said, "You know what's gonna happen to you? One of these days you're gonna get all mashed up. They'll hafta scrape it up and put it in a sack—"

Corey wasn't listening. He was lighting a cigarette. The mugger crossed the street and joined the others and the three of them walked away. The boozehound remained sitting there on the pavement, mumbling incoherently. Corey walked over to him and lifted him to his feet. The boozehound leaned heavily against Corey and said, "I'll tell you what the trouble is."

"No, I'll tell you," Corey said. "You got mugged. They took your last penny."

"Is that a fact?" the boozehound asked mildly. He gazed past Corey and said, "I guess it brings up a problem. It's a good seven miles from here—"

"Where you live?"

The boozehound nodded. Then he grimaced and felt the back of his head. Corey took the six dollars from his pocket, peeled off three and handed the bills to the man. "For cab fare," Corey said. He turned to move away.

"Hey, thanks," the boozehound said.

Corey was walking away.

"Thanks," the boozehound called to him. "No kidding, thanks a lot. You're really all right."

"Yeah," Corey said aloud to himself. "I'm very nice. I'm the original Joe Wonderful."

He walked a few more steps and then, thinking about the boozehound and making a bet with himself, he stopped and looked back. Sure enough, the deal was thirst instead of transportation. The boozehound was weaving slowly but purposefully toward the door of the juice joint. So the three beans go to the houselady instead of the cab driver, Corey thought, and allowed himself a philosophic smile. He was remembering the boozehound's statement, "—trouble is, we just can't get together." And what that means, he told himself, is simply—we just can't get together on what's right and what's wrong.

Now he was walking again, headed in the direction of a certain social center known as the Hangout. The back room of the Hangout was always active on Friday nights and the action was stud poker. Let's get there fast, he urged himself, and his hand drifted to the trousers pocket where the three dollars mingled with some sixty-five cents in coins. It was all the money he had to his name.

Corey Bradford was thirty-four years old. He stood five-nine and weighed one fifty-five. His hair was light brown, his eyes were gray. He seemed to be slightly the worse for wear, in recent weeks he hadn't been eating regularly. What little cash there was went mostly for cigarettes and alcohol, the emphasis on the alcohol. It wasn't because he was worried or depressed. He was never really worried or depressed, not consciously anyway. It was solely because drinking alcohol gave him something to do. He was out of work these days and there was nothing else to do.

Some five weeks ago they'd kicked him off the police force. He was a plain-clothes man attached to the 37th Precinct and they caught him accepting a handout from a houseman. It wasn't carelessness on Corey's part; he was always very smooth and he timed every move. It wasn't treachery, either. He was on friendly terms with all the neighborhood hustlers and scufflers, the numbers writers and unlicensed hooch sellers, the professional females and dice-table bankers. When he was nabbed, it was due solely to the persistence and drive of certain investigators from city hall. There was a campaign going on, aimed specifically at badge-wearing shakedown artists, and Corey was one of many who got busted.

He took it with a shrug. It was bound to happen sooner or later. For three years he'd been getting away with it, but he always had a feeling that one fine day they'd spot him and grab him and take away the badge. When it finally happened, it came almost as relief; the badge was a kind of hindrance, an annoyance. It was like itchy underwear. And aside from the discomfort, it sometimes hit him harder, drilled in deeper. The shining metal face of the badge would somehow come alive. It would look up at him and it would say quite solemnly, who do you think you're kidding?

At times he managed to evade that question. At other times he felt obliged to reply. Without sound he'd say to the badge, what the hell, jim—we ain't tryin' to kid nobody; we sure ain't out to cause grief or suck blood. It's just that we wanna live and have fun and be happy; and we wish all others the same.

That ain't no answer, the shining metal face would say. You'll hafta do better than that.

So then he'd squirm just a little, with perhaps the slightest trace of a sigh. He'd wait a moment, looking off to one side, getting his thoughts lined up in order. Well now, I'll tell ya, he'd say to the badge, his eyes patient and kind as though he was dealing with someone on the square side, someone who just didn't know the score. You see, it's like this—it's a very poor neighborhood, the folks here get hardly any breaks at all. I know that for a fact, I was born and raised in this layout.

The deal is, jim, there's an acute shortage of funds. So let's take whiskey, just as an instance. A legitimate bottle, a fifth, it's four dollars and up. The contraband booze, the cooked corn and goathead, you get it for a dollar a pint. Of course sometimes it's poison, but those times are very seldom. Maybe one batch out of five thousand, and you'll admit that's a tiny percentage. Chances are, when you drink the homemade juice you won't be sick the next day. I've never had a hangover from the corn or the goat, and that's more than I can say for some well-known legal brands.

Or take gambling. You get paid forty to sixty a week and you got a wife and four-five kids to feed. You just ain't got the cash it needs to speculate in the stock market. You can't afford the transportation that will take you to the tracks where the horses run, or join them certain private clubs that are never raided. The membership lists include big names and the big names have the pull and the cash, and that's what counts—only that. So you live in this neighborhood and you wanna gamble. Only thing you can do is play the numbers or pull down the shades and get out a deck of cards. Of course that makes you a lawbreaker, what they call a culprit. Well anyway, you wanna gamble, you gotta have your mind at ease, you gotta be sure they won't come bustin' down the door and breakin' in through the windows. Only way to be sure is to make a deal with some badge-holder.

Another thing, the girlies, the professionals. I don't mean the teasers, the phoneys who drink up all your money and actually it's nothing but tea in shot glasses and later they get their cut from the bar owner. And I don't mean the ones who clip you, the ones who roll you, the ones who get you hurt in some room where Danny comes out of a closet and puts brass knuckles on your jaw. I don't mean them; I mean the real professionals who give you your money's worth and you walk away satisfied. You wanna know somethin', jim? You figure it on the law of averages, them real professionals are more on the plus side than the minus. You can list them in the same groove with the street cleaners and the garbage collectors and the workers in the sewers. It all amounts to the same thing—they're needed. It's what's known as performing a necessary function. And don't give me no argument; it's a matter of statistics. If it wasn't for the professionals, there'd be more suicides, more homicides. And more of them certain cases you read about, like some four-year-old girl getting dragged into an alley, some sixty-year-old landlady getting hacked to pieces with an axe.

The badge made no comment.

So then he went on with it. He said to the badge, I tell you, jim, I know what I'm saying. With all them creeps and freaks and maniacs that walk around loose these days, it's a downright misfortune there ain't more houses where they can go and pay their money and let off steam. Because then nobody gets hurt.

All right, the law says no. But I'd like to have a shiny new dime for every pro skirt in this neighborhood who's pulled the rescue act time and time again, selling him whatever kind of relief he needs to prevent him from going out and doing something weird. Is that good enough for you?

No, the badge said.

You got me labeled bad?

Strictly, the badge said. You accept payoffs from lawbreakers, you're worse than they are.

But listen to me, will you? He begged the badge to hear him out. It's only with the little things, the harmless mischief, the gambling and white whiskey and the girlies turning tricks. Nothing more than that, believe me. I never took a shakedown from dope pushers and store robbers or boosters, and never did business with anyone I knew was really evil. All I did was try to—

Balls, the badge cut in. Don't feed me that mush. You were out for the extra dollar, that's all it amounts to, only that.

You think so?

I know so, the badge said.

He frowned for a moment, and almost gave it some serious thought. But serious thought was like a classroom, and he much preferred the playground. The frown became a grin and he shrugged and said to the badge, maybe you're right, but what does it matter?

Yet even so, the grin was somewhat forced and the shrug

was more or less faked. Under it, he squirmed and twisted as though trying to pull free from hard gripping shackles.

It amounted almost to a favor when they finally caught him and marched him into city hall and took the badge away.

Headed toward the Hangout, he kept fingering the three sixty-five in his pocket. He was walking east on Addison Avenue. It was the neighborhood's main drag.

The neighborhood was known as the Swamp. It was on the outskirts of the big city and on three sides it was bordered by swamplands. The rows of ancient wooden dwellings abruptly gave way to a soggy terrain of gray-colored mud and green-gray weeds and pools of gray water filmed with slime. On the fourth side there was the river and Addison merged with the bridge that crossed it. On any map that showed the city, the Swamp was a tiny triangle that seemed to have no connection with the other areas. It was more or less an island.

Addison was the only two-way street. The other streets were very narrow, some of them paved with cobblestones and others with scarcely any paving at all. For the most part, the thoroughfares were alleys. The Swamp was a labyrinth of alleys, and with an excessive number of oversized cats. The cats were very rugged, but every now and then a loner would be jumped by a pack of rats, and that would be the end of him. The rats in the Swamp were extremely vicious and some of them were almost as large as the cats. On certain nights the noises of cat-rat combat

in the alleys would resemble that of a sawmill going full
blast.

They were at it tonight. As he passed an alley intersection, Corey heard the yowling, screeching, screaming, the
almost human shrieks of agony that mixed with slithering
sounds of lightning-fast four-footed action. He winced
slightly and quickened his steps a little. He'd been born
and raised in the Swamp, but somehow he could never get
accustomed to these sounds.

Of course there'd been worse sounds overseas. He'd
heard some gruesome sounds in Sicily and Italy, especially
at Anzio where the enemy was up in the hills and pouring
down the heavy artillery. And yet the Swamp alley sounds
slashed into him deeper, stabbing through every nerve in
his body and finally making explosive contact with a certain circular jagged scar very high on his thigh near his
groin.

It had happened when Corey was seventeen months old.
He'd been left alone in the first floor back, while his widowed mother and her latest boyfriend were out drinking
wine in some joint on Addison. The baby was asleep when
the rat came in. It was a huge rat, hunger crazed, and it
came creeping in from the alley, entering the room through
a gap in the loose wall boards. Some moments later the
tenants in the first floor front heard the screaming. They
came rushing in. The rat got away, leaping off the bed and
onto a chair and leaping again, went through the open
window.

They tended Corey, knowing what to do about rat bite.
It was a common occurrence in the Swamp. Some newly-

distilled rotgut, over a hundred proof, went splashing onto the blood-gushing thigh. Then they tore the sheet and made a bandage. Inside of a week, the baby was out of bed and toddling around.

And then, when the child was six years old, another rat came in. On that occasion the boy was awake and ready and knew what to do. His mother kept certain weapons within reaching distance, in case some alley prowler happened to venture in. He snatched the six-inch switchblade resting on the chair near the bed. As the rat leaped, there was a clicking sound and the blade opened. It was timed perfectly; his aim was exact. He tossed the dead rat onto the floor, not even bothering to wipe off the blade. He went back to sleep. An hour later, when his mother staggered in, her wine-glazed eyes saw the corpse of the rat and the red-stained blade. She called the boy and he woke up. She said, "What I oughta do is bust your goddam head open. Or maybe it's my mistake. I never shoulda told ya about him—"

She was referring to Corey's father, who had died four months before he was born. A good man, she'd told the boy. The only really good man she'd ever known, and more than just a husband. So decent, so clean, so pure in his heart; it was a privilege just to be near him. Her man. Her Matthew.

Matthew had been a policeman. "Not an ordinary policeman," she had told her son, "even though he'd never been promoted, even though he was listed as just another cop who walked the beat. But I swear to you, Corey, your father was one of the specials. Sure as hell he was one

15

in a thousand. You see, boy, he was an honest policeman.

"And I mean honest all the way. Too goddam honest
for this crummy world, I guess. Something almost saintly
about him, and just like they gave it to the saints they gave
it to him. They played him for a sucker; they kicked him
around and laughed at him. They mauled his body, slashed
at his nerves, and hammered spikes into his spirit. They
worked on him plenty, believe me.

"At the precinct station they had him on the receiving
end of all them scummy underhanded deals that you never
read about in the papers. Time after time he'd risk his neck
to make the pinch, to put the cuffs on some hood caught
red-handed, guilty in spades. But it's one thing to bring
them in and it's another thing to see them walking out free
as the breeze. So you know what he did?

"He went right on bringing them in. And what did it
get him? Lemme tell you, boy, lemme tell you how it is
down here in the Swamp. A policeman who works in the
Swamp has one of two choices. He either goes along with
the game and gets paid off to look the other way, or he
gets the lumps and the bumps, the bleeding and the busted
bones.

"I tell you there were so many mornings when he came
home with a bandage around his head, other mornings it
would be his arm in a sling, or both eyes swollen almost
shut and just as purple as plums. Mornings when he staggered in, holding his belly, coughing up blood. 'Hit with
a crowbar,' he'd say with a shrug. And then he smiled so
I shouldn't get gloomy. But I tell you, boy, it was hard to

take, them certain mornings when he came home all smashed up.

"And then one morning he didn't come home.

"It happened in an alley. He was trailing some thugs and others moved in with iron pipes and baseball bats. Before he had a chance to blow his whistle, they had him down and were doing him in. How it was explained to me, they left him there when they thought he was done. But the bloodspots showed he came out of it and tried to crawl. He didn't get far, and he was too weak to blow the whistle. He was spilling a lot of blood and finally he sat back against a fence post. The blood kept spilling and after a while the smell of it reached the rats.

"That's how it ended, boy. That's what finally happened to your father, the good one, the clean one, the honest policeman. The rats got to him and he was meat for their bellies. You understand now why I gotta have the wine?

"But I never shoulda told ya," she said to the boy whose face was expressionless, who sat there in the bed in the semi-dark room where the wet blade gleamed red and the dead rat stained the floor. "Honest policeman," the woman mumbled, the wine in her head causing her to stumble as she headed for a chair. "They say it pays, honesty pays," she said louder. And then, still louder, "I'll tell you how it pays—I'm a goddam expert on that subject—" but she couldn't go on with it and fell into the chair. She tried to talk again, but then the wine hit her and she passed out.

The boy leaned his head on the pillow and tried to go back to sleep. He couldn't sleep. He sat up and looked at the dead rat. He got off the bed and went to the sink and cleaned the blade. Then he tossed the rat out the window. In bed again, he heard the sounds in the alley and knew that other rats were swarming in to feed on the dead one. The sounds grew louder, they were fighting over the meat. And then the sounds were very loud and the six-year-old boy shut his eyes tightly in a painful grimace and let out a moan.

Now, years later, walking east on Addison and passing the alley intersection and quickening his steps to get away from the sounds, he felt a slight twinge very high on his thigh near his groin. He told himself he was remembering something but he wasn't at all sure what it was.

He passed Third Street, went toward Second. At Second and Addison the lighted windows of the Hangout showed hectic activity inside. The Friday night drinkers were three deep at the bar, and there was considerable jostling and scuffling. At the splintered loose-legged tables, most of the chairs were taken. Several women were skirmishing for possession of one of the tables. A hairy-chested, bulky-shouldered construction worker, wearing a sweat-stained undershirt and a yellow pith helmet, moved toward the women to break it up. One of the women knocked him down.

As Corey walked in, a little man came sailing out, catapulted by the heavy foot of the female bouncer. The little man hit the pavement with expert agility, evidently well experienced at making belly landings. He came nimbly to his feet, his face solemn as he thumbed his nose at the female bouncer.

She doubled her fist and took a step forward. The little man retreated lightly, daintily. As he stepped off the curb, he said quietly, solemnly, "There's other places for me to go."

"I believe it," the female bouncer said. She pointed to the sewer opening across the street. "Try that one."

"I'd be intruding," the little man said. "Your parents live there."

"Do me a favor," she said it almost sweetly. "Come here and let me hit you once. Just once."

The little man's face remained solemn. He glanced at Corey, who was standing just inside the doorway. "She's a mixture," he said, pointing technically at the female bouncer as though she was something on exhibit. "She's one-third Irish, one-third Cherokee, and one-third hippopotamus."

Inhaling slowly, she made a hissing noise. She said to the little man, "You'll get it from me some day."

"Mechanically impossible," he twisted the meaning around. And then, to Corey, "You ever see a rear end jutting out like that? We could use it for a two-handed game of pinochle—"

She lunged toward the little man, whose name was Carp. He moved with reflex action far exceeding that of any sluggish fish. His one-twenty pounds made rapid transit across the street and around the corner. It was no use trying to pursue him; and she walked back to where Corey stood at the side of the doorway. She was muttering aloud to herself, referring to Carp's unique character traits, his family background, and certain plans she had for his future.

Then she looked up and saw Corey standing there. She glared at him, as though he was an accomplice in some Carp-inspired conspiracy against her. He gave her a soft smile, merely to let her know he was friendly. Her mouth tightened and she continued glaring at him.

"And you," she said. "You're another one."

"I'm just a bystander, Nellie. An innocent bystander."

" 'Innocent,' he says." She folded huge arms across forty-four-inch breasts. The breasts were in proportion. She weighed a good two-forty, compressed into five feet six inches. There was no loose fat; it was all solid beef. It amounted to a living missile, braced and aimed, ready for any man who figured he could tamper with her and get away with it.

Corey wasn't tampering. He let the soft smile fade, so it wouldn't be misinterpreted. He gestured casually in the direction Carp had taken. "What's with Carp? What'd he do this time?"

"What he's always doin'," Nellie muttered. "Stealin' drinks off the bar."

Corey sighed. "Some people never learn."

Then he knew he shouldn't have said that. It left him wide open for what was coming. Nellie looked him up and down. Her eyes narrowed with disdain. Her tightened lips twisted with contempt. "You got a right to talk," she said. "As if you think it don't show all over you."

He shrugged, turned away and started through the entrance of the taproom.

But Nellie wasn't quite finished with him. Her thick fingers gripped his arm. She turned him, forcing him to face her.

She said, "Lemme tell you somethin', Bradford—"

"Drop it," he cut in mildly. "You've told me before."

"And I feel like tellin' you again." She held onto his arm. He moved to get away, and she moved with him. It brought them into the taproom. Again he tried to pull free, but she held on. Her grip was very tight; it was hurting him.

"For Christ's sake," he said. Again he tried to get away from her.

She held on. "You're gonna listen," she said loudly, and some drinkers at the tables turned and looked. "You can all listen," she said to them. "I wantcha to hear this—"

And then, facing her audience, "I want it to sink in, I want you to list it and check it and remember. This bastard used the badge to steal bread from people's mouths. They hadda hand it over; they had no choice. Pay him off or get busted; that was the way it went. And who does he do it to? His neighbors, his friends, the very folks he knows from way back, all the way back to when he was a kid. Can you top that for underhanded dealing? I got more respect for a second-story man. Even for a purse snatcher—"

"Say it, Nellie," a skinny white-haired crone sang out. "Say it like it is, girl."

"There ain't nothin' meaner or rottener than a shakedown," Nellie said it with white-hot rage. "And get this ticket—he was always so nice and sweet about it. Knocks

21

so softly on the door and then comes on with that greasy smile. One hand pats you on the shoulder and the other hand is out, palm open. The miserable creep; he even had them thinkin' he was doin' them a favor—"

"Disgraceful," a whiskey-thick voice commented.

"Believe it," Nellie nodded in agreement. She looked sideways at Corey and kept tightening her grip on his arm. Her face twisted in a grimace of disgust as she said to the assemblage, "You know how this makes me feel? It makes me feel like I need soap and water."

"Then why don't you let go of him?" someone inquired quietly, calmly. "What are you holdin' onto him for?"

It was the little man, Carp. He stood in the side entrance, his arms folded, his head inclined, his manner that of an official observer.

"You here again?" Nellie roared at him.

"I guess we could put it that way," Carp said. He sent a thirsty glance toward the bar, then unfolded his arms and pointed stiffly at Nellie and said to all the drinkers, "You see what's happening there? You get the drift? She won't let go of him because she can't let go. It's what we call a dynamic situation, the outward manifestations are utterly superficial."

"Talk English," someone hollered.

"I'll be glad to," Carp said politely. "In plain English, my friends, she's hot for the man."

Nellie let out an animal growl, let go of Corey and made a beeline for Carp. The little man played it with fox-like strategy. He waited until Nellie was just a few feet away, her hands reaching out to grab him. Then with neatness and precision he used his foot to tip over a chair. As Nellie collided with the falling chair, Carp started a circular route that took him swiftly in the direction of the bar. Knowing what was coming, the regulars at the bar reached quickly for their shot glasses and grimly held on. Others weren't quick enough. As Carp flashed past the bar, his arm functioned with the speed of a piston. Before he reached the far end of the bar, he'd snatched and downed a double rye and a single of California brandy. Then he headed for the front door and scampered out.

Corey strolled to the bar. His hand was in his trousers pocket, cupping the combined weight of paper and metal, the three sixty-five. He took out a quarter, put it on the bar. It bought him a single shot of gin. He drank the gin, immediately wanted another, but decided it could wait. As he turned away from the bar, the thirst gave way to what was more important at the moment, the hunger for the poker-table, for delicious aces coming his way.

He moved toward the door that led to the back room. Passing the crowded tables, he was ignored like any casual table passer. They'd forgotten Nellie's tirade and were concentrating on their drinks. But as he neared the door, he had the feeling that a certain pair of eyes were aiming at him. He stopped for a moment, wincing slightly, then continued toward the door. As he reached for the doorknob, something forced him to turn his head.

He saw her.

She was sitting alone at the table near the wall. On the table there was a half-full quart-size bottle of beer. There was an empty glass. Now she reached slowly for the bottle and poured some beer into the glass. While she did it, she looked directly at him.

"Hello, Lil," he said.

Not saying anything, she lifted the glass to her mouth and sipped at the beer. She went on looking at him.

He blinked a few times. He said, "How's it going?"

She didn't answer. She just sat there and sipped more beer and kept looking at him.

"I ain't seen you around," he mumbled. "It's been months now—almost a year, I guess. Or maybe longer than that, I don't know. Where you been?"

She lowered the glass, leaned back in the chair and didn't say anything.

"What's the matter?" he said. "Can't you talk?"

"Not to you." Her voice was toneless. There was no particular expression on her face. "I have nothing to say to you."

He blinked again. Then he started to turn away but for some reason his legs wouldn't move.

"You don't have to stand there," she said. "You said hello and that's it. That's all it calls for, just a hello."

He stood and gazed at her. This ain't easy, he thought. It's like playing checkers with someone who knows all your moves before you make them. She won't give you no openings at all.

And what makes it tougher, he told himself, she's still got it, all of it. That face. That body. She's something, all right. But there's nothing you can do about it. All you can do is stand here like a goddam idiot and give yourself a bad time.

Lillian had dark brown hair, medium brown eyes. Somewhat heavy in the breasts and hips, her body was nonetheless enticing, wasp-waisted and solidly put together. She was an exceptionally good looking woman.

Lil was twenty-six. Some five years ago she was married to Corey Bradford. They hadn't stayed married long. It lasted a little over a year. The split-up was caused by his drinking. At that time he'd been wearing the blue of a beat-walking policeman, and for some reason that he couldn't understand he was drinking very heavily. She begged him to stop, then she warned him to stop. And finally one night when he went over the edge with the rams, she chased him down Addison as he dashed toward the river, intending to jump in. He didn't jump in. What stopped him was the sound behind him, the thud as she hit the ground. She suffered a bruised knee, a severely twisted ankle, and a miscarriage. It was a serious miscarriage. There was considerable pain and some complications and it almost did her in. On his knees beside the bed he held her hand and made a sacred vow that he'd stop the drinking. A month later he was crazy drunk again. That ended it.

He watched her now as she poured more beer into the glass. He frowned slightly, at first not knowing why. Then gradually it came to him. There was something out of kilter in this picture.

He said to her, "What's this with beer?"

She didn't reply. She sipped at the foam, then took a long drink.

"I never saw you drinkin' beer before," he said.

Lillian put the glass down. She gave him a look that said, So what?

"All I ever seen you drink was a lemon pop or a milk shake or just plain water," he said. "How come you've switched to alcohol?"

She shrugged, looking away from him. As if he wasn't there, and as though she was talking aloud to herself, she said, "It gets to a point where it just don't matter."

His frown deepened. "What kind of an answer is that?"

"I don't know," she said, and then she looked at him. "I honestly don't know."

He gave her a side glance. "Come on, Lil. Tell me—"

"Tell you what?"

"What's happening? What's wrong?"

She opened her mouth to say something, then shut her lips tightly. Again she looked away from him.

He leaned toward her. "Tell me, Lil. Let it out. It's better when you let it out."

"Is it?" And then her eyes aimed directly at him. "How would you know?"

He winced slightly. He had no idea what she meant by that, but whatever she meant, it went in deep. It cut like a blade.

He backed away, and mumbled clumsily, "Is that all you're gonna tell me?"

"That's all," Lillian said.

There was a heaviness in his throat. He tried to swallow it. He said, "I hate to see you sitting here alone."

"I'm sitting here alone because I want some privacy,"

she said. She shifted in the chair, turning away from him. For a moment her hands rested limply on the table top. In that moment he noticed something. It glimmered bright yellow on her finger. It was a wedding ring.

"Is that for real?" he asked, pointing at the ring.

She took her hands off the table top, folded them in her lap and didn't say anything.

Corey stared at her. "Well, whaddya know," he murmured. "I guess it calls for congratulations."

"Don't bother," Lillian said tightly.

He smiled thinly, lazily. He was about to say something but just then he sensed that someone stood directly behind him. Turning slowly, he faced a tall man who had thick, curly black hair, rugged features on the wholesome and pleasant side, and the physique of a discus thrower. The man appeared to be in his middle thirties. He wore working clothes. He said quietly to Corey, "Take a walk."

"Who are you?" Corey said.

"I'm her husband."

Corey looked off to one side. He murmured, "Says he's her husband. That's what he says."

"That's the way it is," the man said. He moved closer to Corey but then Lillian was on her feet and she moved in between them. She said to the man, "It's all right, Del. He knows me."

The man looked at her. "He does?"

She said quickly, "Yes, I told you about him. I was married to him."

"Oh," the man said. And then, to Corey, "Sorry, bud.

I didn't know." He smiled pleasantly and held out his hand and Corey took it. They introduced themselves. The man's name was Delbert Kingsley.

He was very pleasant. He invited Corey to sit down at the table. Corey thanked him and refused; then smiled at the two of them and turned away, walking toward the door that led into the back room.

2

It was a fairly large room, a combination of business office and playroom. On a small table set near the wall there were an adding machine, some stacked ledgers and various papers scattered about. Adjacent to the table an ancient slot machine stood on rusty legs. It showed the three black bells of the jackpot, just to let all viewers know it was on the level. Set slantwise, near the one-armed bandit, an age-darkened, rolltop desk leaned wearily on one short-ened leg. At a respectable distance from the outdated desk, there was a brand new filing cabinet, glimmering green, its edges reinforced with brightly shining nickel. On the wall above the filing cabinet were several neatly framed photographs that showed racing rowers in double-oared sculls.

In the center of the room there was a big round table, and seven men were seated at it. They were playing stud poker. Some of them were in undershirts; others were bare to the waist. Despite the breeze from an electric fan, they were all dripping with perspiration. Very intent on the cards, none of them looked up as Corey entered.

He moved toward the table to get a closer look at the action. It wasn't big money, there were less than thirty dollars in the kitty; but even so the action was tense. Some of them were chewing hard on cigar stubs and others were biting the corners of their mouths. While the winner was raking in the money, a loser got up and walked out of the room. Corey glided toward the empty chair. As he lowered himself into it, someone's heavy hand reached out and pushed him away.

"What goes?" Corey asked mildly. He smiled amiably at the big man who'd pushed him away from the empty chair.

"You weren't invited," the big man said. He was very big around the middle, of average height, and weighed around two-sixty. He looked solid, his bulk mainly in the chest and shoulders. The man's name was Rafer.

Corey continued smiling at him, saying, "You kidding me, Rafer?"

"No," Rafer said. "No, I ain't kidding you."

"I don't get it," Corey said. He mixed the smile with a slight frown. "It's a Friday night game and it's open. It's always open on Friday night."

"Not for you," Rafer said. His face was hard with authority; and then as he looked across the table his expression changed to the putty softness of a well trained lackey. "Ain't that right, Walt?"

The man named Walt was sipping from a glass of cold buttermilk. He was concentrating on the buttermilk, his mouth moving in little circles as he tested its flavor. He didn't look up.

Rafer tried again. "He don't believe me, Walt. You say the word and I'll get it across to him. I'll toss him outta here on his head."

The buttermilk drinker glanced up and saw Corey. He grimaced wearily and said to Rafer, "Why do you bother me with these things?"

"I'm just checkin' to get it straight," Rafer said. "You want him bounced?"

"Leave him alone," Walter Grogan said. He drank some buttermilk. "Let him stand there if he wants to."

"Can I sit down?" Corey asked.

Walter Grogan didn't answer.

"Can't I get in the game?" Corey asked.

"No," Grogan said.

"Why?" Corey asked. "Why, Walt?"

Grogan looked at him. That was all, just a look. It caused Corey to take a step backward, as though he was shoved in the face. So this is what it comes to, he thought. And it ain't the treatment; it's worse than the treatment. What it amounts to, is you've been listed minus zero, strictly useless, absolutely worthless. The tip off came when he didn't even bother to have you thrown out. I guess that puts you right at the bottom, even lower than Carp and the other mischief-makers. At least they get some attention, they rate high enough to get bounced. All you're getting is the look; the look that says in no uncertain terms that you've been junked.

Corey took another step backward. Then very slowly he backed across the room until he reached the wall. He leaned back against the wall and stared at the floor. His hand drifted toward his pocket and he fingered the money, the three dollars and forty cents. Let's put it to work, he told himself. Let's drink it up.

But he didn't move. He went on staring at the floor, his head lowered. Then gradually he raised his head and his mouth tightened just a trifle. He focused on Walter Grogan.

Walter Grogan was the owner of the Hangout. He also owned a pawnshop, a poolroom, a dry cleaning establishment and most of the real estate in the Swamp. All his business activities were centered in the Swamp and the same applied to his social life. He seldom was away from the Swamp. Although he had considerable cash—(estimates of his wealth ranging anywhere from one hundred thousand to more than a quarter of a million) it seemed that everything he wanted or needed was in this neighborhood of wooden shacks, tarpaper hovels and narrow alleys. His only recreation outside the Swamp was his membership in the Southeast Boat Club. It was a rather exclusive club and its list included some very important names. But Grogan hadn't joined it for that reason. It was just that he liked to row on the river. He was better than the average rower. Took it very seriously; and he needed the facilities of a good boating club.

He was fifty-six, lean and hard and red-brown from the rowing. His hair was silver, still fairly thick, combed straight across his head so that it glistened. He had a habit of smoothing it with his hand, as though he wanted it to retain the luster. But there was no luster in his eyes. His eyes were a very pale yellow-gray, dull and lifeless, more like lenses.

Lenses that could see through a wall, Corey was thinking. Or inside someone's brain. If they thought he was
really out to win, they wouldn't be sitting at that table
with him. The way it is, they know he's only fooling
around. It's a cinch he ain't interested in their singles and
fives or even their sawbucks. If he actually felt like trying,
he'd have them all flat busted inside a fast ninety minutes.
You can't help but admire him, I mean the machinery in
his head. That's what it is, machinery; and it's strictly precision tooled. You can't remember when it ever made a
mistake. A typical front runner, no two ways about it. But
do you envy him? Do you envy him with his hand-stitched
suits and sixty-dollar shoes? With the limousine from Spain
and the brand new Olds? And while we're at it, we might
as well include that other fancy job he rides, that slinky
platinum blonde he sleeps with every night. So I'm askin'
you, do you envy him?

You're goddam right you envy him. And—

At that moment Rafer was dealing. Grogan was sipping
the buttermilk. It all happened very fast, the back door
opening and two men coming in, showing guns.

The men wore horror masks that covered their entire
heads. One was a werewolf and the other was a stomach-
turning combination of hyena and horned Satan. The werewolf stood near the door and the hyena-devil moved slowly
toward the table.

There was no sound in the room. A few of the poker
players put their arms above their heads. Rafer still held
the card he'd been about to deal, his hand suspended stiffly
in mid-air.

Grogan was gazing calmly at the masked men. He seemed to appraise the masks, as though they were competing for first prize at a costume party and he was one of the judges. He continued studying them for a few moments, sipped some buttermilk, lowered the glass to the table and said, "All right, what do you want?"

"You," the hyena-Satan said. His voice was muffled behind the mask. He had the pistol aimed at Grogan's head. "Just you, Grogan."

Grogan reached for his wallet.

"Don't do that," the hyena-Satan said.

"Then take what's on the table," Grogan told him. "Take it and get outta here."

"We didn't come for that." The pistol gestured toward the money on the table. "I told you what we want. We want you."

Grogan rubbed his chin thoughtfully.

"Get up on your feet," the hyena-Satan said.

Grogan didn't move.

"Get up." The pistol aimed at Grogan again. "Get up or I'll put one in your head."

"No you won't," Grogan said.

"You don't think so?"

"It figures," Grogan said. "You do me in; you'll be slopping up the job. If they wanted me bumped, you coulda shot through the window."

"They?" the hyena-Satan was just a trifle on the defensive. "Whaddya mean? Who's *they*?"

"Whoever sent you," Grogan said. He leaned back in

the chair. His tone was mild, conversational. "Tell me something, buddy boy. How much you getting paid?"

The hyena-Satan made a hissing sound, breathing hard through the mask. He moved a step closer to Grogan, raised the pistol a few inches so that it pointed at Grogan's forehead, just below the hairline.

"Fifty?" Grogan murmured. "A hundred? Let's say it's a hundred and fifty. So what I'll do, I'll double that."

There was another hissing sound from behind the hyena-Satan mask. This time there was a laugh in it.

"Tell you what," Grogan said. He leaned back further in the chair, crossed his legs and folded his arms. "We'll make it five hundred. Good enough?"

The hissing laughter came louder. Then abruptly the laugh was cut off and the mask-muffled voice said, "All right, now we'll time it. I'm givin' you the warning buzzer. You either get up from that chair and come with us or you go to the cemetery."

"Seven hundred," Grogan said. "Seven."

"You like that number?"

"It always pays off," Grogan said. "Well, whaddya say? Make it seven?"

"Sure," the gunman said. "Seven seconds."

He started to count. Grogan didn't move. The count reached three and then the gunman stopped counting and said to his partner, "Lock the front one."

The werewolf masked man moved quickly to the front door leading to the taproom. Above the doorknob there was a slide lock and he set the lock into place. Then he moved sideways, parallel to the wall, his gun pointed in the general direction of the men sitting at the table. As he moved, he turned away from Corey, who remained leaning against the wall.

"We pick it up at three," the hyena-Satan said. "And now it's four seconds—five—"

"All right," Grogan said. "All right. I'll go with you."

Grogan was getting up from the chair and just then Corey lunged at the gunman wearing the werewolf mask. It was a combination move, his left hand going for the gun while his right hand, hard clenched, hit the werewolf mask high on the neck behind the ear. As the gunman sagged, the other gunman fired twice, missed and then delayed for an instant to steady his aim. In that instant the gun was in Corey's hand, spitting flame.

The bullet went into the mouth of the hyena-Satan. Some pieces of rubber sprayed out, mixed with pieces of bone and bloody flesh. From the back of the gunman's skull a thin stream of brains trickled down. He was dead before he hit the floor. The other gunman was trying for the window, at first crawling on hands and knees and then sobbing frenziedly as he fought to get to his feet. He was groggy from the blow that Corey had delivered and as he came to his feet he fell sideways and collided with the wall. Then he was down again, on his knees.

Corey didn't see Rafer coming. Rafer snatched the gun from Corey's hand, and Grogan shouted, "No, don't— don't do that."

But Rafer was pulling the trigger. He shot the gunman

in the spine. Then he shot him in the neck, and sent a third bullet into his head. The corpse was sitting against the wall. Rafer leaned very close and fired twice, the bullets going in through the eye slits of the werewolf mask.

"That fixes it," Rafer said. He turned away from the seated corpse, expanding his chest importantly. He faced Grogan, who'd walked slowly across the room.

"You imbecile," Grogan said quietly. With the back of his hand he hit Rafer across the mouth. Rafer tried to say something and Grogan hit him again. "You imbecile, you," Grogan said.

Excited shouts came from the taproom and people were knocking on the door. Then there was the sound of shoulders thudding against the door as they tried to push it off its hinges.

Grogan moved toward the door and told them to stop. The noise subsided. He went back to Rafer and said, "Tell me something. What's the matter with you?"

Rafer swallowed hard. "I thought—"

"You thought," Grogan said. "With what? Your ass?"

"I figured—"

"No you didn't," Grogan said. "You can't even add one and one." He gestured toward the masked corpse. "Even the dumbest punk would know I wanted him alive."

Rafer blinked several times. "He was makin' for the window. All I done was stop him."

"You stopped him, all right," Grogan said. "You stopped him from talking, that's what you did."

Rafer sighed heavily. He stood there deflated, making a

helpless gesture. Grogan turned away, bent over the sitting corpse and ripped off the werewolf mask. The poker players moved closer to get a look at the face.

"Anyone know him?" Grogan asked. They said no. Grogan crossed over to the other corpse and removed the mask and again it was no.

Grogan frowned, confused. He said aloud to himself, "I don't get this. Just don't get it, that's all."

"It's a cinch they ain't from this neighborhood," someone said.

"Then what's the answer?" another asked, puzzled. "There's gotta be an answer."

"I got it," Rafer said loudly, hitting his fist against his palm. He paused significantly, his chest expanded again. They all looked at him, all except Grogan. The fist hit the palm again and Rafer said, "They were hired by someone who knows about—"

But just then Grogan looked at Rafer. And Corey thought, That look—it's like pressing a button that shuts off the noise!

Rafer stood there stiffly, blinking hard and swallowing air. Grogan went on looking at him. Some moments passed and then Grogan turned away and moved toward the table, sat down and muttered aloud to himself, "I swear I don't know how I manage. What I have to put up with. The people I have around me."

"I didn't say nothin'," Rafer tried to make repairs. "All I said was—"

Grogan looked at him. Some of the men squirmed uneasily. Rafer had his mouth clamped tightly, his features twisted in a straining grimace as he made the effort to remain quiet.

"You want me to really do it?" Grogan said very quietly to Rafer. "You want me to pull your tongue out with pliers?"

Rafer opened his mouth. He started to say something; then forced it back, and his lips locked again.

One of the men said to Grogan, "Whatever it is, you can tell us. After all, we're on the payroll."

"That's right," another put in. "It ain't as if we're outsiders."

And a third one said, "There's somethin' happenin', we'd like to know about it."

"You want me to tell you?" Grogan murmured.

"Sure."

"Well, I'm not gonna tell you."

"But look, Walt—I mean, after all—"

"I'm not gonna tell you," Grogan said.

"That closes it," Rafer barked importantly. He came over and stood at Grogan's side. Again his chest expanded with authority as he scowled at the five men grouped near the table. One of them started to say something and Rafer said, "Cut it, and don't bring it up again."

They didn't talk back. A few of them shrugged. One of them sighed resignedly. It wasn't that they were afraid of Rafer. It was simply that they all drew weekly pay checks from Grogan and they needed the employment. They had wives and children, and they couldn't afford to risk getting fired.

Grogan lifted himself from the chair. For a moment he

looked thoughtfully at the two corpses. Then he said, "All right, now here's how we handle this. We'll hafta call the law and show them what we got here. We tell the law they tried for a heist. They wanted money and that's all they wanted. Not a word about them wanting me."

"That understood?" Rafer frowned sternly at the five men. "You say it just like he tells you to say it."

"They got it," Grogan murmured. He gave Rafer a weary look. "Go on, make the call."

Rafer went to the desk, rolled up the top and reached for the phone. As Rafer dialed, Corey was standing near the table, apart from the group. Corey was thinking, It adds up to a question mark. What's all this cover-up? Whatever it is, it's got Grogan scared. You know he's scared. It don't show in his face, but somehow you can tell he's really scared. So what about that? Well, you've known Walter Grogan all your life, and you've never seen him scared before.

3

About five minutes later the police car arrived. Then more police came in. And after that it was the captain from the 37th Precinct. Finally it was a few plain-clothes men from city hall. Questions were asked and answers given. There were no complications; it went exactly the way Grogan wanted it to go. The plain-clothes men made some notes for their reports and walked out. The police stayed around while the two corpses were placed on stretchers, then hauled away in the morgue wagon. It was cut and dried, it was over and done with in a quarter of an hour.

The captain was the last to leave. At the door, the captain and Grogan stood with their arms around each other's shoulders. They were close friends and Grogan was asking about Sally and the kids. The captain said they were fine. More friendly talk, some chuckling, and then the captain gave Grogan a playful punch in the stomach and said, "Still hard as a rock."

Grogan smiled. "It's the rowing, Tommy. You oughta try it."

"Who's got time for rowing? And who needs exercise? I get enough from Sally."

They both chuckled again. Then they were quiet and looked at each other in a long moment of deep communication. As they shook hands, they smiled warmly.

The captain opened the door and said "Good night, Walt." Then he leaned close to Grogan and added in lower tones, "For Christ's sake, be careful, will you?"

Grogan said, "I'm always careful, Tommy. You know that." The Captain patted Grogan on the shoulder, turned and walked out.

Rafer and the five men had resumed their seats at the table. There were no cards on the table and they were just sitting, some of them smoking and others cleaning their fingernails. Corey stood alone on the other side of the room. He was thinking about the police from the 37th Precinct.

They didn't even say hello, he thought. Aside from the routine questions, they didn't so much as look at me. And the captain. Good old Captain Tommy. He walked right past me as if I wasn't even here.

So what?

So nothing, he told himself. And he shrugged.

At the table, someone produced the cards and started shuffling. Grogan walked to the table and sat down. The shuffling went on and Rafer said, "All right already. Let's have 'em."

The dealer passed the cards around. Grogan leaned back in his chair, ignoring the cards. He was looking at Corey

Bradford. They were waiting for Grogan to bet, he was high with a king.

"Your bet, Walt," someone said. Grogan didn't seem to hear him. Grogan's eyes remained focused on Corey.

Then very slowly Grogan got up from the chair. He moved toward the side door. He opened the door and beckoned to Corey Bradford. They walked out together.

Grogan's house was less than a block away from the Hangout. From the outside, it appeared no different from the other shabby wooden dwellings on Second Street. On one side there was a narrow alley. The other side gave way to a vacant lot littered with rubbish. The windows were grimy; there was no paint on the front door and in places the wood was cracked.

Grogan unlocked the door, opened it and they walked in. Corey had never seen the interior of this house; but he'd heard talk about it and he'd thought the talk was exaggerated. Now he looked around and his eyes widened. The motif was Chinese, extremely expensive and elegant. The furniture was ebony and teakwood; the lamps and vases and ashtrays were rose quartz and jade. On the walls were silk-screen prints that looked like museum pieces. In one corner of the room there was a massive bronze statue of Buddha. From where he was standing, he could see into the dining room. The décor in there was also oriental, and through the dim green lamplight he saw an intricately carved table inlaid with ivory. Then he looked around at the furnishings in the parlor again. It's really something, he thought. It's like what you see in picture magazines.

He sensed that Grogan was watching him, waiting for some comment. He looked at Grogan and said, "Well, I heard about it and now I believe it."

"It all comes from China," Grogan said. "I've always wanted to see China. Never had the chance to go. Too busy. So I do the next best thing. I bring China here."

As Grogan was speaking, there was sound from the stairway. Corey looked and saw a female coming slowly down the stairs. She wore a silver and orange kimono. She was of medium height, very slender. Her hair was platinum blonde. Contrasting with her deep, dark green eyes.

Corey had seen her before, but only from a distance. He'd seen her driving the Olds, and climbing in or out of the Olds when it was parked outside some store on Addison Street. It was always a candy store or a grocery store, and the only item she bought was cigarettes. She never went near the Hangout.

From what he heard about her, she stayed in the house most of the time and seldom spoke to anyone in the Swamp. She'd been with Grogan for more than three years; and that was a long time for Grogan, considering he was fickle with women. The others had lasted only a few months. But she seems to fill the bill, Corey thought. You can tell from the way he looks at her. He's hooked, all right, he's really got it bad. I'd say she's about twenty-four. Another thing I'd say, she ain't no ordinary shack job out for free bed and board. Just look what she's got in her hands.

In one hand she had a pair of reading glasses. The other

hand held a book. Corey could see the title on the cover. He didn't know much about philosophy but he sensed that the book was strictly for deep thinkers. It was Nietzsche, it was *Thus Spake Zarathustra*.

She hadn't yet noticed Corey. She stood talking to Grogan, her voice low but clear, her speech precisely enunciated, her grammar flawless. She was telling Grogan that she'd been in town today, shopping. She bought shoes and a handbag and then went to the beauty parlor. She had dinner in town and attended a lecture at the art museum.

"It was a very interesting lecture," she said. "It concerned the French Impressionists and the lecturer came out with some highly original theories. It was really worthwhile."

"That's fine," Grogan said. "I'm glad you had a nice evening."

"It's delightful at the museum. I wish you'd go with me sometime."

"We'll try to arrange it," Grogan said.

"You're always saying that."

"Well, you know how it is. I just don't have the time."

"You could find the time."

"Not hardly," Grogan said. "Believe me, dear, I'm up to my neck in work."

"It isn't that I'm complaining," she said. "It's for your sake as well as mine. You shouldn't work so hard. If only you'd slacken up a bit. You look so tired."

"I'm not tired." There was a tightness in his voice. "It's just that I'm—"

"Walter, please."

Grogan turned away, his head lowered. He was biting his lip. He muttered, "—tells me I'm tired."

"Don't," she said quietly but firmly. "Don't start that."

But whatever it was, it was started and Grogan couldn't stop it. He went on muttering, "—it's one thing to be tired. It's another thing to be fed up. I tell you it's getting to the point where I'm—"

"Not now," she said warningly, and Grogan looked up and saw Corey standing there.

He was quiet for a moment, then looked at her and mumbled, "All right, all right." It was like a curtain lowered for a change of mood. Grogan rubbed his hand across his mouth, as though to wipe away the tightness and replace it with a soft smile. He went on smiling as he gazed down at the elegant carpet. He murmured, "Lita, this is Corey Bradford."

Lita nodded politely to Corey. Then she took a backward step, as though to get a fuller look at him. It started with his shoes. And he thought, she sees sad looking shoes with the leather cracked, no shine at all and the heels worn down. And pants that need pressing and wouldn't last through another cleaning, with a jacket to match. Now she's looking at the necktie. It's an old necktie, the threads are coming loose. Same applies to the shirt. So all right, so we're not exactly up there with the ten best dressed. Let's let it go at that. But no, she won't let it go, she's looking at the shoes again—

He heard himself saying, "I have a pair of new ones, but these are more comfortable."

"Really?" She folded her arms lightly across her middle. "Do you really have a pair of new shoes?"

"No." He grinned. "I was kidding."

She gave him a side glance. It was ice.

He went on grinning at her. "Just kidding," he said. "Can you take a little kidding?"

Lita didn't answer. She turned her back to him, said good night to Grogan, and moved toward the stairway. Going up the stairs, she put on the reading glasses and started leafing through the pages of *Thus Spake Zarathustra*.

Grogan waited until she was upstairs. Then he faced Corey and said, "You should'na done that. It don't take much to get her annoyed."

Corey shrugged. "So next time I'll know."

Grogan frowned at him. "You take life real easy, don't you?"

He shrugged again. Grogan went on frowning, studying him. Then Grogan said, "Sit down."

Corey sat, leaned back in the chair and watched Grogan pacing back and forth in front of him. It went on that way for some moments, and Corey thought, don't say nothing, just wait it out. And whatever you do, don't play tag with him. You can see he's in no mood for games. The man is having aggravation and aside from his other worries he's got himself a bedroom problem. It's fifty to one he ain't getting much these days.

Grogan stopped pacing. He sat down in an ebony armchair, facing Corey. "All right, here it is," he said. "I like to give credit where credit is due. What you did tonight at the Hangout, it took talent. It was clean and fast and I guess you got as much style as I've ever seen. And I've seen the best."

Corey leaned further back in the chair. He thought, well, that's nice to hear. But I can't put it on a plate and eat it. And then he saw Grogan reaching into a pocket and taking out a wallet.

"Here," Grogan said, and handed him some ones and fives and tens. It amounted to seventy dollars.

Corey said, "Thanks."

"Thanks nothing. You're gonna work for that. That's your first week's salary."

"Doing what?"

"Investigation," Grogan said. "I want to know who hired them."

Corey looked down at the money in his hand. He murmured, "Well, it's bread and I damn sure need it. Except—"

"Except what? What bothers you?"

"Well, it ain't like steady employment. I come up with the answer; I'll be out of a job."

"You come up with the answer, you won't need the job."

Corey's eyes widened slightly.

Grogan said, "It's like this—the seventy is just a drawing account. If you score, you're in for velvet. You get fifteen thousand dollars."

"Fifteen *what?*"

"Thousand."

Corey sat motionless. Fifteen thousand dollars, he thought. The man said fifteen thousand. Should we tell him to say it again, just to make sure we heard him right? No, we heard him right. He said fifteen thousand dollars.

"Well?" Grogan murmured. And then, a trifle louder, "Well?"

"It's velvet, all right." Corey gazed past Walter Grogan. "I'm wondering why it's worth that much to you."

The silver haired man slowly lifted himself from the ebony armchair. Annoyance came into his eyes. "I don't like it when they start getting cagey."

"It ain't that," Corey said. "I just want a little briefing here."

"That's out," Grogan said. "Ain't nothing I can tell you."

"How come?"

"I just can't."

Corey smiled dimly. "You can't or you won't?"

Grogan gave him a look. Just a look. The look said, you want this job or don't you?

The dim smile faded. Corey shrugged and said, "After all, I'm not a cat. I can't operate in the dark."

It was quiet for some moments. Grogan moved slowly toward the other side of the parlor, stood facing the massive bronze Buddha. Then he moved closer to it as though he was consulting the Buddha. Finally he turned and looked at Corey; his eyes slits like the eyes of the Buddha.

"Well now, you got me thinking. Just standing here wondering how much I should tell you. If I tell you too much, you'll know too much."

Corey decided not to comment.

"On the other hand," Grogan went on, "you can't go to work if I don't give you nothing to work with."

Then it was quiet again. Corey sat and waited.

Walter Grogan came across the room and stood beside the ebony armchair. He ran his hand along the glistening black wood. And then, his voice low, the words coming slowly, "Whoever hired them hoods, it was someone playing for high stakes. Someone who knows—" and he stopped.

Corey said, "Knows what?"

Grogan took a deep breath, let it out. "Some lettuce. I got some lettuce put away."

"In a vault?" Corey asked. "Safe deposit?"

"Safer than that."

"Stashed?"

Grogan nodded. He kept rubbing his hand along the back of the ebony armchair. He said, "It's what they call unlisted assets. Or let's call it unreported income. From certain deals I've been in on. All paid off in cash."

"It's warm money?"

"It's very warm," Grogan said. "Piled up over a period of years. If the government ever gets wise, I'd pull ten to twenty or maybe even twenty to forty."

"Just for tax evasion?"

"They get me for tax evasion, that's only the beginning. Then they really go to work. Them Federal agents, they get onto something, it's like white on rice. So one thing leads to another. Some joker gets scared and opens his mouth and that drags in some other joker and so on. And finally they wrap it up; they get all the money tabulated—who paid off and why."

"It comes to a lotta money?"

"Plenty."

"How much?"

"I'm not gonna tell you how much," Grogan said. "You got a gleam in your eye already. Next thing you'll ask me where it's stashed."

Corey ignored that. He thought aloud, "A bundle of money hidden somewhere—"

And then they looked at each other. Grogan said, "You thinkin' what I'm thinkin'?"

"Well, it's an angle."

"You're damn right it's an angle," Grogan said. "There's people who know my financial setup. People close to me and maybe others not so close to me. So let's say one of them latches on to an idea. Just plays around with it. Tells himself that Grogan don't live in a mansion and Grogan don't play the races and what it all comes down to, Grogan ain't a big spender. So what does Grogan do with all his money? Christ's sake, of all the money Grogan's been making, there's gotta be more than what's in the bank and what's in stocks and bonds. Sure, there's gotta be a lot more than that. But where?

"And that's the question. And there's only one way to get the answer. Get it from Grogan. Get Grogan in some nice quiet place and sit him down and have a friendly conversation. Then maybe a little pressure, and sooner or later Grogan spills."

Corey was gazing at the floor. "It's possible." He rubbed

his chin thoughtfully. "It adds, anyway. I mean, it checks with what them hoods did. The way they played it. They wanted to get you outta there alive."

Corey kept gazing at the floor. Then he slowly got up from the chair, started walking around, not looking at Grogan. His forehead was creased and he was biting his lip.

"You're letting it show," Grogan said.

Corey looked at him.

The silver-haired man was smiling thinly, knowingly. "You're wishing," he said. "Wishing you had the badge."

Correct, Corey thought.

Grogan went on smiling. "With the badge it would be a breeze. You could go around knocking on doors and asking questions. In no time at all you get a lead. And then another lead. And then another lead. And still another—"

"*If* I had the badge," Corey cut in dryly.

"If you had the badge," Grogan said, not smiling now, "I wouldn't give you the job."

"How come?"

Grogan's voice was toneless. "I don't trust anyone who carries a badge. Not even my good-time buddy Captain Tommy; and I been doing business with the captain for years. In his heart he's a thug and that's why we get along. Up to a point, that is. It comes to anything important, I remember his badge and that's the stoplight."

"But why?"

"You oughta know why," Grogan said. "You and the captain are in the same groove; both out for the extra dollar. But tell me," his eyes were lenses probing deep, "weren't there times when you saw the badge lookin' at you? When you heard the badge talkin' to you?"

Corey blinked hard.

"Get what I mean?" Grogan murmured.

"Let's drop it." He looked away from Grogan.

There was a soft chuckle. "It kinda tickles me," Grogan said. "No matter what he does on the side, a cop is always a cop—until they take the badge away. Then he is what he is."

"Look, whaddya say we drop it?"

"Sure, sure." Grogan patted Corey's shoulder. "Sure," and his tone was soft with understanding.

His hand stayed on Corey's shoulder. Then he was guiding Corey toward the front door. As they neared the door, Corey took out his wallet and inserted the seventy dollars. He pocketed the wallet, made a move to open the door, and heard Grogan saying. "There's one more thing."

They looked at each other.

"This deal is you and me," Grogan said. "Just you and me. That understood?"

Corey frowned thoughtfully. He muttered, "We better get our signals straight. So I'll know what to tell your people. They know you brought me here to offer me a job."

"It ain't no problem," Grogan said. "They start askin' questions, you can tell them you're on the payroll."

"Collector?"

"Make it watchdog."

"Watchdog? That's Rafer's job."

"All right, let's say you're Rafer's assistant."

"Will he go for that?"

"Don't worry about it," Grogan said. He opened the door for Corey. But Corey closed the door and said, "There's another item. I'm gonna need a gun."

"Wait here," Grogan said, and went through the parlor and into the dining room. Corey heard him opening a drawer. He came back with a .38 and a box of cartridges. Corey loaded the pistol and slipped it under his belt and pocketed the cartridge box. And just as he was doing that, he heard something.

It wasn't loud, barely audible; but he heard it as clearly as the slamming of a door. It came from upstairs. It was just a tiny clicking noise and he knew it was the bedroom door. The door had been open and Lita had closed it. Closed it very quietly, he told himself. Quietly and carefully. Which means that all this time she wasn't in the bedroom. Or in the bathroom. You're a former plainclothes man and you add it up in a jiffy. You know where she was all this time. She was in the hallway up there, listening in.

Grogan hadn't heard it. Or maybe he was pretending he hadn't heard it. His face showed no reaction. His tone was technical as he said, "Keep in touch. That means at least once a day. If I'm not at the Hangout, try me here."

Corey nodded. He said good night and walked out of the house. He crossed the street diagonally, and when he was on the other side he turned his head quickly, just in time to catch a glimpse of her face in the bedroom window. She'd pulled at the side of the shade to have a look, and now the shade was in place again. Is that important? he wondered. Well, it could be important. Then again, maybe it's nothing. Maybe she lives a very dull life in that house and this eavesdropping and peeking out of windows is just to break the monotony. But then, on the other hand, I mean if you wanna look into it deeper—

Cut it, he told himself. You start with the digging, you'll wind up way over your head. Better stick with what you know. And all you know is, her name is Lita and she's Grogan's woman.

And what do you know about Grogan?

Well, let's see. It goes back a long way. You were just a kid when Grogan started running things in this neighborhood. He was born and raised here in the Swamp and according to what you've heard from the talkers, he started his career as an ordinary hoodlum. So before he was twenty he'd done some time at the Industrial School For Boys. But that was the only stretch. He came out very educated, and even though they grabbed him time and time again, they couldn't get a thing on him. It was either lack of evidence or lack of witnesses, especially lack of witnesses. You look back through the records, it shows quite a few names that suddenly left town. At least it was said they left town. The fact that they were never seen again is something else. It sorta ties in with that old saying, that friendly suggestion— if you live in the Swamp and you wanna keep living, don't tangle with Grogan.

All right, that's one thing. And the other thing is the money. Where does all the money come from? Well, the list of properties shows the taproom and the poolroom, the dry-cleaning shop and the pawnshop. And the rent that comes in from damn near every rent payer in the Swamp. So put all that together and it mounts up. But it's only part of the money. A very small part.

The real money is the haul from the other activities— the transactions and manipulations that nobody talks about. Not when they're sober or in their right mind, that is. But there were times when some poor fool would have one drink too many, and then it would slip out. So you remember hearing talk about such matters as extortion and strong arm protection. And some smuggling. And hijacking. All big-time operations ranging from truckload to carload to shipload. That's money, all right. That's heavy gold.

So come to think of it, he didn't hafta tell you that he's got a bundle stashed away. You coulda guessed that. Or decided that. And you're only one of many. It amounts to a long list, this list of people who can guess or decide that Grogan ain't been paying the income tax he ought to be paying. You can't start checkin' the names of that list. You wouldn't know where to start; there's too many names and this ain't like using an index. There's no way to classify or narrow it down to just a few. I think that fifteen grand is very far away. And I think—

But just then he stopped thinking. His brain became a measuring gauge as he heard the sound behind him. It was momentary, a very slight crunching sound, a sort of grinding, then nothing more. The measuring gauge indicated a distance of some thirty feet. It stated further that someone had accidentally stepped on broken glass. The someone had been tailing him, doing it very carefully and without any noise of footsteps, and then the broken glass had functioned like radar and he knew for sure he had company.

He didn't look behind him. He didn't change his pace. He was headed south on Second, moving at medium stride, going toward Addison. His arms swung loosely but his right hand was ready, each swing of the arm brought his fingers closer to the gun under his belt.

But there was no sound behind him, and he smiled dimly, seeing it clearly on the radar screen, knowing that the follower was slackening to increase the distance between them. Also, the follower was probably scanning the pavement for more broken glass, evading the noisemakers. Very neat, Corey thought. Whoever he is, he's an expert.

Then again the measuring gauge was working. The intersection of Second and Addison was less than sixty feet away. About twenty feet away there was an alley entrance. Across the street from the alley entrance a lamppost gave off a fairly bright glow. Corey headed for the alley. He did it slowly, casually, as though this was the route he always took.

As he entered the alley he moved fast. The loose boarded fence of a backyard was in front of him. He went up and over, then ducked low and waited. There was no sound. Through a gap in the boards he could see the glow coming in from the lamppost on the other side of Second Street. That oughta do it, he thought. That light is just about bright enough.

A shadow ribboned through the glow. The shadow became larger. Corey's eyes narrowed and he peered through the slit in the fence. Then it wasn't a shadow; it was a man standing in the entrance to the alley.

The man was leaning forward, his jutting head moved slowly from side to side as he peered through the alley. The glow from the lamppost lit the man's face and it was the face of Delbert Kingsley.

4

Nothing happened. Kingsley just stood there, his face expressionless in the glow from the lamppost. For a moment his gaze rested on the loose boarded fence; then again he peered through the darkness. He made no move to enter the alley. But gradually his features tightened and it seemed he was trying to make up his mind about something.

Corey breathed very slowly, crouching behind the fence. Through the slit in the boards he studied Kingsley's face and thought, It's sorta like stud poker; the man knows it's his bet and he's figuring the odds. He knows there ain't no hurry; he can take all the time he wants. It amounts to the fence. He's wondering if it's worth the chance to come over here and look behind the fence.

Sure, he's thinkin' maybe there's nothing behind the fence. And then he's thinkin', maybe there is, and if he makes the move he'll come out second best. Well, we'll just let him sweat it out. But we hope he decides to play it safe. We don't want no showdowns now. It's a cinch he wouldn't spill anything, not even with the gun pointing at his belly. You read his face, you know he ain't the type to spill.

What makes you say that? I mean, what do you know for sure? So all right, he tailed you from Grogan's house. But what else do you know about him? Before tonight, you never saw him; you never even heard his name. As it stacks up now, all you know is he wears working clothes and he's married to Lillian. And that's it, that's all—no, wait. There's one more thing—

I mean Lillian. She's hitched to this big good lookin' healthy lookin' man; but she ain't exactly jumpin' for joy. He's got polite manners and a pleasant smile and all that, but you know Lillian; at least you can read her to an extent. And what you read tonight was something on the minus side, something downright dismal.

Does that tell you anything? Not hardly. You'll just hafta sleep on it. That is, if you get any sleep tonight. The way it looks, it's stalemate and it's gonna stay that way until one of us moves.

Another minute passed. Then Kingsley turned slowly and faced toward Addison. He moved away from the alley entrance, and Corey heard his footsteps going toward Addison. The sound of the footsteps receded and then faded altogether. Corey waited another few minutes, decided it was all right now and climbed over the fence and headed down the alley toward Third. Some five minutes later he was in his room.

It was on the second floor of a rooming house a few blocks north of Addison. It was four and a half a week. As he came in, he saw the note from the landlady; she'd slipped it under the door. It stated that he owed thirteen-fifty and she was sick and tired of waiting for it. If she didn't get it before the end of the week she'd toss him out. He reached for his wallet, took out three fives, and folded the note around them, like an envelope. Feeling kindly toward the landlady, he went from the room down to the first floor and put the envelope under her door.

In bed, wearing only his shorts, he yawned a few times, then felt the sweat dripping down from his brow and his chin, and wished that a breeze would get started some-where and come through the window. It's an oven in here, he thought, then rolled over on his side and told himself to fall asleep. The damp sheet became damper and he kept changing his position and cursing without sound. Then gradually he drifted into sleep.

He slept for less than ten minutes. The noise of the knuckles hitting the door woke him.

He got out of bed and turned on the light. The gun was on the dresser and he picked it up, holding it loosely and looking at it as he heard the knocking again. He said, "Who is it?"

"Police."

"Whaddya want?"

"Open the door."

Corey opened the door, still holding the gun and step-ping back as two men walked into the room. They wore plain clothes, both were rather tall, and one was semi-bald. The other was dark-haired and sad-faced, with heavy shad-ows under sunken eyes. He gazed gloomily at the pistol in Corey's hand. He said, "What's the gun for?"

"General welfare."

"Put it away," the balding one said.

Corey had the gun pointed at them. He lowered it just a little but it was still ready. "Let's see the credentials."

They looked at each other. Then they took out their wallets and showed the badges clipped onto the leather. Corey leaned over and read the names on the identification cards. The semi-bald one was William Heeley. The other card read Louis Donofrio. Both names meant nothing to Corey, but he kept looking at the cards in the wallets. He was focusing on something stamped slantwise on the cards. His eyes burned and behind the burning there was freezing. The stamped lettering read "Night Squad."

Night Squad, he said to himself. And then, looking at the two men, "Night Squad?"

They didn't say anything. They stood waiting for him to put the gun away. Heeley showed his teeth and Donofrio looked very sad. Corey told himself not to mess with them; they were really Night Squad.

He put the gun in a dresser drawer and faced them and said, "You sure you got the right party?"

Heeley kept showing his teeth. "All right, let's check it. You Corey Bradford?"

He nodded slowly.

"Get dressed," Heeley said. Corey opened his mouth to say something and Heeley spoke through his teeth. "Just get dressed and don't ask no questions."

Corey started to put on his clothes. He was aching to ask them what they wanted him for, but again he reminded himself they were Night Squad and it didn't pay to tamper with them. Just go along with it, he told himself. You get involved with the Night Squad, there's no telling what they might do, even though they work from city hall and are listed officially as policemen.

But you know damn well what they really are. He was sitting on the edge of the bed, leaning over and tying his shoelaces. He was remembering editorials that referred to them as barbarians, and petitions circulated by various civic groups which had branded them butchers. On street corners and in various bars and poolrooms the local hustlers and hoodlums were always stiff with indignation as they talked about the Squad. "You get no breaks at all from them," some two-bit thug would say. "You know what they amount to? They're gangsters."

Now he was dressed and Donofrio opened the door and Heeley motioned him out. Again he wanted to ask what they wanted with him, and if it was any other branch of the police department he would have demanded to know what was happening. He grinned inside himself, genuinely amused at his own fright. He kept telling himself that this was the Night Squad.

Then they were outside and there was a car waiting. It wasn't a police car. Heeley got in behind the wheel. Then Donofrio climbed in and beckoned to Corey. So this puts me next to the door, Corey thought as he got in. If they were taking me in, they'd have me sitting in the middle. What goes here? What do they want?

The car moved off, made a turn onto Addison, stayed on Addison and crossed the bridge. There was no talk. Corey lit a cigarette and kept looking out the window as the car headed south on Banker Street going toward city hall. In the city hall courtyard Heeley parked the car next to a row of police cars. They got out and went into the hall and took the elevator up to the fifth floor.

It was room 529. A few squadmen were questioning a woman and two men. The woman was gasping with fear. The men were trying to hide their fright, but their faces were pale and one of them was beginning to tremble. Donofrio lit a cigarette and sat down on a bench near the window. Heeley pointed to the door of a side room and said to Corey, "In there."

Corey walked into the adjacent room. It was a small office with a single desk. An electric fan was whirring but it needed oiling. It didn't stir up much of a breeze and the man at the desk was perspiring. He was chunky, in his middle fifties. There was some white in his straw-colored hair and his face was seamed with deep lines. A few of the lines were scars. The right side of his face was a trifle out of line, and running down from the right eye almost to the lip there was a wide jagged scar. It wasn't a knife scar, Corey decided. It looked more on the cudgel side, as though some very heavy, blunt weapon had smashed into the man's face and split it wide open.

The man was wearing a short sleeve sport shirt and in places it was dark with sweat stains. He was rubbing his forearm across his sweat-dripping brow. "Close the door," he said to Corey. "Bring a chair over."

Corey closed the door, brought a chair near the desk and sat down. He saw that the man had mild grey eyes, and aside from the scars there was nothing hard about his face. He'd seen the man before, but he'd never been this close to him. It was surprising to see the mildness in the eyes, the softness in the lines of the mouth. The man had a reputation for brutality; it was said he was utterly merciless. He was Detective-Sergeant Henry McDermott, and he was head of the Night Squad.

Corey sat and waited. The only sound in the room was the slow whirring of the faulty electric fan.

McDermott sat slumped in his chair, looking off to the side as though Corey wasn't there. From the screenless window a fly came looping in, made tentative passes at the inkwell on the desk pad, then settled down on the desk top and rubbed its feelers contentedly. McDermott gazed at the fly; it stayed on the desk top. It seemed to be saying, don't mess with me and I won't mess with you. But the fly's presence was a challenge for the detective-sergeant and his eyes narrowed with strategy, his hand moving very slowly, closing in on the insect. Like any other fly, its policy was passive resistance. It didn't move. McDermott's cupped hand came down on it, scooped it up but didn't crush it, just held it in the space between bent fingers and palm. Then McDermott raised his closed hand, peeked through a gap between his fingers and said aloud to the fly, "That's the lesson for today. Class dismissed."

He opened his hand and the fly took off. It was wised up now, educated to the ways of the world, understanding fully that if you stroll in where there's happenings, you're gonna get involved. It flew toward the ceiling, saw there was no exit in that direction, then circled down and found the window and flew out.

Corey stood up.

"Sit down," McDermott said.

Corey remained standing. "Look, you wanna kill time, do it alone. It's half-past three in the morning and I wanna get some sleep."

"Sit down," McDermott said. "This is official."

"Then get to it," Corey said. "Don't play with me."

He sat down. McDermott was leafing through a stack of reports, taking out one from the top of the stack, glancing at it for a moment, then saying, "It says here you were attached to the 37th Precinct—plain-clothes man. Says you were fired from the force for accepting bribes. That right?"

"That's right," Corey said.

McDermott put the paper back on the stack. "Tell me about it."

"Why should I?"

McDermott grinned at him. "You getting tough?"

He grinned back. "Not yet."

Again it was quiet for some moments. Then McDermott said, "What bothers you, Bradford?"

"Not a thing." He went on grinning.

McDermott sighed and looked up at the ceiling. Then he frowned clinically and said, "I'm trying to connect with you, that's all." He looked at Corey. "Come on, lemme see that hole card."

"It ain't for inspection," Corey said. He held onto the grin. "You wanna check on me, they got it all on paper at the Hall of Records. You can start with my birth certificate."

"I've already done that," McDermott said. And something in his tone caused Corey to stiffen inwardly. Mc-Dermott seemed to sense the stiffening and his eyes narrowed just a little and he said, "You're thirty-four years old. You were born here in this city."

"So?"

But McDermott went on with it. "Your mother's name was Ethel. She died when you were seven."

"So? So?"

"Your father's name was Matthew. He died before you were born. He was a policeman."

Corey blinked a few times. He squirmed slightly. He felt a twinge very high on his thigh near his groin. It was only for an instant, it faded before he could wonder about it. But in that instant his eyes were shut tightly, his mouth tight and twisted with something close to pain.

But now he grinned again at McDermott. He said, "Go on, I'm listening."

"He was a policeman."

"You said that already."

"I want you to hear it again. He was a policeman."

Corey mixed the grin with a scowl. "Whatever hurts you, Sergeant, you really got it bad."

McDermott smiled softly, almost tenderly. "I guess that makes two of us," he murmured. And then abruptly the smile faded and his voice was crisp and technical. "All right, here it is. I heard the talk about that party tonight, with them two hoods barging in and showing guns and so forth. The talk is, you stopped the show and you did it very fancy. So that gets me to thinking—"

"Forget it," Corey said.

McDermott didn't seem to hear him. "I'm working with six men, and I need a seventh."

"Just forget it," Corey said. He stood up and started toward the door. Then something stopped him. He was thinking in terms of fifteen thousand dollars. Specifically he was thinking that in order to maneuver toward the fifteen thousand, he needed a certain tool.

That certain tool was the badge.

He heard the detective-sergeant saying, "You wanna be reinstated?"

He nodded slowly.

There was the scraping sound of wood against wood as McDermott opened a desk drawer. Then there was the clinking sound of metal hitting wood. Corey turned his head and saw it shining on the desk top. Before he knew what he was doing he reached for the badge and when he had it in his hand he stared at it.

"And here's your card," McDermott said.

Corey took the card. He saw his name typed under the printed designation, police department, and stamped slant-wise across the card was the lettering. It read "Night Squad."

Corey muttered, "You had me reinstated before you knew I'd say yes." He looked at the detective-sergeant. "What made you so sure I'd say yes?"

"I wasn't sure," McDermott said. "I was just hoping you would."

"That grooves it sorta deep," Corey muttered. "What this all amounts to, you got some special reason for wanting me on the squad."

McDermott didn't reply to that. He sat motionless for some moments; then got up from the desk chair and moved toward the window. He stood at the window with his back to Corey Bradford. There's something missing, Corey thought. There's something missing here, all right.

The detective-sergeant turned and went back to the desk. He didn't sit down. He gazed at the desk top and said, "There's a job I want done. It's a big one. It's the biggest on our list. We been on it for years and we're nowhere. I'm thinking maybe you can handle it."

"Why me?"

Again McDermott was quiet for a long spell. He gazed down at the desk top. Finally he said, "We know who we want but we can't move. We got nothing on him. He's listed as a solid citizen, honest tax-payer and respected member of the community and so forth. He's got money, he's got connections, he's got a lot of people scared. The ones he couldn't scare, you don't see around no more. You don't see them because they're in boxes; buried."

Corey stiffened slightly.

"What we need is evidence," McDermott said. "We need tangible proof that he's a lawbreaker. And I don't mean jaywalking. It's gotta be something big and it's gotta be airtight and—what's the matter?"

Corey was shaking his head.

"What's the matter?" McDermott said. "You backing out? You don't wanna know who he is? You afraid to know?"

That just about says it, Corey told himself.

The detective-sergeant spoke very softly. "You got the

jitters, there's no use talking further. We'll call it off and you can walk out."

Corey moved his hand toward the trousers pocket where he'd put the badge and the card. His hand went in and he told himself to take out the badge and the card and toss them onto the desk and go for the door. Do it, he begged himself. Get out while the getting is good. Like that fly got out. That fly who didn't hafta be told twice.

His hand moved deeper into his pocket and came in contact with the metal of the badge. In that instant he felt a twinge very high on his thigh near his groin.

He grimaced. He took his hand from his pocket and there was nothing in his hand. He heard himself saying, "All right, I'll go to work on it. Who is he?"

"I'm trusting you with this," McDermott said. "You come in on this, you're in all the way. You're under oath—"

"All right, all right," Corey cut in irritably, impatiently. "Lemme have it. Who is he?"

McDermott said quietly, matter-of-factly, "His name is Walter Grogan."

5

It was ten minutes later and Corey sat in the rear of a taxi headed toward the Swamp. He asked the driver what time it was and the driver said twenty after four. Then the driver yawned. The taxi was moving very slowly and the driver steered with one hand, his free arm resting languidly across the top of the backrest. Ahead a signal light showed green and the driver made no effort to get through it before it flashed red. But when it was red the taxi went past it. A milk truck was crossing the intersection and the truck and the taxi almost collided. The driver of the truck leaned out and yelled, "You louse!" and the taxi driver waved wearily and said, "Go shove it—" and then let out another yawn.

"You sleepy?" Corey asked the taxi driver.

The driver didn't answer. The taxi was crawling, doing less than twenty miles per hour.

"You wanna sleep, do it in bed," Corey said.

The driver turned and looked at him.

"You heard me," Corey said.

Facing the windshield, the driver muttered, "I like when they tell me how to drive."

"You call this driving?"

The driver gave him another look. "Why don't you relax?"

"All right," Corey smiled dimly. "Let's both relax."

The taxi made a turn. Corey saw two tiny points of light sliding across the rearview mirror, then vanishing. Some moments later the points of light showed again in the rear-view mirror. The taxi made another turn and it happened again.

The driver said, "I'm not hard to get along with. I'm just tired, that's all."

"Look, I'm not pushing you," Corey said mildly. "Just get me there, all right?"

"Sure." The driver sat up straighter and steered with both hands. The taxi picked up to thirty miles per hour. The rearview mirror showed two tiny points of light. The taxi made a turn; the points of light faded from view. Corey waited to see it again and it showed again. Now the taxi was nearing the bridge that connected the city with the Swamp. In the rearview mirror the twin lights were the eyes of a goblin saying, peek-a-boo, I see you. And then, crossing the bridge, the interior of the taxi was slashed with the ribboned reflections of the bridge lights and it interfered with the pattern in the mirror. Corey turned and looked through the rear window and saw the headlights far behind. The taxi was doing thirty-five. He said to the driver, "Slow down just a little."

"What's the matter now?"

"Just slow down. Not too much."

The taxi continued across the bridge at a little over twenty-five miles per hour. Corey looked back at the headlights of the other car. The distance between the two cars remained the same.

Then the taxi came off the bridge and onto Addison Avenue and Corey said, "Make a turn. That next little street."

"You said Fourth and—"

"Forget that," Corey said. "Just make the turn."

"Left or right?"

"Either way."

As the taxi made the turn onto the narrow side street, the driver said, "What's happening here? What the hell's happening?"

"Don't worry about it," Corey said. Just then he saw the headlights of the other car showing in the rearview mirror. Against his side he could feel the pressure of the police pistol, issued to him just before he'd walked out of Room 529 in city hall. The pistol was loaded and for a moment he allowed his fingers to glide along the leather of the holster under his shirt. The taxi was slightly more than halfway down the narrow street and he looked at the meter and saw it read a dollar-twenty. He said to the driver, "Stop here."

The taxi came to a stop. Corey gave the driver two dollars and got out of the taxi, slowly, not looking backward. The driver started to hand him the change and he said, "That's all right."

"Thanks." The driver looked as if he was caught between worry and curiosity. Then it was only worry, and he was in a hurry to get away. He faced forward, his grip tight on the steering wheel. The taxi moved off.

There were no lampposts and no lit windows along the narrow street. The only glow was the light from the headlights of the car which came slowly toward Corey as he walked near the curb. His back was to the car. It's like a shell-game, he thought. You pick up the wrong shell, you're done. And the odds are always two-to-one against you. At least two-to-one, that is. In this case it's more like fifty-to-one. But that's the gamble you gotta take. There just ain't no other way to play this deal.

He kept walking along, near the curb. He heard the engine of the car coming closer. The glare of the headlights splashed onto him but he still kept his back to the car. Then the car moved up alongside Corey and came to a stop. A voice said, "Hello, Corey."

He turned and looked. There were two men in the car. He recognized them, members of Grogan's outfit. Earlier tonight they'd been in the poker game in the backroom of the Hangout.

"Hello," he said, and started to walk on.

"Wait, Corey. We wanna talk to you."

He stopped. They got out of the car and came toward him. One of them was medium sized and long jawed, an ex-con in his middle thirties named Macy. The other was tall and close to fifty, also an ex-con and a former minor league ball player who still kept himself in shape. His name was Lattimore. They were both specialists in strong arm and liquidation and they took their occupation very seriously. These ain't the ordinary hoodlums, Corey thought. These are the experts.

They were standing very close to him. Lattimore said, "We seen you gettin' out of a taxi. Where were you comin' from?"

"City hall."

Macy leaned in toward him. "How come city hall? What were you doing in city hall?"

"They took me in for questioning."

"About what?"

"Them hoods," Corey said. "The ones we handled tonight at the Hangout."

Macy turned to Lattimore. "Whaddya say?"

"I'm satisfied," Lattimore said.

"Same here," Macy muttered. He smiled at Corey, a tinge of apology in his tone as he said, "You understand, don't you? It's part of the business. We gotta check all the moves."

"I understand."

"Good boy," Macy said, and went on smiling at him and patted him on the shoulder. Then Macy turned away.

"See you later, Corey," Lattimore said.

"Later," Corey said. And just when he wasn't expecting the move, it came. It had all of Lattimore's talent and experience behind it, the timing perfect, the gauging accurate, and no wasted motion. Lattimore's hands held Corey's wrists, Corey's right arm pulled up high, bent behind his back, his left arm stretched out to the side. Lattimore forced him to his knees as Macy pivoted with the move and came in fast for the frisking. Corey told himself to accept it, there was nothing to do but accept it. He felt Macy's hand going under his shirt, saw Macy's hand coming out with the police pistol. Macy looked at the police pistol, then looked at Corey and smiled. The smile widened as Macy's other hand hit Corey's trousers pocket and then went in and came out with the badge and the card. Macy's smile was very wide as he looked at the card. He held it up for Lattimore to see. The parked car's glowing headlights seemed to spotlight the card, to focus directly on the words stamped slantwise: "Night Squad."

"Let him up," Macy said.

Lattimore released Corey's wrists. Corey, his knees on the pavement, now lifted himself slowly, grimacing slightly as he rubbed his right arm. He wondered if some of the ligaments were torn. From his shoulder to his elbow it felt as though white hot wires were twisted and knotted along the inside of his arm.

Macy continued to smile at him. The three of them stood there for a long moment, Lattimore behind Corey. Then Macy said to Lattimore, "Put a rod on him. Let him feel it."

Corey sighed, looking down at the pavement and shaking his head slowly. He felt the muzzle of the gun pressing against his back, a little to the side of his spine. "Let's move it," Lattimore said, and they walked toward the car.

In the car, Macy took the wheel, Corey and Lattimore sat in the back. Lattimore was sitting sideways, displaying the gun and holding it aimed at Corey's chest. They sat at opposite sides of the seat, and Corey was slumped forward with his hands loose in his lap. The car moved slowly along the narrow street.

Nothing you can do, Corey told himself. You had a chance to do something and you let it slide past. I mean you coulda got rid of the badge and the card and the police pistol before you climbed outta the taxi. But you didn't figure on a frisk, and it's a cinch you didn't figure it was Grogan's people. Grogan said the deal was just him and yourself and the way he said it you were sure he meant it. And the weird thing is, you still believe that he meant it. Or maybe that's just confusion in your head. Maybe if you'd straighten out your thinking you could add this up and see it for what it is.

The car made a left hand turn. Corey looked up and he frowned slightly. He knew it ought to be a right hand turn if they were going to Grogan's. Some moments later the car made another turn and he told himself it didn't look as though they were going to Grogan's.

He said, "Where you takin' me?"

They didn't reply.

"At least you can tell me." He put a whine into his voice.

"Tell him," Macy said, and looked over his shoulder at Lattimore. "Go on, tell him."

Lattimore spoke softly to Corey. "It's the windup."

"What?"

"You're done," Lattimore said. "We seen that badge and we seen that card and the card reads Night Squad. That's all we hadda see."

"But it ain't like you think," Corey said. "If you'll take me to Grogan—"

"We can't do that," Lattimore cut in. "Not on this particular deal. On this particular deal we ain't workin' for Grogan."

Corey waited a long moment. And then, very quietly, "You're with the other outfit?"

"That's right."

"Then take me to the boss man."

"That wouldn't help you none," Lattimore said. "And besides, he's got a nasty disposition. Likes to hear screams. At least from us you'll get it fast."

The car was moving slowly, going down the bumpy slope. The slope gave way to a vacant lot. On one side there was a warehouse with most of its windows broken. It looked out of business. On the other side a concrete pier had most of its concrete chipped away, the pier office just about ready to fall apart. The vacant lot was littered with rubbish and there were some deep, muddy crevices near the edge of the river. The car crossed the crevices and came to a stop just a few feet away from the edge of the river.

Macy shut the engine and climbed out. Lattimore said to Corey, "All right, move."

"Jesus Christ," Corey said, giving Lattimore a pleading look.

"Go on, move," Lattimore said, pointing the gun at Corey's throat.

Corey sat there and intensified the pleading look. "Gimme a break. Cantcha gimme a break?"

"No," Lattimore said.

Corey shut his eyes tightly, as though trying to keep from weeping. "I can't go through with it—"

"You'll go through with it," Lattimore said.

Corey kept his eyes shut and let out a groan.

"Get outta the car," Lattimore said.

Corey groaned again and remained sitting there. Then he lowered his head and covered his eyes with his hands.

Macy was standing near the front fender and he called to Lattimore, "What's all the delay?"

"He's cracking up."

"Get him outta there," Macy said.

Lattimore leaned close to Corey and put the muzzle of the gun against his neck. His other hand clenched and sent in a kidney punch. Corey grunted, gasped and groaned again.

"Open the door and get out," Lattimore said. "I'm not gonna tell you again."

Corey sat there. He let out a sob. Lattimore moved close, punching him again in the kidney, then shifting the gun so that he held it by the barrel. Lattimore raised the gun and aimed the butt at the side of Corey's head. Bent very low, Corey had his eyes halfway open. Looking to the side and seeing the gun's butt raised and coming down, he rolled sideways, going inside the arc of the clubbing weapon, his elbow bashing Lattimore in the testicles. Lattimore let out a scream but didn't let go of the gun. He tried to shift it in his hand to get his finger on the trigger. Corey used the elbow again, driving it into the same place, and then with both hands took the gun away from Lattimore. At that moment Macy was at the car window and aimed a gun at Corey's head. Both guns went off at the same instant. Macy stood outside the car window with a red-black cavity gushing bright red where his left eye had been. As he stood there he died, and then on rigid legs he went sliding down sideways, out of sight under the car window.

There was no sound from Lattimore. Corey turned and saw the tall ex-con sitting with his head thrown far back, his mouth and eyes wide open. There was a bullet hole in his chest. The slug from Macy's gun had gone through his heart.

Corey opened the door and got out of the car. Now Macy's corpse was face down in a deep muddy crevice. Corey turned the corpse over, went through the pockets, and took back the badge and the card and the police pistol. Then he used his handkerchief to wipe his prints off Lattimore's gun. He leaned inside the car and put the gun in Lattimore's hand, forcing Lattimore's fingers onto the butt and barrel. When he let go of Lattimore's hand the gun slipped loose and fell onto the seat at the side of the dead man.

That should do it, Corey thought. That sets it up so they shot each other. You sure you want it that way? Well for Christ's sake of course you want it that way. You can't do it no other way. I mean if you were a policeman you'd call in and make a report, but the deal is you're not a policeman.

The badge was in his hand; he looked at it. As matters stand, he said to himself, that is to say according to the records, you're a policeman, you're a member of the Night Squad.

The badge's shining face looked up at him and said, that's correct.

He said to the badge, you go to hell. You don't tell me nothing.

Then he said to himself, now look, let's get it straight once and for all. You're a member of only one organization. It's got only this one member and it's known as the Friends of Corey Bradford.

You slimy worm, the badge said. You zero you—

Get outta my way, he said to the badge, and quickly slipped it into his pocket. But as he walked away he could feel its weight. He grimaced with discomfort and the weight of the badge was heavier. He tried to pull his thoughts away from it; but it continued talking to him.

In his room the going was easier. He opened the small closet and found some loose boards in the wall. He took out the boards, arranging a place of concealment for the badge and the card and the police pistol. He put the boards back in position and then got undressed and climbed into bed.

As he drifted into sleep, the only thought in his mind was the bonus money offered by Grogan—the fifteen thousand dollars.

6

He slept until two in the afternoon. At 2:10 he was seated at the counter of a hash house on Addison. The counter girl had served him a cinnamon bun and coffee. He was biting into the bun when a voice beside him said, "The problem for today is nourishment."

Corey turned his head. It was the little man, Carp. His sparse black hair was slicked down sideways with cheap pomade. The high starched collar was ripped at the edges and the rummage-sale clothing showed several patches. The jacket was a thick woolen material, the wearer seemingly unmindful of the 90° weather. Corey muttered, "Don't know how you can stand it. You ain't even sweating."

"I'm too busy starving," Carp said. "It's a state of affairs known as stark malnutrition."

"You really want food?" Corey muttered. "I thought you live on alcohol."

"The needs of the body are various," Carp said. He looked down along the counter, his eyes aiming cravingly at the heaping plate of lamb stew that the counter girl was serving to a customer. He called to her, "How much is lamb stew, Terese?"

"Thirty-five cents."

"Including the bread?"

"That's right," Terese said.

"Excellent," Carp said. "Excellent in all respects." He looked at Corey. "Except I lack the necessary funds."

Corey sighed. He called to Terese, telling her to bring Carp a plate of lamb stew.

"A truly noble gesture," Carp said. "It calls for an expression of gratitude. Or let's say a favor in return."

"A favor?" Corey glanced sideways at the little man. "I don't need no favors."

"That's debatable," Carp said. He called to Terese, "I'll have the beverage later, if you please. A demitasse." And then, aloud to himself, "Let's hope and pray it's in the proper cup. The proper cup for a demitasse is pure white porcelain, paper thin."

Corey frowned at him. "You got something you wanna tell me?"

Carp didn't answer. He was gazing into a small mirror, stained and cracked, set against some cereal boxes behind the counter. Carefully appraising his appearance in the mirror, he smoothed his greasy hair and adjusted his scraggly necktie. Terese arrived with the lamb stew and bread. Carp picked up the fork, holding it delicately with his little finger curved daintily. Tasting the lamb stew, he nodded slowly and approvingly, then took another taste and frowned carefully like a gourmet. "Perhaps a dash of thyme, to give it nobility. And a mere suggestion of marjoram—"

Terese shook her head hopelessly and turned away. Carp continued to eat the lamb stew; using a delicate gourmet style as he manipulated the fork from platter to mouth, then deftly broke bread. His etiquette was perfect as he paused now and then to apply the paper napkin to his lips. There was nothing affected in the performance, and it seemed to Corey that the little man was utterly oblivious of the impression he created. It just comes natural to him, Corey thought. As if he was born and raised in a high class setup. Come to think of it, them big words he sometimes uses, it gives you the notion he musta went to some fancy school, I mean it's the way he pronounces them words—

Carp finished the lamb stew, called to Terese and gave her precise instructions for the preparation of the demitasse. At first she told him to come out of the clouds, then decided to go along with it and served him the black coffee in a small toothpick container. He sipped it very slowly, savouring the flavor and nodding appreciatively to Terese. She muttered, through her teeth, "It pleases you, sir?"

"It's delightful," Carp said.

"Thank you, sir," Terese said. "I'm so glad it meets with your approval, sir."

She went off to serve another customer. Carp took a few more sips of black coffee. And then, without looking at Corey, he murmured, "You understand the issues involved?"

"What issues?" Corey frowned.

Carp turned and looked at him and didn't say anything.

"Come on, come on," Corey said. "You got a point to make, make it."

"I intend to do that," Carp said. "But first I must establish my position. I wish to cooperate in every way possible."

There was a long silence. Corey decided there was no use trying to guess what the little man had in mind. The little man was a walking question mark. No one knew Carp's age or anything at all about his background or what he did with his time when he wasn't snatching drinks off the bar at the Hangout. The only known facts concerning Carp were that he'd come to the Swamp about four years ago, drifting in with the fog from the river. Another lost soul with nothing in his eyes and nothing in his pockets. Until now Corey had never given a thought to the why and the wherefore of this particular Swampcat; but as he studied Carp's eyes he felt uneasy. He muttered with a touch of annoyance, "Don't gimme the buddy-buddy routine. Whatever it is, just state the terms."

"It calls for an agreement of mutual trust and confidence."

"Concerning—?"

Carp leaned a little closer to Corey, his voice close to a whisper. "If you've heard the talk, you already know."

Corey stiffened. He said quietly, "I ain't heard no talk."

"According to talk, they shot each other," Carp said. "They were found on a vacant lot near the river."

Corey gazed past the little man. His lips scarcely moved as he said, "Do I know the people?"

"You know the people," Carp said. "We both know the people. It was Mr. Macy and Mr. Lattimore."

Corey kept gazing off to one side. He said to himself, you're dealing with a manipulator. Whatever else he is, he's a slick manipulator and I have a feeling this is gonna cost you some U.S. currency.

He heard Carp saying, "At present, my living quarters are on Marion Street."

Corey blinked a few times. Marion Street was where the taxi had come to a stop and he'd climbed out and the headlights of the other car had come closer and closer.

"I'm a rather light sleeper," Carp said. "The slightest noise and I'm awake. In this case it was the noise of an automobile. I came to the window and saw you getting out of the taxi. Then I saw the other car. Shall we have more coffee?"

Corey nodded. Carp called to Terese. She served the refills and went away. Then Carp said, "I watched it from the window, from the second floor. At first they just stood there and asked you some questions. Then Mr. Lattimore grabbed you and forced you to your knees and held you there while Mr. Macy went through your pockets. I'm relating this in detail so you'll know I saw it as it happened."

Corey spooned some sugar into his coffee. He stirred it very slowly.

The little man said, "What Mr. Macy took from your pockets was a pistol and some kind of identification card and a shiny metal object shaped something like a badge. I assume that's what it was, a badge, a police badge."

"You got good eyes," Corey said. He was gazing down at the coffee cup. "You check them items from a second floor window, you got damn good eyes."

"Of course I couldn't read the printing on the card," Carp said matter-of-factly. "You understand I'm only guessing it was an identification card. If I'm not mistaken, there were words stencilled diagonally across the card. Or maybe it wasn't stencilling. Maybe the words were applied to the card with a rubber stamp."

"That's right," Corey said. "The words were stamped."

"I perceived two words," Carp said. "Each word had five letters. From that distance I couldn't make out the lettering."

Corey kept looking down at the coffee cup.

Carp leaned very close. "What were the two words?"

"If I tell you, you're in hot water," Corey said. Then he looked at the little man. "I think you're in hot water already."

But Carp looked dry and cool and his tone remained matter-of-fact. "What were the two words?"

"Night Squad."

Carp showed no reaction. It was as though he hadn't heard it. He said, "I saw them putting you in the car. Then the car drove away. It occurred to me I wouldn't see you around anymore. Then today I heard some talk that Mr. Macy and Mr. Lattimore have dispensed with each other. At any rate, that's the accepted theory."

Corey smiled lazily. He aimed the smile at the coffee cup. He sighed sadly. You feel sorry for Carp? he asked himself. You feel sorry for this little man because he knows too much? Or maybe you feel sorry for yourself. Could be this deal winds up with you the loser.

He heard Carp saying, "As to what actually happened, I have my own theory."

"Let's hear it," Corey murmured, still smiling down at the coffee cup.

Carp said, "I don't think Mr. Macy and Mr. Lattimore shot each other. I'm quite sure it didn't happen that way. It's my conclusion that you did the shooting."

Corey widened the smile just a trifle. He gave Carp a side glance, then looked again at the coffee cup.

"I'm positive you did the shooting," Carp said. "And yet, I must admit, I'm rather puzzled. It stands to reason you did it in self-defense, that's one factor. The other factor is, you're a policeman. It would seem that you'd report the matter. I'm wondering why you didn't report it."

"You wanna report it?"

"I can't do that," Carp said.

"Yes you can." Corey gestured idly toward the pay phone on the wall near the door. "All you hafta do is make a call. Just ask for the police. Then tell them what you saw last night."

"But I can't do that," Carp said solemnly. "It's against my principles."

"What principles?" The smile faded from Corey's face. He turned and looked at the little man. "What are you giving me here?"

"I'm not an informer."

"You're not an informer providing you get paid to keep your mouth closed."

Carp looked off to one side. "You embarrass me."

"Yeah, I know. You feel awful about it. So what's your price?"

Carp sighed heavily. "What a world we live in."

"Come on. We're talking business. What's this gonna cost me?"

"Nothing," Carp said. "Nothing at all."

Corey winced. "Say what?"

The little man shrugged and said, "I was offering friendship and trust and confidence. Such things are priceless commodities. I thought perhaps you'd understand."

"You gotta be kidding," Corey frowned. "Or maybe I'm on another track. I just don't get this line of talk."

Carp sighed again. He turned away and started toward the door. Corey stood there frowning, then darted toward the little man and took hold of his arm and spoke in a whisper through tightened teeth, "Let's check this once, just to get it straight. You see anything last night? You hear any noise that got'cha outta bed and made you look out the window?"

"Not that I can recall," Carp said.

"That's good," Corey hissed softly. "Keep it that way."

"You needn't worry," the little man said. His voice was toneless, yet a certain dignity was on the edge of it. The unspoken message came across: it isn't because you scare me; nothing scares me, really. I can't even feel your grip on my arm. All I can feel is pity for your troubled soul. You must be very deeply troubled. You can't believe that anyone would extend a helping hand for no purpose other than trying to help. Well anyway, I tried.

Corey released the little man's arm. For a moment they stood looking at each other. Then Carp said, "Thank you for the luncheon, it was most enjoyable," turned away and walked out of the diner.

About fifteen minutes later, Corey entered the seething, sweating mass of Saturday afternoon drinkers at the Hangout. He looked for an empty spot at the bar, but knew there was no use looking. It was the same at the tables, and the standees were packed in close, jostling the sitters. He heard Nellie cursing. Then came a sound like a .38 as her open palm connected with the face of someone who talked long and talked wrong. Turning to look, Corey saw the man sailing away from the bar, leaving a space open at the bar rail. Corey moved fast, put a foot on the bar rail and an elbow on the bar, and ordered a double gin.

The gin came; he put it away in one fast gulp and ordered another. There were times when he drank slowly and chased the gin with water. But this ain't one of them times, he told himself, downing the second gin and ordering a third. This is a time for heavy thinking, which means, of course, heavy drinking. And I got the notion it's gonna take a lotta gin to set your mind straight.

Or maybe that ain't what you want at all. What I mean is, if you really wanna concentrate, you wouldn't be needing the gin. Might as well say it like it is. It's actually the other way around; it's the gin that keeps you from thinking and that's the only reason you're drinking. What it all amounts to, things are piling up on you all of a sudden and you wanna get that load off your brain; wash it away; flood it out with alcohol.

He pushed the empty shot glass toward the bartender. The refill came and he poured it down his throat. While he waited for the liquor to hit him, another hitter got there first, an invisible finger nudging him, gently urging him to turn his head. He turned slowly, not fully knowing why. For an instant he focused on an empty wall, and then gazed blankly at the door leading to the back room. The invisible finger kept nudging and his head kept turning. Finally he was looking at the table in the far corner near the door leading to the back room.

She sat at the table, alone, drinking beer. Her head was lowered as she set the glass on the table and reached slowly for the quart-size bottle. That ain't nothin', he told himself. That's just another thirsty skirt who likes to sit alone and drink beer. Ain't a damn thing there for you to look at.

But he went on looking at Lillian. The invisible finger was pointing at her and saying, there she is, that's your wife.

You better check the calendar, he said to the unseen pointer. That broad ain't been my wife for a long time. That broad and me, we're a long way off from each other.

Then why you lookin' at her?

He didn't try to answer that. He sat looking, as though there were no other faces in the room. The feeling in his chest hit harder than the gin hitting his head. He said to himself, we get just one short life to live, and ain't it a wonder the way we louse it up? The deals we make, it adds up, I swear, to one big joke that gets no laughs at all.

You come right down to it, there's some of us who oughta be wearin' dunce caps seven days a week. We're like them double-jointed clowns who got that special talent for twistin' themselves all around so they finally kick their own teeth. But this don't hurt in the teeth. This hurts in the blood, and it hurts real bad in the thing that pumps the blood.

"Fill it," he said to the bartender. When the gin came he drank it with his eyes shut tightly, grimacing in a kind of anguish and surrender, as though he was drinking cyanide.

Quit lookin' at her, he shouted at himself. You got no right to look at her. That woman is another man's wife. And even if she wasn't, you still wouldn't have the right. You ain't in her league, that's why. She's a good clean package and you're nothin' but a Swampcat with dirty claws, a double-dealin' operator who only knows from cagey capers, angles—

"Perchance a wine?" from a mild voice at his side, and before he looked he knew it was Carp. But the little man was speaking to someone else, a tall, lean sun-darkened construction worker who preferred to show his money on the bar, a ten and two fives and a flock of ones.

"A wine, perchance?" Carp coaxed again. The construction worker looked down at the little man and said, "Don't bother me, and that's final." Carp sighed wistfully, gazing at the man's money and said aloud, "A wine, a whiskey, or any nectar at all to spread some cheer—"

"I said don't bother me," the construction worker muttered. He raised his hand to strike Carp, aiming a backhand blow that didn't go anywhere. He stared with amazement at Corey's fingers gripping his wrist, then stared at Corey's face and said, "Who asked for you?"

"Let it ride," Corey said. He released the man's wrist, began to turn away, then felt the hard tug as the man pulled him around. The man leaned toward him and gritted, "You wanna get your face pushed in?"

Corey smiled lazily. His eyes were half-closed. He didn't say anything.

The construction worker lifted a hard-muscled arm and showed Corey a big fist. "You see this? You know what it can do?"

"No," Corey said. "Show me."

"You really want it, dontcha?" The construction worker spoke louder now, and stepped back to give himself room. Corey didn't move. A moment passed and nothing happened, except that the construction worker was studying Corey's eyes, his own eyes blinking and his expression somewhat uneasy. Then without saying anything he faced away from Corey, bending low over the bar and staring past a double rye.

Carp still stood there, placidly rubbing his hands together, like a fly rubbing its feelers. Over the top of the little man's head Corey saw Lillian getting up from the table and starting toward the side door. In his brain he pressed a button that had no connection with a woman named Lillian, the name on the button was Delbert Kingsley.

The button was wired to the deal last night in the alley off Second Street, when he hid behind the fence and saw the face of Delbert Kingsley, the man's eyes scanning the alley.

He took hold of Carp's shoulders and turned the little man so that he faced the side door. At that moment Lillian was approaching the door. Corey said to Carp, "You see that dame? The one walking out? You know her?"

Carp shook his head.

"That offer you made," Corey said. "That trust and friendship. You wanna prove it?"

"Most assuredly," the little man said.

"Follow her," Corey murmured. "Find out where she lives."

Carp glided away. As he neared the side door, he lifted someone's double bourbon. Nellie made a try for him and he slithered away from her clutching hands. He was gulping bourbon as he exited from the taproom.

Corey turned and faced the bar. He ordered more gin. But when it arrived he didn't grab for it. He reached for it slowly and then sipped it absently, not really needing it any more. His thinking was all mechanical; he was telling himself that these were working hours and he ought to be working. He ought to be making a report to his employer.

He finished the gin and walked from the Hangout and headed north on Second Street, going toward Grogan's house.

His finger pressed the doorbell. It was the fourth time he'd pressed it. Now he kept his finger on the button. Finally the door opened and a girl wearing a maid's uniform with the collar ripped and her dark hair mussed stood there breathing hard, her eyes wet. She was in her early twenties and there was something Far Eastern in her features. He guessed she was East Indian. On the slim side, her hips very narrow, she seemed just a bit too fragile for whatever action had caused the tears. As he looked closer, he saw a cut near the corner of her mouth. It was bleeding slightly.

"Yes?" she murmured, looking away from him while pressing a fingertip against her cut lip. "What is you want, please?"

"Mr. Grogan."

"You are who?"

"Bradford."

"Bradford what? You give me full name, please. You tell me—"

From behind the girl, fingers pulled at her and she was yanked backward, then shoved aside. Now Lita was standing in the doorway, the platinum hair only slightly out of place, the dark green eyes tiny green-yellow torches. She was wearing a two-piece outfit that left her midriff bare. It was a pale green silk halter and toreador pants. "Very nice," Corey murmured, looking at her navel.

"What do you want?" Lita asked impatiently. She seemed anxious to get back to her discussion with the girl.

"Is he here?" Corey asked.

"He's occupied right now. He's upstairs."

"So I'll wait. I'll just come in and wait. I can wait a few minutes."

"It'll be longer than that," she said.

"How long?"

"At least an hour."

"What's he doin'?"

She didn't answer. She glanced backward at the East Indian girl. The girl was leaning against the wall of the vestibule, making whimpering noises.

"You wait," Lita promised her. "You just wait." And then to Corey, "Look, I can't talk to you now. Can't be bothered—"

She tried to close the door but he kept his hand against it. He said, "What happens upstairs?"

She heaved an exasperated sigh. "If you must know," she said, "he's getting an irrigation."

"A what?"

"An irrigation," she said. "A high colonic."

Corey thought about that for a moment. The gin he'd consumed was swirling in his head and he heard himself saying, "That ain't what he needs."

Lita stiffened. She breathed in through her teeth and made a hissing noise.

"You know what he needs," Corey said. "He needs it and he ain't getting it."

She studied him. She said, "You've been drinking."

"That's right."

"You're drunk."

"Just a little."

She smiled thinly, contemptuously. "You don't amount to much, do you?"

Corey grinned. "That calls for another drink. You got anything to drink?"

"You've had enough," she said. And then, turning away

from him, as though he had no importance, no meaning at all, she released her hold on the door. Corey opened it wider and walked in.

As Corey passed through the vestibule, the East Indian girl made a move toward the open doorway. Corey looked back and saw Lita reach out and grab the girl's wrist.

"Please no. Please," the girl said. Lita pulled her away from the door, then kicked the door shut and shoved the girl through the vestibule. The girl bumped into Corey, they both staggered backward into the parlor and the girl fell to her knees.

Corey bent over to help her up. Lita quickly came in and pushed him aside. The gin was rocking him now and he looked for a place to sit down. He lurched across the expensive Chinese rug and fell into the ebony armchair near the massive bronze Buddha. On the floor around the Buddha there was an overturned jade lamp, the pieces of a broken vase, an ashtray upside down and scattered cigarette stubs and ashes. Corey turned his head and looked at the Buddha, as though expecting some comment from the impassive bronze face. The slit eyes of the Buddha had nothing to offer except the soundless utterance, problems of the earth not mine these days. Am merely an observer.

We'll go along with that, Corey decided. The gin was throwing left hooks at his senses. He leaned back, his legs sprawled. Through gin-clouded vision he saw Lita and the girl. They were moving around considerably. A chair was knocked over. Then another chair fell over. The girl cringed under Lita's upraised arm.

"You no can do this," the girl whined. "You no have right to do this."

Lita's arm came down and the girl blocked the blow with crossed open hands. Lita used her other arm and her fist hit the girl on the shoulder. The girl went down on her side, rolled over and got to her feet and dodged another blow. She couldn't dodge the next one. It caught her on the temple and she fell sideways, then landed on the rug sitting down. She sat there weeping softly, her face in her hands. Lita aimed another blow with her fist, then seemed to change her mind and looked around the room, finally focusing on the brass-ornamented fireplace. In a holder there was an intricately carved brass poker, its handle a dragon's head. Lita crossed to the fireplace and picked up the poker and tried the weight of it in her hand. She said to the girl, "Now tell me the truth."

"Is like I say before," the girl wept. She started to get up from the floor. Lita moved quickly with the poker raised high. The girl sat down again and covered her head with her arms.

"You're a thief," Lita said.

"Why you call me a thief? I no take nothing."

"Perfume."

"What perfume?"

"A five-ounce bottle," Lita said. "Thirty dollars an ounce."

The girl looked up, bewildered. She shook her head slowly. She said, "Is wrong for you to say this. Is very unfair—"

"You went out last night. You sneaked out."

"Is like I say before."

"I don't want to hear that," Lita said. "You'll tell me why you went out."

"To go for walk," the girl wailed. "Is like I say before. To go for walk."

"At half-past four in the morning?"

"I no could sleep. Too hot in room. No could stay in bed."

"Keep telling me that and you'll stay in bed for a month, in a cast."

"You no can do this. Is not right."

Lita swung the brass poker and it came down on the girl's back just below her shoulders. The girl yowled, fell forward and was face down on the floor as Lita raised the poker again. Corey got up from the chair and lunged forward. Then he had the poker in his hand and tossed it onto the floor behind him. Lita grabbed for the poker but he blocked her path.

"Get away," she hissed. "You're not in this."

He smiled lazily. His eyes said, don't come any closer.

She stepped back. It wasn't retreat. She was coiled, her arms bent stiffly and her fingers hooked, the fingernails aiming. Then she came at him with the fingernails going for his eyes.

He caught her wrists. She brought up her knee, trying for his groin. He pulled away and she tried again and came close, then made another try. This time it was closer and he let go of her wrists. She let out a low rattling sound, like a snake, and came at him with fingernails and teeth. This dame is really outta control he thought. You're gonna hafta—

Her teeth missed his hand. Her fingernails missed his face, almost found his throat. She backed away and came in again and he let her have it, a very short stiff right that caught her high on the jaw, just under the ear. She sagged, her eyes closed. Before she hit the floor, he moved fast and grabbed her around the middle. He saw she was out.

He lifted her in his arms and carried her to the sofa. It won't show, he thought, looking at her jaw where he'd hit her. You didn't really hurt her. You measured it and you can see it wasn't an overdose of knuckles. You know it won't show, and there ain't no damage. But even so, it's a pity. You hadda do it, though. What else could you do?

The East Indian girl was standing at his side, looking down worriedly at the platinum blonde sleeping on the sofa. The girl said, "Is terrible thing."

"She'll be all right."

"Is really a terrible thing." The girl was getting ready to weep again.

Corey turned and looked at her. "She sure put it on you with that poker."

"What hurts is not that. What hurts is name she calls me. She calls me thief. In front of you. Now why she do that?"

"I'm wondering."

"I work here long time. Almost two year. Never anything like this. This is something I no understand."

Corey gazed past the girl. His eyes narrowed and he murmured, "What started it?"

"Was not about perfume."

"I know that."

"Before you came in, was no talk about perfume. Was just that she gets upset about something. Walks up and down and makes noises like she is speaking to herself. Is very upset. Never see her like that before. Is nervous sometimes, but never like that. And then she jumps at me."

"For what?"

"For nothing."

"She said you went out last night."

"Just to go for a walk. I no can sleep and I go out for a walk. To get some air. Only to get some air. But she says I no tell truth. And then she hits me in mouth."

"So what it amounts to," Corey said, "something happened that caused her to flip and she took it out on you."

The girl opened her mouth to speak, then checked it. On the sofa, Lita stirred, letting out a slight moan. The girl frowned and spoke in a whisper, "Better I say no more. She wakes up, she will hear."

"She ain't wakin' up yet. Come on, say what you wanna say."

"Is perhaps not important."

"Say it," he urged.

"Well—at first today, when she comes downstairs, everything is pleasant. Like always, she says good morning."

"What time was that?"

"Just a little while ago. Always she sleeps until middle

of day. So then she sits at table and I bring the coffee and toast and she starts to drink the coffee and read the newspaper. Is something she sees on front page."

"You sure it was the front page?"

The girl nodded emphatically. "I was standing near table. She sits there looking at front page with her eyes coming out of her face. She jumps up and knocks over chair; and coffee spills all over the floor. She walks around saying terrible things, dirty words."

"Where's that newspaper?" Corey cut in.

"In wastebasket. In kitchen."

"Wait here," Corey said. "If she comes to, tell her I went to the kitchen to get her some water."

He hurried from the parlor. In the kitchen he reached into the wastebasket and took out the crumpled newspaper. The pages were disarranged. He leafed through them, came to the front page and scanned the headlines. The banner headline told of another flare-up in the Middle East. There was a three column write-up dealing with a plane crash costing seventeen lives. And a prominent politician was accused of embezzling public funds. In the lower left hand corner of the page there was a single column headline. It read, "Two Die In Gun Battle." He focused on the first paragraph, and then the short paragraphs that followed. The final paragraph stated that the two men who had obviously slain each other were mobsters with criminal records and it gave their names. Macy and Lattimore.

Corey tossed the newspaper into the wastebasket, then went to the sink and filled a glass with water. He returned to the parlor, where the East Indian girl was straightening up the room, setting the chairs in their proper places and cleaning the littered carpet. On the sofa, Lita was slowly coming to her senses, grimacing with genuine confusion as she managed to sit up. Corey handed her the water glass. She sipped some water, took several deep breaths, then murmured, "Thank you."

He didn't say anything. With his eyes he said something to the East Indian girl. The message got across to her, and she walked out of the parlor. Lita sipped more water, then dipped her fingers into the glass and applied her wet fingers to her temples. She put the glass on a small table adjoining the sofa. Then she was on her feet, crossing to the other side of the room, and faced a wall mirror. She had her hand to the side of her jaw.

"Does it hurt?" Corey asked.

"Only a little."

"I hope it ain't swollen."

"Slightly," she said. "It's hardly noticeable."

She turned away from the mirror, pressed the half-smoked cigarette into an ashtray. For some moments she walked around the parlor, not looking at Corey. Then she came back to the sofa and sat down. Two pillows were between them.

For a while it was quiet. Then from upstairs there was the sound of glass breaking on a tile floor. With it came Grogan's voice, "What the hell are you trying to do?" There were a couple of nurses working with the high colonic expert, and they were jabbering excitedly. The high colonic expert shouted, "Hold it—be careful."

Grogan shouted again, "Wait—wait!" He was shrieking

now. "Wait, goddamit—" After that, the nurses, the high colonic expert and Grogan all were yelling as something very heavy hit the tile floor. There was the sound of more glass breaking; then another stretch of silence. Finally Corey said, "You gonna tell him?"

"Tell him what?"

"That I socked you."

She leaned back in the sofa, facing front with her arms folded across her bare midriff. "You want me to tell him?"

"It don't matter. Not to me."

"Then why did you ask?"

"I just wondered," he said.

She unfolded her arms. Her hands came up in front of her face and she hit her fingertips together. She did that several times. Then she said, "No, I won't tell him."

"Why not?"

"He'll only worry," she said. "He worries too much as it is."

"About you?"

She turned her head very slowly and looked at him. Then she faced forward again. "He'll be fifty-six. I'm twenty-five."

"What's that got to do with it?"

"You'll know when you're fifty-six," she said.

"I won't make it to fifty-six. Not the way I live." And as he spoke, he was thinking, it's sorta like short wave. You use the right frequency, you can tune in on this dame. To some degree, anyway.

She was looking at him. "What do you mean, the way you live? You mean the drinking?"

He didn't answer. He looked at her bare middle, looked away. Then he got up from the sofa, took a few steps and came back to the sofa and sat down. Now there was one pillow between them.

She was still facing forward. Her features were impassive, but he knew she was wondering what he'd do next. He thought, you're gonna take it step by step, it's gotta be timed and that timing better be damn near perfect.

He stood up again. He moved very slowly across the room and stood near the big bronze Buddha. He looked at the Buddha, took a very deep breath, put a troubled frown on his face, then faked an impulsive move toward the front door. All the while he hadn't looked at her, and he wasn't looking at her now as he put his hand on the doorknob. He was thinking in that instant, it's like in Italy, we had a C.O. who took some awful chances.

He turned the doorknob, and heard her saying, "Where are you going?"

Standing there at the door with his back to her, "Just getting out, that's all. I gotta get outta here."

"But why? What's wrong?"

"Damned if I know," he muttered. He let go of the doorknob. Then with another synthetic deep breath, expelling it with a hiss through his teeth, "—just can't take this."

And again his hand was on the doorknob, and he was opening the door. She said, "Wait, don't leave." He hesitated a moment, then opened the door and heard her saying, "No, don't."

He stepped back, slowly closed the door. You think she's buying this? he asked himself.

"Come here," she said.

"What for?" He spoke wearily. "What's the percentage?"

"If you mean what I think you mean—"

"Look, it's no use."

"Please," she said. "Tell me."

He turned and looked at her. "Can't you see what's going on?"

For a long while she sat still studying him. He put a blaze into his eyes and shot it at her. Without sound he said to her, this hurts. I'm really hurting. In deep.

She got up from the sofa. Moving toward him, as though drifting toward him, she looked him up and down. Then as she came close she murmured, "Tell me. Why can't you tell me?"

He pushed her away, letting her feel the trembling in his hands as they gripped her shoulders. He tightened the grip, made a hissing sound, then let go of her shoulders and muttered, "I'm trying to control it. Can't let it get started."

"Why not?" and she leaned toward him, but he pulled back and said, "No, don't. For Christ's sake, don't."

"Buy why not?"

"We let it get started, we're in for grief."

"But if we—"

"Look, let's forget it," he cut in. "We need each other like gasoline needs a lit match."

He was facing the bronze bulk of the Buddha. The

statue's slit eyes seemed to say, what I observe these days is considerable scheming and bluffing.

Believe it, Mac. Corey winked at the Buddha.

She came close behind him. She didn't touch him. In his brain he heard her telling herself that this one would be easy. He winked again at the Buddha.

Then he felt her hand on his side, just under his ribs. Her hand moved across and down, going toward his belt line.

"Don't do that," he pleaded in a hoarse whisper, but made no move to get away from her fingers sliding under his shirt. Her hand kept going down and he grimaced slightly and the grimace wasn't faked. What's happening here? he asked himself.

His head was spinning as the answer hit him. You ain't pretending now, he told himself through the giddy feeling that was almost like floating. She's actually got you.

She took her hand away. Upstairs a door had been opened and Grogan's voice barked very loudly, "—don't tell me about prune juice. I don't like prune juice. I ain't gonna drink no prune juice. Now leave me alone and beat it!"

Footsteps moved across the second floor hallway going toward the stairway. Then the high colonic crew was coming downstairs and they saw Lita seated on the sofa with a picture magazine in her lap, Corey in the ebony armchair scrutinizing a thumbnail.

Corey glanced up, wanting to see what a high colonic crew looked like. The two nurses were scrawny, unhappy looking. One of them appeared to have been weeping. The high colonic expert was a short pudgy middle-aged man with a gray-yellow complexion that indicated some internal trouble. He carried a large calfskin satchel. With the back of his hand he wiped perspiration from his forehead. He said to Lita, "A difficult patient, Mrs. Grogan. Very difficult indeed."

"And he insulted me," the nurse with the wet red-rimmed eyes added. "He called me an imbecile."

"I told you to beat it," said Grogan, rapidly coming down the steps. The nurses and the high colonic expert headed for the front door. They managed to make a dignified exit, but it was hurried.

Grogan looked at Corey. "How long you been here?"

Corey shrugged. "Not very long."

Lita put the picture magazine aside. She got up from the sofa and moved toward Grogan. "How did it go?"

"It was hell," Grogan muttered. "They damn near busted me open. They really had me scared, the way they were getting their signals mixed. D'ja hear all that racket up there? You shoulda seen them. Like the Three Stooges."

"You look weak," Lita said. "Washed out."

"I'm washed out, all right," Grogan said. "They call it irrigation, it's more like a flash flood." He turned to Corey. "What they do is, they take this hose and ram it—"

"Please," Lita interrupted. "Not the details."

Grogan glanced at his wristwatch. "Think I'll go out for awhile."

"Why don't you get some rest? That's what you need. You should get in bed and rest."

"I'm not tired," Grogan said. "I could use a half-hour on the river."

"Rowing? You're in no condition to go rowing. After what you've just been through—"

"Look. I'm going rowing," Grogan said with quiet finality. He moved toward the vestibule, looked back, and beckoned to Corey.

Corey got up from the armchair and started to follow Grogan, who was already out of the house. As Corey neared the front door, Lita came close beside him and he felt her hand sliding down across his ribs, going down further and still further. Then she had him there. She held him.

He didn't look at her. But somehow he could see the green of her eyes. It was inside him, a green flame. It lanced through his thinking. It was her green web; he was in it.

"No," he hissed. "Damn it, no." He pushed her away and moved quickly out of the house. Going down the front steps he stumbled and almost fell. He felt dizzy and it seemed everything was that green color.

You jerk, he said to himself. He scowled at the mirror inside himself. The scowl was set hard for a moment, showing his gritting teeth. Then his face relaxed as he came up beside Grogan, who was walking across the street toward a parked car.

7

It was a six-passenger custom-made sedan, dark green, conservative in styling, with very little chrome. It was imported from Spain and the original purchaser was a member of the boating club to which Grogan belonged. The original purchaser was fickle with cars and had paid seventeen thousand for this one. The first time it needed minor repair he sold it to Grogan for nine thousand. Grogan was very proud of the car and had a habit of caressing its fenders, its hood, as though the car was alive.

Grogan stood beside the car and patted the front fender, murmuring aloud to the car, "You doll you." He spotted a slight blemish on the gleaming waxed fender, took out a handkerchief and carefully wiped the surface. He stepped back, inspected his work and said to the car, "You doll. You sweetheart."

Corey coughed lightly, just to let Grogan know he was there. Grogan didn't look at him, but said to the car, "You know the way it is, don't you? I don't hafta explain it to you. All I gotta do is look at you and I know you'll never let me down."

A dirty-faced boy, about ten, came up to Grogan and said, "I'll put a rag on her. Wipe her down real good. Cost you fifty cents."

"I'll pay you a dollar," Grogan said, not looking at the boy.

"A whole dollar?"

Grogan took a roll from his pocket and peeled off a bill. As he handed it to the boy, he said loudly and fervently, "I'm paying you this dollar to stay the hell away from her."

"Right," the boy said, pocketed the dollar and scurried off. Grogan took out the handkerchief again and applied it to some dust on the hood. While doing so, he said to Corey, "You see the front page today?"

Corey didn't answer.

Grogan continued to rub at the dust marks on the hood of the car. Corey looked to one side, his eyes narrow and precisely aimed, as though he was studying the tiny numbers on a slide rule.

"I asked you something," Grogan said quietly, still rubbing the handkerchief on the hood. Corey remained silent. Grogan whirled around and stared at him and shouted, "You gonna tell me or ain't you gonna tell me?"

Corey stood relaxed, his expression placid. He said softly, "What's all the commotion?"

Grogan opened his mouth to shout again. He checked it, then let out a grunt and gritted his teeth. He lifted his hand to his head, smoothing the silver hair. "It's Macy and Lattimore. It says in the paper they bumped each other. Happened on a vacant lot alongside the river."

"Is that how you got it? You read it in the paper?"

"Christ no," Grogan said. "I get a call from the precinct station, from the captain. That's early this morning, a little after five. So then I'm in the station house and from there we go to the morgue. After that it's the Hall and they're making a ballistics check. And sure enough—say whatcha lookin' at me like that for?"

"I'm just listening," Corey said mildly. "Go on."

Grogan took a deep breath. "I don't know," he said aloud to himself. "I just don't know." He looked at Corey. "I mean, I just can't buy it."

"Did Homicide buy it?"

Grogan nodded. "They wrapped it up and filed it away. A double shooting, period. But goddamit, I just can't see it that way."

"Why not?"

"It just don't add," Grogan said worriedly. "Macy and Lattimore, they always got along. They weren't buddies exactly; and maybe now and then they'd have words. But never anything serious. So why the hell would they shoot each other?"

"They didn't," Corey said.

Grogan was quiet for some moments. And then, "What was that you said?"

"They didn't shoot each other."

There was a long silence. Grogan turned away, took a few steps, came back and said, "If you know something, why do you hide it from me?"

"I'm not hiding anything," Corey said. "It's just that you weren't ready to hear it."

112

Grogan's eyes were high-powered lenses. "Whaddya mean—ready?"

"To handle it. Be braced for it. This ain't no ordinary development. This is something that when you hear it, you gotta have a good tight hold on yourself."

Grogan smoothed his hair again. He took a slow and deep breath. "All right, let's have it."

Corey spoke matter-of-factly, "It was me who drilled them. Then I set it up so it'd look like they drilled each other."

Grogan took several backward steps. He looked up at the sky. Then he looked down at the cobblestones. "One of these days I'm gonna have a stroke."

"I hadda drill them," Corey went on with it. "It was them or me. They had me slated for the river. They'd tailed me from the Hall."

"The Hall?" Grogan started to walk backward again, then came close to Corey. Grogan was pale as he said, "What the hell were you doing at the Hall?"

"They had me there for questioning."

"About what?"

"The party last night. At the Hangout, in the back room. And them two hoods—"

"But that's a closed case," Grogan muttered. He turned his head a little giving Corey a side glance. "How come they opened it up again?"

Corey shrugged. "They musta figured I'd have something more to tell them."

Grogan kept looking at him sideways. "So?"

"So they sat me down and asked how it happened and I told them. Said it just like you said it. And that's all."

"You sure that's all?"

Corey nodded slowly, wearily. And then, "It goes like this—I come outta City Hall and get in a taxi. We're coming toward the bridge and there's a car in back. I see it's a tail and I wanna know what's happening; so I'm outta the taxi on Marion Street. Then this car cruises in, and they get out, and it's Macy and Lattimore. They wanna know what I was doing at the Hall. So right away I figured you musta told them to check all my moves."

"I didn't tell them anything," Grogan said. His voice was mechanical, his eyes lenses. The lenses were aimed past Corey.

He's adding it up already, Corey thought, then went on, "They ask what I was doing at the Hall. I tell them, and they look at each other like it ain't good enough. Next thing I know they have me in the car. Not that I was worried. Not right then, anyway." He shrugged. "I thought they were doing what you wanted them to do—just driving me over to your house."

"And instead?"

"It's that vacant lot along the river front. Lattimore has a gun on me and tells me to get outta the car. So then I know they ain't workin' for you no more. It hits me they're signed in with the other outfit."

Grogan showed no emotion, no reaction at all.

"You expected that?" Corey asked.

"No," Grogan muttered. "But then, in this game, you never know what to expect." He opened the car door and got in behind the wheel. Corey turned away, heard the powerful hand tooled Spanish engine catching spark and make the noise of a hundred kettle drums going full blast. Then as the noise decreased to a silk-smooth idling purr, Corey walked away from the car, saying to himself, you'll take three or four more steps and then he'll call you back, you'll see.

He took three more steps away from the car and heard Grogan calling to him.

Facing about, he walked back to the car. For a moment Grogan merely gazed at him. Then he asked, "Wanna come along? Just for the ride?"

"I don't mind," Corey shrugged. He walked around to the other side of the car and climbed in beside Grogan.

The custom-built Spanish automobile made a u-turn and went south to Addison gliding along while various Swamp citizens yelled hello to Grogan. Through the open car window, he waved back. Then the car headed away from the Swamp, climbing along the arc of the bridge, high above the river. Grogan turned on the radio and got a ball game. The car came off the bridge and joined the slow-moving Saturday afternoon traffic on the six-lane highway that bordered the river. They were moving past factories and coal yards and freight yards. In this area the river was scummy. There was a half-sunken barge near the river bank and some boys in swim trunks were using it for a diving board. The traffic heading north gradually thinned out. It was a residential section, the street lined with expensive apartment houses. Then it was just the green of the municipal park and some statues of Revolutionary War generals, a few of the generals saluting, one of them brandishing a sword. At the base of that statue, under the shadow of the sword, an old colored man was sleeping peacefully on the grass. Heading further north along the highway, going through the park at the side of the river, the aquarium came into view; then the immense art museum designed like the Parthenon. It had cost the city some thirty million dollars and it was used mostly as a nesting place for pigeons and flocks of nine-year-old boys who came at night to play hide-and-seek in the labyrinth of marble columns. Past the art museum there was a traffic circle, then the highway curved in very close to the river. There were some people on the banks angling for catfish and carp, some park guards on horseback and a few men wearing sweat suits practicing for walking races. Further ahead some very old but solidly constructed and well kept houses appeared and pennants were flying above their roofs. These were the boat clubs, the members all rowers or former rowers and the boats were racing shells. In this area, the river water was clean and there were fences preventing fishermen and swimmers and any trespassers. The city was very proud of the boat clubs, some of which boasted rowers who'd made the Olympics. Also, many of the members were from families whose names were a tradition in the city, the lineage going back to the Seventeenth Century. The fences made certain that only the properly qualified got in. A blueblood could get in. A ditch digger could get in provided he was a first rate rower, capable of winning silver cups. There was no way for a man to buy his way in. In the city there were multi-millionaires who'd been trying for years to get in and never would. On very rare occasions a man got in because he had something on one of the bluebloods. Like a photograph showing the blueblood in an off-beat situation. That was how Grogan got in, some twelve years back. The photo had been taken at night in the zoo, and it showed the blueblood involved with a full-grown zebra.

Grogan's car came to a stop in the parking area adjacent to a large four-storied, colonial-style structure, its orange and white pennant reading Southeast Boat Club.

"Wait here," Grogan said, the first words he'd uttered since they started the ride.

Grogan got out of the car. "How long you gonna be?" Corey asked.

"Thirty-forty minutes," Grogan said. "You mind waiting?"

Corey shrugged. "I'll listen to the ball game."

Grogan walked across the parking area and entered the clubhouse. For a few minutes Corey listened to the radio. Cincinnati and Philadelphia were tied three-three in the fifth. Robin Roberts was pitching for Philadelphia and he gave up a single. Then an infield error sent the man to third. The next man walked. The announcer said, "Now Robin's in a lotta trouble—"

Got my own trouble, Corey told the radio. He wondered why Grogan had brought him here. He switched off the radio and tried to think in analytical terms. It was no use. He was thinking in terms of the platinum blonde hair and the dark green eyes.

On the river a four oared shell was coming toward the

dock of the Southeast Boat Club. A single sculler was heading out. On the dock eight men in their late twenties and early thirties were hoisting a gleaming mahogany racing shell high above their heads. The tiny coxswain yapped instructions. They carried the shell across the planks and down the ramp to the water. Now some older members of the boat club came out the side door, walked across the parking area and along a gravel path leading to the dock. They were in their fifties and sixties, and one of them, Corey judged, was over seventy. Some wore orange jerseys and orange striped white shorts. Others were stripped to the waist. Arriving on the dock, they moved briskly, diligently, readying their racing shells for the water. Corey shrugged and thought, some people never give up. I guess you gotta hand it to them. It's like watching Archie Moore climbing into the ring. Archie would enjoy this demonstration. He'd understand it. Be damned if I can understand it. Well, that's how it goes. Every cat to his own alley.

He saw Grogan coming out the side door. Grogan's silver hair was mirror-bright in the sun. Under one arm, Grogan carried two long oars, the blades painted orange and white. There was a white sailor's cap in his hand, the brim turned down. His chest was bare and he wore bright orange shorts, white socks and spotless white sneakers.

Grogan walked past the car, not even looking toward it. He went onto the dock and chatted a few moments with some other rowers. They clustered around him, all nodding as he said something while pointing to the river. Some technical point about the current, Corey guessed. One of the white-haired rowers patted Grogan on the shoulder.

Grogan said something and they all guffawed. He's a fa-
vorite here, Corey decided. They actually look up to him.
These bluebloods.

Grogan walked down the ramp to the water and got
into his racing shell. He rowed out toward the middle of
the river. His strokes were smooth, seemingly effortless.
Corey stepped out of the car and went onto the dock. He
watched Grogan rest the oars for a moment. Then Grogan
was rowing again.

Now it was serious rowing and the single scull cut
cleanly through the water; the blades of the oars domi-
nating the water. There was no splashing, no deviation of
boat motion; the shell responded to Grogan's strokes like
an eager steed flawlessly handled.

He's a rower, all right, Corey said to himself. You don't
hafta know about rowing to see that he's good. It's better
than good. It's really pretty.

He watched the single scull as it picked up the increasing
tempo of the oar strokes. It flashed past other rowers. Some
of them rested their oars and just sat and looked. And he's
fifty-six years old, Corey reminded himself. The man is
fifty-six years old.

The single scull passed under a railroad bridge more
than a mile away from the dock. Then it turned and started
back. Corey strolled off the dock and along the gravel path.
He got into the car.

About twenty minutes later Grogan came out of the
clubhouse wearing his street clothes and climbed into the
car and started the engine. There was no talk. The car
backed out of the parking area and maneuvered onto the

highway. There was no talk. The car passed the art museum, passed the aquarium, the statues of the Revolutionary War generals and still there was no talk. They were passing the expensive apartment houses when Grogan said, "Gimme a rating."

"On what?"

"The rowing."

"You knew I was watching?"

"Gimme a rating," Grogan said.

"It was nice," Corey said. "It was something to see."

"They all say that," Grogan murmured. He glanced at Corey. "You think I do it to show off?"

"I wouldn't know."

"Well, I don't do it to show off. I don't do it for the exercise, neither. I mean the exercise is secondary."

There was silence for a while. Then Grogan said, "You wanna know why I do it?"

"I'm sorta wondering."

"All right, I'll tell you. It's more than just pulling the oars. It's sorta like pumping the machinery. Up here," and he pointed to his head. "The faster I move that boat, the better I can think," Grogan said. "I mean real thinking. With real thinking it's just the brain that's talking, there ain't no interference from the muscles and the glands and the nerves. Or what they call the feelings."

"You mean when you're rowing you don't feel nothing?"

"That about tells it," Grogan said. "When it comes to real thinking, it's gotta be arithmetic and nothing else. If the feelings interfere, it ain't thinking no more; it's just worriment and the blues and a lotta confusion. You follow that?"

Corey nodded slowly.

Grogan said, "I'm rowing on that river, the numbers start to add, and sooner or later I get the total. Like today."

The car pulled over to the side of the highway. Grogan switched off the engine. He looked at Corey Bradford in silence. Then Grogan murmured, "I'm waiting, Corey."

"For what? I told you everything."

"You sure?"

"All right, let's check it. I told you about City Hall. And the party I had with Macy and Lattimore. And that's it. That's the full report."

"For last night only," Grogan said. He let a pause drift in. And then, "What about today?"

"Whaddya mean, today?"

"In my house. While I was upstairs. And you were downstairs. With her."

There was a long pause.

Grogan said, "Here's how it adds. I come downstairs and she's sitting on the sofa. You're on the other side of the room. In the armchair. Now back to her again. She's got something in her lap. It's a picture magazine. It didn't hit me then, but when I'm rowing on the river I get to thinking about it.

Corey's eyebrows went up slightly. He wondered if he looked relaxed. He was trying very hard to appear relaxed.

"I get to thinking she's a fussy reader," Grogan said. "She don't go in for picture magazines. Always complains when I bring one home. Says it's just a lotta trash."

"So?"

"So the magazine was in her lap and it was open. That means she was reading it. But she wasn't wearing her reading glasses."

Corey grimaced, puzzled.

Grogan said, "She never reads without her reading glasses."

"So what?" Corey mumbled. "What are you giving me here?"

"I'm telling you what you already know," Grogan said. "She was bluffing. She wasn't reading no picture magazine while I was upstairs. And while I was upstairs there wasn't no twelve feet of carpet between you and her."

Corey gazed past Grogan and smiled lazily. He said, "You putting me on the grill?"

"Without grease. Now let's have it."

Corey tightened his lips. He told himself it needed cold anger, and of course the less he said the better. He put cold anger in his eyes, looked at Grogan and said, "Look, let's forget the whole thing."

Then he had his hand on the door handle. He turned it, opened the car door and started to get out. Grogan took hold of his arm and held on. "Now wait," Grogan said. "We ain't finished."

"Take your hand off me."

Grogan let go. He said softly, "Don't be a damn fool. You can't walk out on me. Nobody walks out on me."

Corey closed the car door and settled back in the seat.

"What the hell's wrong with you?" Grogan asked. "Whatcha all upset about?"

"I'll just tell you this," Corey spoke through his teeth. "I didn't touch her."

"You wanted to?"

"Now listen, Grogan," and he shifted in the seat and faced the silver-haired man. "In the first place, she's your wife and I'm not a creep. In the second place, she's a teaser and I'm not a chump. In the third place, I'm out to score for loot, not gash."

"All right," Grogan said.

"It ain't all right. Christ's sake, you forget I damn near got bumped last night. This job I'm doin' for you, I'm playin' tag with the undertaker. So it ain't enough I got that on my mind. I gotta sit here and hear about your woman. What do I care about your woman? The hell with your woman."

Grogan chuckled very softly, somewhat bitterly. "I wish I could say that." And then for a moment he closed his eyes and was alone with himself, muttering, "God damn her."

Corey slumped low in the car seat. He gazed through the windshield. He told himself not to say anything. He put a sullen look on his face and kept it there.

Grogan said, "Don't pay me no mind, Corey. It's just that I been takin' it and takin' it and—it's chokin' me, that's what it's doin'. Like a knotted rope around my neck. And every day it gets tighter. So why do I keep takin' it? Why do I put up with her?"

Grogan's voice was twisted with anguish. He bent low and his forehead was pressed against the steering wheel. "Whaddya do in a case like this?" he asked nobody in particular. "You know what it amounts to? She got me hexed, that's what. It's gotta be that. She puts the hex on me."

"You believe in that?" Corey murmured.

"Corey boy, I'll tell you. I don't know what the hell to believe. If I could only reach her, you know? But I swear it's like reachin' for an eel in the water. You can touch it, but you can't hold on. That's what I live with. In my own house I gotta live like that."

Corey glanced at the silver-haired man. The thick rower's fingers were hooked around the rim of the steering wheel. The hands that had controlled the oars so precisely were quivering.

"Three years now," Grogan spoke through the soft chuckle laced with bitterness, anguish. "Three years I been living with this goddam question mark. Ain't a day in the week she don't throw another riddle at me. Like today with that picture magazine. Sitting there reading it and not wearing her reading glasses." He raised his head and looked pleadingly at Corey. "Can'tcha gimme the answer to that? Can'tcha help me a little?"

"Ain't nothing I can tell you," Corey shrugged. "I can't look inside her head."

"You called her a teaser." Grogan's eyes were lenses again, adjusting and probing. "Why'd you call her a teaser?"

"It's the way she moves around. She sorta flicks it at you and then pulls it away. You know what I mean?"

Grogan looked to one side. He nodded slowly, grunting as though someone was jabbing him with a blunt weapon, giving it to him in the kidney. "Yes, I know whatcha mean. I oughta know. There's been nights I just plain wished the wagon would come and take me away."

Corey blinked.

Grogan went on, "But lemme tell you, Corey boy, there's been them other nights when I climbed into that bed, and it was there and it was fabulous. How many nights like that? I can count them nights on my fingers. And maybe that's why I hold onto her, just hoping for more of them nights."

There was a long silence. Then Grogan started the car engine, pulled away from the side of the highway and joined the stream of traffic. Several minutes later the car came to a stop across the street from Grogan's house. Grogan walked toward the house. Corey Bradford walked south on Second going toward Addison.

On Addison, approaching the Hangout, he spotted Carp across the street. Carp was with some winos, sharing a bottle wrapped in newspaper. The little man glanced at Corey, then strolled away from the winos and went around the corner.

Corey waited a few minutes. Then he crossed Addison, tossed a dollar bill to the winos, and rounded the corner onto Second. Carp was sitting on a doorstep a few houses down on Second. The little man had picked up a rag from the littered pavement and was using it to polish his rummage-sale shoes. The leather was cracked and, in places, torn wide, and his socks showed through. He continued to polish industriously, meticulously, as though the shoes were the finest quality and merited the best care. As Corey's shadow fell over him, he didn't look up. His complete attention was on the shoes.

"You do what I told you to do?" Corey asked.

"Exactly as specified," the little man murmured, not looking up.

"Where'd she go?"

"First a meat market on Seventh Street," the little man said, rubbing the rag across his left shoe. He raised the rag, examined the shoe, wasn't satisfied, and resumed the rubbing. "Then back to Addison and into a grocery. After that she went home."

"You sure it was home? She might have been visiting someone."

"No," Carp said. "I checked that possibility. I checked it quite thoroughly. She entered her own place of residence."

Corey frowned slightly. "Whaddya mean you checked it?"

"I watched through the window," Carp said. "She put the meat in the icebox. She opened some cans of vegetables, peas and creamed corn, then unwrapped a loaf of bread—"

"Was she alone?"

Carp nodded.

"All right," Corey said. "Gimme the address."

"Six-seventeen Ingersoll Street," the little man said. "First floor back."

"Thanks," Corey said. And then, without thinking, he

put his hand in his pocket, his fingers going for paper money. Carp looked up at that moment and his eyes said, Please don't insult me. Corey's hand came out of the trousers pocket empty, and the little man smiled with approval. He looked down again and went back to polishing his shoes. Corey walked away.

Six-seventeen Ingersoll, Corey was thinking. He was in his room, getting into a clean shirt. He decided to take it all the way, and put on clean shorts and socks, then opened the closet and took out the only suit he owned. It was a $19.50 rayon acetate that needed pressing badly. He wished he had time to get it pressed. There were four neckties dangling from a nail on the inside of the closet door. He reached for the dark green one, got it under the shirt collar, started to tie it and then realized what color it was. You don't want that color, he told himself.

He pulled off the dark green tie and put it back on the nail. For some moments he stood looking at it. What's all this see-saw routine? he wondered, and tried to back away from it, thinking. It's just that you don't like that color—

He snatched the dark green tie and quickly slipped it under his collar and knotted it.

After that he loosened the wall boards in the closet, took out the badge and the card and the police pistol. He put the card in his wallet and was placing the pistol under his belt when he heard the soft sound of someone tapping on the door.

"Who is it?"

"McDermott."

He went to the door, opened it and McDermott walked in. Corey frowned and deepened the frown as he watched the detective-sergeant move purposefully toward the window and pull down the shade.

"Just so nobody can see us in here together," McDermott said.

"Nobody's looking."

"We don't know that."

"If they're looking, they saw you come in."

"I came in through the alley," McDermott said. "And besides, there's other roomers here. No way of telling what room I'm visiting."

"They could check with the landlady."

"She didn't see me. The back door was open and I just slipped in."

"For Christ's sake," Corey muttered irritably. "In broad daylight—"

"Quit worrying," McDermott said.

Corey laughed lightly.

"What's comical?"

"He says quit worrying."

"So?"

"You don't know this neighborhood."

"I know every neighborhood."

"Not this one," Corey said. "To know this layout you gotta live in it. And not for a week or a month. You gotta be born and raised here. This is the Swamp and to know it, really know it, you gotta be a Swampcat."

"I'm wise to that fact."

Corey looked at him. There was something in the man's

voice that chilled the room. And from the man's eyes, ice came out and sliced into Corey. It lasted for only an instant, but in that instant Corey had the feeling that he'd seen McDermott somewhere a long time ago.

The detective-sergeant looked around for a chair. There was no chair, so he sat down on the edge of the bed. Corey moved past the bed and leaned against the dresser. There was a long pause. Then McDermott said, "Got anything to tell me?"

"No," Corey said.

It was quiet again.

McDermott looked at him. "I just thought you had something to tell me."

"If there was anything to tell," Corey said slowly and quietly, "I wouldn't be sitting around waiting. I'da phoned in or reported in."

"All right," McDermott said mildly. "All right, Bradford."

"You sure it's all right?"

McDermott smiled at him. "Don't get annoyed."

"I'm not annoyed," Corey said. He told himself to be extremely careful. He looked away from the detective-sergeant. "It's just that I'm curious, that's all. I just don't get this routine."

"But that's all it is. Just routine."

Tell that to the birds, Corey said to himself. He glanced at McDermott, then looked away and murmured, "You do this all the time, Sergeant?"

"Do what?"

"Come checking."

McDermott's eyebrows went up just a little. "Is that what I'm doing?"

"That's how I read it."

The detective-sergeant leaned back on the bed, resting on his elbows. He squinted up at the ceiling, looked around at the walls, focusing on the places where the wallpaper was ripped and the plaster showed through. He murmured, "Whaddya pay for this room?"

"Four-fifty."

"That's a dollar too much."

"It don't bother me," Corey said. "I'm a spender."

McDermott chuckled softly. And then, cutting it off, "Well, I don't know. Maybe you are, at that."

What the hell is he saying? Corey wondered. What's it signify? Could be he's been drinking. He's got that hazy look, as if he's high on something. But it don't hafta be liquor; it don't hafta be weed or pills or anything like that. It could very well be that he's high on just plain oxygen. There's some who can do that, you know. They set their minds to it, and all they gotta do is breathe air, and in no time at all they're high. I'll give you fifty-to-one that's the way it is with him. And that makes it a problem for you. I mean, he can climb up there and float around and bomb away from any angle.

The detective-sergeant said, "You sure you got nothing to tell me?"

"All I got is a question."

"Let's have it."

"How'd you like to go to hell?"

McDermott chuckled again. "Now you're really annoyed."

"Now I'm plenty annoyed." Corey spoke more tightly, exaggerating the annoyance, faking a scowl. "You sign me in, you gimme a badge, and the very next day you come snooping."

"It ain't that."

"Then what is it?"

"It's just that you're new on the squad and I wanna get to know you better."

Corey thought about that for a moment. He smiled inside himself. He said, "Let's try that again."

"I wanna get to know you. This is just a social call."

"Then why the grilling?"

"Don't pay that no mind," McDermott said, and he smiled gently. "That's just a habit I got. Like some of them dentists when they're away from the office. They wait for you to open your mouth and right away they're looking at your teeth."

There was another lapse of silence.

Then the detective-sergeant said, "You got a girl friend?"

"No."

"How come?"

"There's nothing around."

"Maybe you ain't looking."

Corey scowled again. This time he wasn't faking. He said, "What about yourself, Sergeant? What do you do for relief?"

"I buy it," McDermott said.

"You ain't married?"

"Yes, I'm married," McDermott said. "I been married twenty-seven years."

"And?"

"She can't do it. She won't let me come near her."

Corey looked at the detective-sergeant, then quickly looked away.

"It ain't that we don't get along," McDermott said. "We get along fine. It's one of them situations, and we make the best of it. At first it wasn't easy; she wanted to leave me. One time she tried to knock herself off. Then gradually I sold her on the idea we could get adjusted, learn to live with it."

"Live with what?"

"Her condition."

"She crippled?"

"In her head," the detective-sergeant said. "Not all the way. It's just that one mental block. She's incapable, that's all."

Why is he telling me this? Corey wondered, and heard himself asking, "What happened to her?"

"She was jumped. A bunch of thugs jumped her and took her into an empty house. There were nine of them. They had her there for a little less than forty-eight hours. Some people found her in an alley. She didn't have no clothes on. There was blood running down her legs and later in the hospital they said it was fifty-fifty, she'd lost an awful lot of blood."

"She talk?"

"She couldn't talk. That is, she couldn't talk at all. For

over a year she wouldn't say a word. She wouldn't eat, neither. They hadda feed her through a tube. And then when she was able to talk, she wouldn't say anything about it, and the doctors told me not to ask her. They let me have it straight. They said she was on the border line and only time would tell. They said I'd hafta be very careful not to bring it up again. Another thing, they sat me down and counseled me. Said I'd better call it off—"

"Call what off?"

"The engagement."

Corey blinked a few times.

McDermott said, "You thought all this happened recently?"

"Well, I figured—"

"It happened six years before we were married," McDermott said. "It happened thirty-three years ago."

Corey blinked again. He grimaced slightly, then sensed that more was coming and braced himself. And for some unaccountable reason, he wasn't able to look at the detective-sergeant. He just stood there stiffly and stared off to one side and waited.

He heard McDermott saying, "You wanna know where it happened?"

He nodded slowly, not knowing why he was nodding.

"It happened here in the Swamp," McDermott said.

Corey turned his head slowly. He looked at the detective-sergeant.

"I'll tell you something else," McDermott said. He was still relaxed on the bed, leaning back on his elbows. He spoke softly. "I'll tell you why they did it to her. Not because they were hopped up, or juiced, or anything like that. It was a carefully planned maneuver. They did it to get back at me."

In Corey's brain a screen showed Henry McDermott at the age of twenty-two. McDermott was wearing a policeman's uniform. There was no action on the screen, just the image of the young McDermott, the rookie policeman.

"Here's how it was," McDermott said. "I was attached to the Nineteenth Precinct; the city was smaller then. Now it's the Thirty-Seventh. All right, they had me on the night shift; the beat was Addison to Munroe, Second Street to Seventh. Every time I walked the beat I passed the house where I lived. I was born and raised in that house; so don't tell me I don't know this neighborhood. I know this neighborhood like I know the taste inside my mouth.

"I lived on Fifth. On Third there was this bunch of thugs. They called themselves the Third Street Dragons. Late teens, early twenties. The worst. I mean the very worst. They had every store owner on Addison pissing in his pants. The Third Street Dragons. They wore baseball caps; the emblem was a dragon's head. You asked them what the angle was, they said it was just an athletic club. You tried to get anything on them, it was nothing doing. They were slick and tightly organized, and there was nothing to go on. And people were getting robbed, getting slugged, getting butchered.

"Finally I made up my mind. Comes a night I sneak up on one of them, and just on general principles I use the club. He goes to the hospital and damn near dies and nobody knows who did it. So all right, that's fine. That's just how I want it, hitting them in the dark so they can't see who the hitter is. A week later another one goes to the hospital, then a third and a fourth. And that was all. It wasn't dark enough that night and that fourth Dragon musta seen who'd hit him just before he passed out. A few nights after that they slip a note under my door. It's black crayon and it reads 'You ask for it you get it,' and that's all it reads.

"And what they did, they made me wait. It was a week and then another week and I was sweating every minute. One time I passed an alley and a voice says, just loud enough for me to hear, 'We ain't in no hurry, McDermott,' and I rush the alley. But there ain't nobody there. He musta crawled through some cellar window.

"So they made me wait for it to happen. And after three weeks I'm just about ready to call for help, to tell the precinct captain exactly how it is. But I do that, I lose the badge, and then face trial for aggravated assault and battery, four counts. I'm thinking what I should do. I'm eating away at myself with the thinking. And then, before I can decide, the Dragons decide it for me. But it ain't McDermott they get. It's McDermott's girl."

There was a long pause. Then Corey said "D'ja hit back?"

McDermott smiled dimly, somewhat contently.

"How many?" Corey asked.

"Five," McDermott said. "One at a time. Over a period of years."

"Dead?"

McDermott nodded.

"Slow?" Corey asked.

"Very slow," McDermott said. "And they were gagged. I used pliers. When they fainted I brought them to with smelling salts. It was very, very slow."

Again in Corey's brain the screen was lit and it showed McDermott with his shirt collar open and his sleeves rolled up. He was holding the pliers. The pliers were bloody. Nearby a man was sitting in a chair, his wrists and ankles tied and a gag across his mouth. On the floor, between the man's naked legs, there was a pool of blood, and more blood was dripping down. The man's eyes were closed and his head sagged to one side. McDermott used the little bottle of smelling salts and the man regained consciousness and then McDermott smiled softly and resumed the business with the pliers.

"All right, I got five," the detective-sergeant said. "I was out to get all nine, but two of them died a natural death and one fell in the river and drowned."

"That's only eight accounted for."

"There's one still alive," the detective-sergeant said. The dim smile was fading. He gazed at the wall across from the bed. "The leader," he murmured. "The leader of the Third Street Dragons."

And then he turned his head and looked at Corey. His eyes said, only now it ain't the baseball caps. And the meeting place ain't Third Street, it's been shifted to Second. It's the corner of Second and Addison. Specifically it's the back room at the Hangout.

The detective-sergeant looked away from Corey Bradford. He sat up on the edge of the bed. Then he stood up, moving toward the door, opened it and started to walk out. Then stopped. He turned slowly and gazed at Corey for a few moments. There was a certain sadness in his eyes. After that the door was closed and Corey was alone in the room. He shivered. A blade of ice was stabbing him, going deep, very high on his thigh, near his groin.

8

Several minutes passed and Corey Bradford didn't move from where he stood, staring at the closed door. There was a baffled look in his eyes, as though he was confronted with the pieces of a jig-saw puzzle, not one of which fit the other.

Come off it, he urged himself. You keep standing here trying to figure it out, you'll wind up giggling with your brains all outta joint.

The jig-saw puzzle wouldn't go away.

Thirty-three years, Corey muttered without sound. For thirty-three years a policeman named McDermott has been out to get the leader of the Third Street Dragons. And then outta nowhere a hook makes a grab, and you're pulled into the deal. You're handed the card. You're handed the badge. You're given the assignment.

The hook was aimed at you. At you alone. There's gotta be a reason—

You're nowhere near the reason, the only thing you got here is a certain creepy notion regarding McDermott. You got the feeling there's some special connection between you and him, a connection that has you standing here like some goddam statue—

Now listen, for Christ's sake. You're just gonna hafta come off it. Only way to look at it is don't look at all. It don't mean nothing, and chances are this cat McDermott is way out there on Track 73 with all them other mixed-up, shook-up, messed-up cats who got hit on the head just once too often.

All them sad-faced cats on the Night Squad.

That's where they are, all right, way out there on 73, that dismal track that aims straight at the booby hatch. And the only stops along the line are the graves.

That's it, that's how it is with the Squad, with McDermott. And jim that lets you out, absolutely. Lets you out and takes you clean off the hook. Or to see it another way, to see it like it really is, there ain't no hook at all. You're a loner and you can't be hooked.

Yet in that same moment he had the wallet out and he was looking at the badge.

You make me laugh, he said to himself, and managed to force a chuckle. Then quickly, almost spasmodically, he closed the wallet and put it back in his pocket.

Come on, he prodded the cagey manipulator who was out for gold and nothing else. Come on, let's haul this freight. It goes west on Addison and south on Sixth to Ingersoll.

Six-seventeen Ingersoll.

*　　*　　*

Ingersoll Street was little more than an alley, much too narrow for cars to pass through. It was located at the edge of the neighborhood, the six-hundred block gave way to the swamplands. Greenish water from the swamplands was always seeping into the cellars of Ingersoll houses; and in the street there were weeds growing between the loose cobblestones. Fumes from the swamplands formed ribbons of green-gray vapor that floated in circles above Ingersoll roofs, at times gliding down to drift past the first floor windows. There was little or no paint remaining on the two story wooden dwellings; the fumes had eaten it away. The dominant color along Ingersoll was the green-gray of the swamplands.

As Corey came onto Ingersoll it was getting dark. It shouldn't be getting dark this early, he thought. It's just a few minutes past seven, and this time of year it don't get dark until around eight-thirty.

Then he looked up and saw what was happening in the sky. There was no sun, just a thick blanket of rain clouds. The clouds were getting ready to burst, and he heard the rumblings of thunder. It's gonna come down in buckets, he decided, but didn't bother to quicken his pace. When the first drops fell, he was moving slowly along the narrow alley adjacent to the house numbered six-seventeen.

The backyard had no fence. It was muddy and only some weeds were growing; but somehow it looked cleaner and neater than the other backyards. That's to be expected, he thought. That's how it is with her; that's how it always was. You remember when you were married to her, she knocked herself out with all the scrubbing and the mopping and dusting. You remember she used to say, "All right, if you're poor you're poor, but that's no excuse to be dirty."

He stood in the backyard, thinking about her and how it was when they were married. The rain came down faster, but he didn't feel it. Then it was really coming down and he was drenched. He went to the back door and hit his knuckles against it. There were footsteps coming toward the door and he waited for it to open.

It didn't open. He heard her calling, "Who's out there?"

"Police."

She hadn't recognized his voice. She said loudly, firmly, "You got the wrong address."

"This six-seventeen?"

"That's right."

"You Mrs. Kingsley? Mrs. Delbert Kingsley?"

"That's right. So what?"

"So open the door. This is the police."

"If it ain't, you'll be sorry."

He pictured her standing there behind the door with something heavy in her hand, ready for any Swampcat who had nothing better to do than go around knocking on doors, pretending to be the police.

The door opened slightly. She stared at him. The shock was too much for her, and for a moment she couldn't say anything. And then, to let him know that it meant nothing, that he was just another Swampcat pulling a caper, she displayed an iron frying pan and gritted, "You wanna get your head caved in?"

"Calm down," he murmured, then made a move to walk in; but she put her weight against the door. He stepped back and shrugged. For an instant she was off guard, and he moved very fast, pushing the door wide open, and went through and took the frying pan away from her. As she ran toward the stove to reach for another, he took the wallet out and when she pivoted with her hand gripping a larger, heavier frying pan, he showed her the badge.

Lillian gaped at the badge. She reached backward slowly, putting the frying pan on the stove. She stood rigidly, her eyes bolted to the badge. Corey walked toward her, to let her get a closer look at the badge. She continued to gape at it, then slumped into a chair and looked at the floor.

Corey went to the door and closed it. The rain water was dripping from his head and shoulders. He wiped his brow and murmured, "It's kinda damp out there."

She sat still, gazing dully at the floor. She can't believe it, Corey thought. She can't believe they reinstated the shakedown artist. And aside from the seeing the badge, another item she gandered in the wallet was the card that reads "Night Squad." Maybe that accounts for something else you see in her eyes, a certain uneasiness.

He glanced around the tiny kitchen, seeing the neat arrangement of glasses and jars and pots and pans. On the stove there was something cooking. The aroma was appetizing, and he remembered how it was when they were married. She liked to cook. She was really a wonderful cook.

And then he looked at her and saw the dark brown hair, the medium brown eyes, the pink and olive complexion

that never needed rouge or powder, and he remembered
she never used lipstick, either. Never put her hair up in
curlers, never spent a thin dime on face creams or cologne
or any perfume at all, not even them deodorant sticks. Just
soap and water, and she took a bath every day, and that
was it. When you got near her, that flower scent was Lillian
herself, and not some fancy junk from a fancy bottle.

Another thing, she liked to sew. She made her own
dresses and never from them paper patterns, never copying
anything she saw in a store window. It was always her
own inventions and you remember that time we went to
the Policemen's Benefit Ball and she wore that evening
gown she made. Them other dames wanted to kill her.

Yes that's how it was, that's what you had. You had
yourself a woman. I mean a real woman, not some pho-
nograph record or sappy sweet chippy or one of them
glamor broads who, when you add it up, comes to nothing
more than a pain in the ass. With this one you had something on the plus side, and I swear you start to think about
it, you get upset, remembering—

Like in bed. The way it was them nights when you
weren't drunk or let's say too drunk. You check back, it
amounts to very few nights when you were sober enough
to really know her, to realize what you had. It was more
than just her face and body. It was so much more than
that. I mean the feeling deeper than the fire.

Five years ago.

Five goddam years you been without this woman. Five
years of nothing. And not caring. That is, until last night
when you saw her in the Hangout sitting alone at that

table, drinking beer. This woman who'd never gone for any kind of alcohol; she sat there filling the glass again and again, and you knew the kind of drinking it was. The weary drinking, the dreary drinking, the drinking that says, there's trouble here.

All right, let's find out why.

What I mean, goddamit, it ain't that you're gettin' detoured. You didn't come to this address to offer assistance. In the first place, she don't want your assistance. In the second place, her personal problems got nothing to do with your money problems. You're out to score for a stack of G-notes and that's all.

He couldn't look at her. He mumbled, "I got some questions—"

"Like what?" and she stiffened slightly, defensive.

"Your husband—"

"What about him?"

"Does he work?"

"Whaddya mean, does he work? Sure he works."

"Where?"

She didn't answer.

"Where?" Corey repeated. Then he looked at her and said softly, his expression solemn and official, "Now look, you know you gotta tell me. This is police business."

"Maybe."

"No maybes about it. You saw the badge—"

"I didn't see the warrant."

"There ain't no warrant," he said. "I'm not here to make an arrest. Or search the rooms. All I want is some information."

"Get it someplace else. I'm not talking to you."

"All right," he shrugged. And then, "Better bring an umbrella."

"What for?"

"So you won't get wet."

She took a deep breath. Her mouth tightened.

He shrugged again. "That's how it is," he said. "You won't talk here; you'll talk at city hall."

Lillian shifted her position in the chair. "Just tell me one thing," with her voice dull, the glint gone out of her eyes. "Why do they want him?"

"I didn't say they wanted him. They're just investigating, that's all."

"Investigating what?"

"This neighborhood," he said. "Some goings on in this neighborhood."

She blinked several times. Corey picked up a chair and brought it close to where she was sitting. He sat down, leaned back and said, "Where does he work?"

"Chatworth Leather."

"What's he do there?"

"He's a shipper."

"Nine to five?"

She nodded.

"What's he make a week?"

"Why?"

"Look, it's a question. Answer it. What's he make?"

"Fifty—fifty-five. Some weeks it's sixty."

"For overtime?"

"He don't get much overtime. Most weeks it's fifty."

"Fifty a week," Corey murmured, looking around at the tiny kitchen, then past the kitchen at the combination parlor-bedroom with a sagging ceiling and cracks showing in the walls. He leaned back further in the chair and said, "What's the rent here?"

"Twenty-nine fifty."

"A year?"

"That ain't clever," she said. "It ain't even funny."

"Sorry."

"No you're not. You hadda get that in."

"Let it ride."

She stood up. "I'll tell you why we live in this trap. On fifty-sixty a week we could live in a better place, except it ain't just him and me. He's got his mother in a convalescent home. He helps to support two sisters—"

"All right, all right."

"—and never spends a dime on himself. Walks to work every day to save carfare. And—"

"All right," he cut in. "Let it ride already—"

"No," she said. "You wanna know about him, I'll tell you. He's a clean-living, hard-working man. He's got a load to carry and he carries it. Last week he had a cold, and he shoulda been in bed, and he went to work anyway. Wouldn't even let me buy cough medicine. Said it cost too much. It's less than a dollar in the cut-rate store, and he said it cost too much. Then the very next day he gives me this," and she indicated a bracelet she was wearing.

It was a cheap bracelet, about a dollar-fifty. Corey glanced at it and saw it was on the conservative side, just a plain metal band with a simple design.

"Went out that day and bought it for me," she said. "For my birthday. You hear what I'm saying? He had that bad cold, coughing his head off. So instead of medicine for himself he remembers it's my birthday and goes out and buys me this bracelet."

"Like in them shows," Corey murmured.

"What shows?"

"Them picture shows. You know, them tear-jerkers for the women."

She turned away from him. "It's no use telling you anything. You're too far away from what's real."

"Or maybe too close."

She took a very deep breath and put her hands on her hips. For a moment she stood with her back to him, her head lifted and her shoulders erect. Then her arms fell limply at her sides, her shoulders drooped. It was as though something heavy was pressing down on her.

Corey lifted himself from the chair and went to the window. He stood looking out at the rain. He said, "How long you been married to him?"

"Seven months."

"And before that—?"

"Well, I hadn't known him long."

"How long?"

"A few weeks," she said.

Some mist was clouding the window. He wiped it away with his hand and peered out at the rain. It had subsided and there was a slow, quiet drizzle that sounded like fingers tapping softly on drums. Ain't nothing jazzy in that sound, he thought. That sound is on the heartache side. Goes along with the color of the sky up there, that dark gray making everything dark gray down here.

And through the dreary drumming of the rain he heard her saying, "—met him one day in a restaurant across the street from Chatworth Leather. I was working there then. So anyway, I was in the restaurant sitting at the counter and having coffee and he sits down beside me and—"

"Skip that," Corey cut in. "I didn't ask how you happened to meet him."

"I thought maybe you wanted to know."

"Why should I wanna know?" he muttered. "What the hell do I care how you met him or where you met him? I don't even wanna hear about that."

"Why not?"

Corey couldn't answer. He kept looking out at the rain.

"Why not?" she asked again. "Ain't that what you're here for? To find out about him? To check on him?"

He winced. He said to himself, you walked right into that one. And then, turning away from the window, wanting to look at her but knowing he couldn't, knowing he mustn't show what he was feeling, he affected a detached frown and said, "I'm checking only what I think is important."

"For city hall."

"That's right."

"For the records only."

"That's right."

"For the official report on the investigation—"

"That's absolutely right," he said, and turned and looked at her and saw she was smiling thinly. Her eyes were drills going into his head. He turned quickly and faced the window again.

He heard himself saying, "All right, go ahead and tell it."

"Well, like I said, we met when I was working at Chatworth Leather—"

"Hold it," he cut in. "How come you're not working there now?"

"He don't want me to work."

"Any special reason?"

"Like what?"

"Like maybe you're knocked up."

"You asking me?"

"I'm asking you," he said. "You knocked up?"

"No," she said. And then, "You wanna make a note of that?"

"For what?"

"For city hall. For the records. For the official report on the investigation."

Corey winced again. Then he turned slowly and showed her the lazy smile. He murmured, "I'll tell you why he don't want you to work. It looks better this way. It always looks better when the wife stays at home where she belongs."

Lillian moved toward a chair and sagged into it.

The lazy smile thinned just a trifle as Corey queried, "How long has he been out?"

She didn't answer.

"How long has he been out?"

"Over a year."

"What was he in for?"

"Manslaughter." Her head lowered. And then, looking up, "But he wasn't guilty—"

"Of course not."

"He swore to me—"

"Of course."

"He was only trying to protect himself."

"Sure, sure," Corey purred. Then his voice tightened. "What was the weapon?"

"His hands. Just his hands. He's never carried a weapon. He's not a thug."

Corey chuckled softly.

"Damn you," she gritted. "I'm telling you he's straight, he's decent—"

"You think so?" The lazy smile probed ever so gently. "You really think so?"

She started to get up from the chair, then slumped back into it and stared at the floor. Her eyes were saying, I don't know what to think. She made another effort and managed to lift herself from the chair. She breathed in through her teeth and said, "A factory worker, a man who sweats for every nickel he earns, who slaves in a tannery from nine to five—"

"In the daytime," Corey said. And then, jabbing lightly, "What happens at night?"

She stood there breathing hard.

Corey said, "You can't answer that. You don't have the answer. You got no idea where he goes at night, and night after night you sit here wondering. You look at the floor, you look at the walls, and you wonder."

"Stop it."

"You wonder what goes on while you look at the clock, let's say it's midnight already, and he ain't home yet. Then it's two in the morning and then it's three—"

"Stop it."

"And maybe three-thirty or four, he comes walking in, and you're waiting up. You ask him where he's been. Chances are you don't get an answer. If there's any answer at all, it's just some words coming out of his mouth; like he went for a walk or he went to play dominoes and lost track of the time. Or maybe he tells you—"

"No matter what he tells me, it's all right."

"She stands there and says it's all right. Then later she'll be at the Hangout, sitting alone and drinking beer."

"God damn you," she hissed. "Get out. Get outta here."

He went to the door and opened it. The sound of the rain came in. "Be seeing you," he said.

Then he was in the backyard, stepping over muddy puddles, going through the rain toward the alley leading to Ingersoll Street.

In the alley he saw them coming. There were three. They seemed to appear from nowhere; but he knew they'd been waiting in a doorway, waiting until he was halfway down the alley.

They were coming slowly. In the semi-darkness he squinted through the curtain of rain, focusing hard on their faces. He told himself he didn't know these three, he'd never seen them before.

As they came closer, one of them showed a gun, not aiming it, just lifting it for display. Corey sighed, then looked behind him. Sure enough there were two more coming from the other end of the alley, and one had a gun.

I think we got a problem here, Corey said to himself.

He lifted his hands shoulder high, palms open. Then he turned, faced the two and walked toward them. They came to a stop and stood waiting for him. The one with the gun was tall and heavy and looked in his middle twenties. Corey had never seen him before. The one who stood beside him was colored, also tall, not quite so heavy. Corey peered at the Negro man and decided he'd never seen him before.

Walking slowly toward the two, Corey heard the footsteps of the three coming in behind him. He kept the same pace, but lengthened his stride just a little to give himself more time before the three arrived. He came to where the two were waiting and pasted a grimace of cold fury onto his face, aiming it at the colored man.

Corey said to him, "I been lookin' for you, Creighton."

"My name ain't Creighton," the colored man said.

"Don't gimme that—"

"He said his name ain't Creighton." The one with the gun spoke quietly, then raised the gun so that the muzzle was just a few inches away from Corey's chest.

Corey didn't seem to notice the gun. He showed his teeth to the colored man and said, "You're Creighton, and you and me are gonna talk—"

Then he made a move toward the colored man and the one with the gun reached out to push him back. He feinted a swipe at the man's hand, still looking at the Negro, making it appear that his only thought was an obsession to get back at the man named Creighton. This happened very fast. The three coming in from behind were still moving slowly and were about twenty feet away when Corey started to lunge toward the colored man. The one with the gun said, "What are you doing? You a lunatic or something?" and Corey swerved in that instant, his fist hitting the gunman in the throat, his other hand closing on the gunman's wrist, twisting it hard. The gunman gurgled and the gun fell from his hand. The colored man made a grab for Corey and missed, then yelled at the three who were coming in running, "Don't—don't—don't shoot."

There was no shooting. There was no way to get a shot at Corey without the possibility of the bullet hitting the other two. Both of them were grabbing for Corey, but he wriggled away and ran down the alley.

He ran very fast, cut around the corner of the house, then across the backyard. He was thinking, you gotta make it to Ingersoll, gotta find another alley and get through it and make Ingersoll before they—

At that moment he heard them shouting and cursing in a conference, the loudest voice declaring, "—do it my way. We split and you two get on Ingersoll. You see him comin' out of an alley, you'll be ready and you'll get him."

That's intelligent, Corey approved. Then he switched his own thinking away from Ingersoll and looked in the other direction where all the backyards gave way to the swamplands.

You can't go in there, he thought. You get in them swamplands it's a hundred-to-one you won't get out. You know them swamplands.

Sure as hell you know them swamplands, and you know what can happen in there. Especially when it gets dark and you can't see where you're going. Another thing, this rain. This rain, it ain't no light drizzle anymore. It rains like this, it's really raining; and the swamplands sit lower than the neighborhood, so all the water from the gutters goes into them holes and slimy pools out there, along with the overflow from the goddam river. You remember one time some years ago there were kids out playing in them swamplands, and it started to rain, and then it was a heavy rain, and it got dark. And a few days later a searching party went in, and the search went on for weeks, but it was no use. Then another time some grown-ups, who shoulda had more sense and woulda had more sense if they were sober, got to fooling around. And for some idiotic reason they wandered in there; it was six of them, or seven I think. Anyway you remember it was during a spell of heavy rain and again the searching party went in and again it was no use. So according to that—

His thoughts were interrupted. He heard a shot and he threw himself into the mud, landing face down, then twisting and looking back to see three of them running across the backyards. He pulled the police pistol from his belt and fired without aiming, just to let them know he had a gun. He fired again, and they fired back at him. All three of them fired as they scattered for cover behind trash barrels, rubbish cans.

It's gonna hafta be the swamplands, he told himself. You can't try for Ingersoll, and you can't try for no back doors, either. It's a cinch all them back doors are locked. Just look at the lights goin' out in them windows, like they're tellin' you they don't wanna know from nothin'. They got their own worries.

So it's gonna be the swamplands. It's gotta be the swamplands, jim. There ain't no other place for you to go. But Jesus Christ, what a setup. What a mess.

He grimaced wryly, shaking his head slowly as he rested, face down in the mud, about thirty yards away from the edge of the swamplands.

Some mud got into his mouth and he wiped it away from his teeth. He thought about the two who were waiting on Ingersoll. But they won't just stay there and wait, he told himself. What they'll do, they'll join the party when the deal goes down and you make your break for the swamplands. They'll hear the shooting in there, and they'll come running to put in their two cents. You mean their two guns. And two added to three makes five. It's gonna be five guns on your tail, and you won't be no rabbit in there. You can't move fast like a rabbit in all that ooze and muck and guck. You're gonna hafta move like a night crawler. Like a blind night crawler, considering how dark it's getting now.

Well, maybe that's a break for you, that dark sky getting darker. Them five guns can't aim at what they can't see. But you know they can aim at what they hear, and you go stumbling into a ditch or tumble into one of them pools, they'll hear that and they'll—

All right, cut this noise. Just cut it, will you? You'll handle the aggravation when you come to it. What you better do now, and I mean right now, is get rolling, and fast.

He was up on his feet, running hard toward the swamplands. He heard the shots and wanted to throw himself down again but knew it wouldn't delay them this time. They're out for meat; they're really hungry, he thought and told his legs to keep running.

At the edge of the swamplands, there were mostly weeds and low bushes. He heard the buzzing of a bullet. It was close and he wished the bushes were higher so he could throw himself down behind cover. He kept running, going deeper into the swamplands and heard one of them shouting, "There he goes." Next he heard a flurry of shots, and he pleaded with himself to run faster. In this section the ground was fairly solid, but he was slowed down because he was zig-zagging. Ahead the bushes were higher, the vegetation thicker, and he could make out the silhouettes of trees.

He heard someone shout, "You see him?"

Another voice answered, "Can't see him now."

Just as Corey was getting a lift from that, a third voice yelled, "I see him—headed for them trees."

"Them trees won't do him no good," the one who'd shouted first predicted, and then there was heavy firing. The buzzing of the bullets came closer. Corey sprinted for the nearest tree, got behind it, realized it wasn't wide enough to offer cover. He heard the bullets buzzing very close, much too close, and got away from the tree and ran deeper into the swamplands.

He zig-zagged for about forty yards, looking for anything that offered cover. None of the trees was wide enough. There were some mounds of dead wood and decayed vegetation but that wasn't cover. You need something bulletproof, he told himself as a slug thudded into one of the mushy mounds, went through, came out the other side and smashed into a tree. Some splinters from the tree hit him in the face and he came to a stop. Irritated, he cursed to himself.

Then he was running again. He ran another fifteen yards, but after that it was like trying to run through glue. Now you're really in it, he thought. This is why it's called the swamplands. It was up above his ankles. Moments later it was up past his knees. He kept moving ahead and it came up to his waist. Behind him the firing had stopped, and he decided they'd lost him in the increasing darkness.

Or it could be they're reloading? he wondered. He stood in the moldy, gucky pool, thinking if he moved ahead he'd only sink in deeper. In the immediate area there were no trees, no bushes, nothing to hold onto. He looked around; about twenty feet ahead and slightly to the left something appeared to be solid and hard, glittering grey in the rain and darkness. He squinted and studied it, then headed toward it.

It was a rock, a very large rock, rising a good four feet above the surface of the pool. It's high enough, he told himself. It's also wide enough. It's a barricade, all right.

That is, if you can get there. You might go in over your head before you get there and remember this ain't just water. You go down in this, you stay down.

Moving very slowly on a diagonal, going toward the rock, he felt the slimy glutinous ooze of the pool pulling him down. It was above his waist; it was coming up to his chest. He started to take another step forward, hesitated, took the step and went in deeper. Gauging the distance to the rock, he estimated it was at least twelve feet. He stood wondering what to do. He was holding the gun above his shoulder so it wouldn't get wet. He looked at the gun and told himself that maybe now was the time to tighten up and force the issue. But you only got four bullets, he cautioned himself.

He stood with the gucky surface of the pool coming up higher on his chest. Some dead twigs floated past and flicked gently at his chin. The only sound was the splashing of the rain.

Then he heard the yell, "I see him—there he is."

"Where?"

"There—right there."

"Ain't nothin' there. Ain't nothin' movin'."

"He can't move. He's stuck."

"You sure it's him? Maybe it's—"

"It's him, all right."

"So watcha waitin' for? Shoot him."

"With what? I'm outta clips."

"Of all the dumb—"

Corey moved forward, his arms pumping as he fought against the downward pull of the bog. There were moments when he couldn't feel anything solid under his feet, but he knew that if he kept working his arms and wriggling his legs, he could keep his head above the surface. You're getting tired, though, he told himself. You're getting very tired—

And then he reached the rock. He got behind it, climbed onto it where it offered a ledge, and crouched there, breathing hard.

Bullets were hitting the rock and ricocheting. He waited a few minutes and then decided it was time for some counterpunching. Above his head there was a gap in the rock. He raised himself up just a little and looked through the gap and saw the five of them on the other side of the bog.

It had stopped raining. There was moonlight now, and he could see them clearly.

They were set up for him, standing close together. Corey thought, it's almost a pity, it's strictly slaughterhouse, they're just waiting to get chopped down.

His eyes narrowed and measured the distance. He raised his right arm and started to take aim. Just then something occurred to him. He didn't have the gun.

9

You goofer. You butter-fingered, wrong-way artist. If they hand out awards for lousing things up, you're a cinch to get first prize. And don't gimme no excuses, either. Don't tell me you had other things to think about. Don't tell me you only got two hands and that's why you hadda let go of the gun. You clown; you can't remember letting go of the gun. It just slipped away from your fingers and now it's down there somewhere at the bottom of the pool and you can forget about it. But jim I swear you really irk me sometimes.

He shook his head slowly, crouching low again. Bullets were hitting the rock and bouncing off, others whizzed through the gap where he'd shown his face.

Then suddenly the firing stopped, as though someone had given them an order to stop firing. He waited a minute, but there was no further firing. So now they're getting clever, he thought. Now it's strategy and they'll try a flank maneuver. They know they can't get you with frontal shooting and they'll hafta figure some way of crossing the pool. They do that, they'll be coming in from the left flank or the right flank or both flanks and it's the end of the line. You know, it's almost enough to give a man the blues.

Well anyway, they got that pool to cross and how they're gonna cross it is their headache. Maybe they won't be able to cross it. Maybe they'll be stymied and—

Or maybe they're crossing it already.

You better take a look and check what they're doing.

He lifted his head and peered through the gap. The moonlight cast a blue-white glow on them. They were assembled in a tight circle at the edge of the quagmire. Then the circle broke up and Corey frowned, puzzled. He counted them, focusing hard to make sure he was counting correctly. There were six.

First five and now six. He stated the fact to himself, narrowing his focus to exclude the five faces he'd seen before, his eyes slitted and straining, aiming like twin needles at the sixth man.

The sixth man was tall and had wide shoulders. The moonlight lacquered his curly black hair. His features were rugged, yet wholesome and pleasant, and he could have posed for an ad captioned, "He Takes Vitamins," or smokes X brand of cigarettes. Or wears a certain type of elastic-waisted shorts. Or uses a certain cologne that lists him positively as a man of merit, a specimen of quality.

And that's what she saw when she saw him for the first time, Corey reasoned. She saw them big fine shoulders and all that bulk packed in nice and solid, some two hundred pounds on a six-foot frame. So a female, any female, would naturally take a second look and what Lillian saw with that closer inspection was something she musta been hoping for or let's say starved for. She musta caught the vibration that under all that muscle and power there was what they call the true blue, the clean thoughts and the honest striving and so forth. It musta come across to her that his pleasant smile and the wholesome look in his eyes were a hundred percent for real. And you can understand her buying that. Considering the run of available roosters in this neighborhood, or any neighborhood for that matter, all she hadda do was make a comparison and it hits her that this is it. This is the genuine merchandise.

What she did, of course, she sold herself a bill of goods. Not that she's a fool. Not that she's inclined to move without thinking. It's just that she's a woman and she's hot-natured and at the same time she's pure-minded. It's hell on a woman like that when she ain't married. Especially when she's been married, and she knows what it is to have it there when she needs it. So then when she's alone, she tries not to think about it; but she's flesh and blood. You can see her squirming in bed, twisting her head on the pillow, finally getting up to drink a glass of water, as if that can do any good. It goes on like that for weeks, for months, for years and you'll give odds there weren't no one night stands, not even them nights when she was absolutely desperate. But finally it gets to the point where she just can't bear it no more; she's gotta have a man or have fits.

So then she meets this two hundred pound six-footer with the wide shoulders and black curly hair and the rugged wholesome pleasant face. Let's say he levels with her right from the start and tells her he's an ex-con and the rap was manslaughter. But then of course he swears it was self-defense. And she believes him, or forces herself to believe him. Or maybe she finds it easy to believe him because he's holding her hands, he's looking deep into her eyes. He's saying it slow and quiet and it's getting across. Some of them can do that, you know. The old soft sell. The sound of sincerity. He's saying something like, sure I've made mistakes. I'm not an angel and I know my faults, but what really counts is knowing what I want. And all I want is to live a decent worthwhile life—

And say a month later the parole officer is writing out his report on Delbert Kingsley and it's all on the plus side. It states that in addition to holding down a steady job and reporting for work every day and working efficiently and diligently, Delbert Kingsley is now married. The report goes on to say that the bride is a girl of clean habits and polite manners. She's a good housekeeper, does her own sewing, doesn't spend money on trifles and never uses make-up and—

You get it? The report on Delbert Kingsley recommends that he be released from parole. And that's just what they did; they released him. You ain't guessing, either. You heard her saying he stays out late at night; and you know he wouldn't do that if he was on parole.

There you have it. That's why he married her. He musta been frantic to get released from parole, to move around freely and not hafta answer questions. To get released from parole he hadda do something to impress the authorities, to give them some guarantee that from here on in he'd be playing it straight. And what he gave them, what he actually showed them, was a living guarantee. He showed them the grade-A material he'd chosen for a wife.

She came in handy, all right. She got baited and pulled in and then like a trophy she was placed on exhibit.

Corey Bradford sighed heavily. Then his eyes were slits again and he peered through the gap in the rock, seeing Delbert Kingsley and the others on the far side of the quagmire. Kingsley was facing them, gesturing as though giving orders. Two of them moved off, going fast along a route running parallel to the quagmire. Then two went running in the opposite direction. Kingsley stood with the fifth man and seemed to be urging him to do something. Corey couldn't hear their voices, but it appeared that the man was reluctant. He shook his head and turned away from Kingsley. A moment later the man was on the ground, and Kingsley reached down and lifted him up, punched him in the face, and he went down again. Kingsley kicked him in the head. He got to his knees. Kingsley made a gesture, telling him to get to his feet. He obeyed, but he seemed to be pleading. Kingsley moved close to him and punched him in the stomach. Then Kingsley shoved him toward the quagmire.

The man moved forward slowly, his head lowered. He appeared very unhappy. The mushy slime was up to his knees and he came to a stop and looked back at Kingsley, who stood at the edge of the bog. Kingsley motioned him to keep moving across the bog and head toward the rock.

And he'll do it, Corey thought. Or at least he'll try to do it. That ain't the traffic manager who's issuing the orders. That ain't the vice president, neither. From all indications that's the top executive, that's the boss man.

That's the driver, all right. That's the brain. He musta spotted me through the window when I was in there talking to Lillian, and told his people to be ready for me when I come out. He stayed in the background while all the shooting was taking place, but now he figures he can show himself. He figures he can let me see his face and it won't matter. I mean it won't matter because I'm not gonna get outta here alive. That's what he figures.

Corey focused hard on the face of Delbert Kingsley. The moonlight shone brightly on the surface of the bog. Then Corey looked at the man who was trying to get across. The man was in it up to his waist. The moonlight showed something glistening in his hand. It was a gun. Corey quickly lowered himself under the aperture in the rock.

He crouched there and listened. He heard the man yelling to Kingsley, "It's getting deeper—"

And Kingsley's voice, "Keep going."

"I can't."

"Don't tell me that. Don't tell me nothing. Keep going."

"I'll sink."

"It ain't all that deep."

"It's plenty deep. Keeps getting deeper."

"You're almost there."

"It's damn near up to my neck."

"You'll make it," Kingsley shouted. "Just keep going."

"It's pullin' at me," the man yelled. "It's draggin' me down."

Corey raised his head to venture another look through the gap in the rock. The man was less than six feet away from the rock. He was sinking slowly but still trying to move forward. He didn't see Corey. His head was down as he strained with the effort of pushing himself against the viscous mass.

Gasping and grunting, the man looked up and saw Corey. But instead of pointing the gun he just stared with his eyes getting wider and wider. He was sinking.

"No," the man said. "No, no. Please. No, no." He went under.

Corey gazed at the green-gray surface of the quagmire. He looked across to the other side where Kingsley stood at the edge. Without sound, he said to Kingsley, well you lost that investment. You were using him for a decoy. You figure I still got the gun and you sent him in to draw fire so the gun would be empty when them others move in from the flanks. So what it amounts to, he was used and now he's useless. That's what bothers you. Just that and nothing more. You're something, all right. You're really a sweetheart.

Kingsley stood there studying the rock. He had a gun in his hand and he took a shot at the rock. Corey ducked under the gap. Kingsley used another bullet and it went through the gap and sliced air just a few inches above Corey's head.

Corey crouched lower. Kingsley tried another shot and the slug screamed through the gap and smacked into a tree about twenty yards behind the rock. Corey turned his head slowly and looked in the direction of the tree. It appeared to be rooted in fairly solid ground but in order to get there he'd be gambling on the depth of the quagmire. He didn't feel like taking that gamble.

He stayed crouched. It was quiet now, real quiet, for almost a minute. Then, in the distance and off to the left, there were squishy noises. He shifted his position on the rock and squinted toward the left. He saw the two men who'd been sent to flank him from that side. They were about seventy yards away and a little more than halfway across the quagmire. It was below their knees and they were making rapid progress. Then suddenly they were slowed down. They were in it up to their waists. They kept moving forward and went in deeper. Then they just stood there.

Corey took a deep breath. Again he shifted his position and aimed his eyes at the opposite flank. He saw the other two moving across the quagmire, not more than fifty yards away. It was up past their knees. It stayed at that level as they advanced another fifteen feet. They were nearing the point where they'd be on a line with the rock and Corey thought, they reach that point, that's it. That's the finish. They'll take aim and fire and you're done.

"Hold it," a voice shouted. It was Kingsley's voice.

The two men stopped and faced about. One of them called to Kingsley, "Whatsa matter?"

"Just hold it there—wait."

"For what?" the man whined loudly. "What the hell's wrong?"

For a few moments there was no reply. Then Kingsley yelled, "Come back, come back."

"What's happening?"

"Come back." Now it was a shriek. "Don't stand there, we gotta get outta here. Come on, make it fast."

The two men headed back toward the other side of the quagmire. There was something frantic in the way they were moving. Corey turned and looked at the two on the left flank and saw them wading through the thick slime, going back to the other side.

Then he lifted his head and peered through the gap. He saw Kingsley running back and forth along the edge of the quagmire, beckoning feverishly, urging them to hurry.

And it ain't no fake maneuver, Corey told himself. What musta happened, Kingsley thought he heard something, and then he listened again and knew he'd heard something. And it wasn't no four-footed drifter coming in to get chummy. Whatever it is that's coming in, it's got Kingsley snapping his lid. Just look at him hopping around.

"Move it," Kingsley was screaming to the men. "Move it move it!"

The two who'd been flanking from the right arrived on the other side of the quagmire. They ran toward Kingsley. Then the two on the left came in. The four of them stood close to Kingsley, and it appeared he was giving them in-structions. One of them backed away and made a gesture of protest. Kingsley reached out, grabbed him and hit him in the face. Then Kingsley went on with the instructions. Another one started to argue and Kingsley clouted him in the ribs with the butt of his gun. There were no further arguments. The group stood there for another moment, then split up, going out fanwise toward the trees in the distance.

Corey watched them as they ran off. They merged with the darkness. Well they're gone, he thought. And you're alone here. And believe me, jim, this is one time when it's nice to be alone.

He let out a heavy sigh. Then slowly he climbed up on top of the rock and rested flat, face down. He said to himself, it's velvet. It's a chunk of jagged rock but I swear it's velvet.

He closed his eyes. He smiled dimly, floating out with the waves of weariness, going out farther and farther.

All at once he opened his eyes, sat up and listened. Then he squinted in the direction of the gunfire. He saw tiny points of yellow light winking in the darkness. The gun flashes were a few hundred yards away. As the firing became more intense there were shouts and screams. Some were screams of panic and other screams were like the howling of animals getting eaten alive.

The exchange of gunfire was spreading over a wider area. Watching the gun flashes, he saw that a considerable number of pistols were in action. Nine or ten or eleven, he estimated. And you can tell from the noise they're all .38s. And just listen to them screams.

Can you guess what's actually happening? Well, not hardly. But there's one thing you know for sure. You know that things don't look too cozy right now for Delbert Kingsley and company.

But who's the opposition? Would it be the blue boys from the 37th Precinct? No, it wouldn't be them. They're busy with more important assignments. They're raiding penny ante poker games and issuing tickets for parking violations. Them fearless law enforcers from the 37th, they're out taking all kinds of chances and putting the pinch on each and every harmless vag and painted-up fag and liquored-up hag. They got all that to do. They can't be bothered with a little fuss involving .38s.

So the question remains, who's the opposition? You think it's Grogan's mob? Well, it could be. It very well could be. But on the other hand—

His thoughts were cut off. The shooting had stopped and he sat up straighter and listened for any noise at all. There was complete silence. A minute passed. Another minute. And then he heard a voice calling his name.

He got down behind the rock, crouching.

The voice came closer, calling his name. It was an unfamiliar voice, and he crouched lower. The voice kept calling, coming closer to the other side of the quagmire.

He breathed very slowly, telling himself not to move, not to make the slightest sound.

"Bradford—Bradford—"

Go away, he said to the voice.

"Bradford—you there? Where are you?"

Go away, mister. I don't know who you are and I'm not sure you're a friend.

"Bradford."

Will you do me a favor and go away?

The voice continued to call his name. Then the voice receded and finally stopped calling.

He remained motionless behind the rock waiting several minutes, listening for the slightest sound; but there was no noise and he told himself to move.

Maneuvering carefully, he lowered himself from the rock, going into the quagmire, holding onto the rock with his feet, searching for a foothold. Some minutes later he arrived on the other side of the bog. Far in the distance he could see the bright yellow face of the clock in the tower of city hall. The hands pointed to nine-ten.

In the bathroom on the second floor of the rooming house there was a small clock on top of the medicine cabinet. The hands pointed to nine-thirty-seven. Corey was sitting in a tub of warm water, soaping himself, scrubbing hard to get the slime off his body. It clung to him like axle grease and he wished the water was warmer. The rooming house lacked a hot-water heater, and he didn't feel like making a trip down to the kitchen to fill the kettle and put it on the stove. He stayed in the tub more than a quarter of an hour, changing the water several times until it finally drained out clear.

He shaved, put on clean clothes. As he left the rooming house it occurred to him that he'd forgotten something. He went back to his room, opened the dresser drawer and took out the .38 that Grogan had given him. He put the gun under his belt, the polo shirt over the gun, the lower edge of the shirt flapping loose around his thighs. He went out of the room and was going down the stairs when he stopped and bit the corner of his mouth. He was wondering if he really needed the gun.

It ain't like you're gonna go lookin' for targets, he told himself. You'll just drift over to the Hangout and socialize awhile. But even so, you better hold on to the gun.

He continued down the stairs. Just before he opened the door to walk out of the rooming house, he tapped his fingers against the fabric of the polo shirt where it covered the gun. As his fingers felt the hard metal under the fabric, he grimaced with annoyance. For some unaccountable reason, he was bothered about the gun. Not about the possibility that he might be forced to use it. The uncertainty went beyond that. He wished he knew the reason for it. His grimace tightened as he wondered about the gun for another instant. Then he shrugged, opened the door and walked out.

They picked him up at Third and Addison.

He was crossing Third when the noise of the car came close and the brakes squealed. He started a move, his right hand going under his polo shirt. Then he heard the voice, "Hold it—this is Squad."

His head turned and he looked at the squad car. It was Heeley and Donofrio. They just sat there looking at him for a long while.

Donofrio opened the car door, got out and beckoned to Corey.

"Me in the middle?" Corey murmured as Donofrio held the door open for him.

"That's right," Heeley said from behind the wheel. "You in the middle."

Corey got in. Donofrio climbed in and closed the car door and they started off. Heeley turned on the siren and went through a red light at First and Addison. The siren was humming low. Heeley raised it a few octaves as they moved faster on Addison going toward the bridge.

"What's the rush?" Corey asked.

They didn't answer. They didn't look at him. Now the car was on the bridge, doing sixty, and the siren was up another octave. Coming off the bridge the car was doing close to seventy and Heeley had the siren going full blast.

What gives here? Corey wondered. He turned his head and looked at Donofrio. For a moment the Italian's face stayed in profile. "Hey you," Corey said softly.

Donofrio looked at him and muttered, "You talkin' to me?"

Corey winced slightly, seeing something in the squad-man's eyes that spoke in terms of claws and fangs, a big cat crouched and ready to leap.

"Look, I wanna know what's happening," Corey said.

Donofrio looked past Corey, saying to Heeley, "So whaddya think? You think Fullmer?"

"Sure," Heeley said. "It won't go five rounds."

"I don't know," Donofrio frowned and bit the corner of his mouth. "It looks like Fullmer and yet—"

"He can't do nothing with Fullmer. He's made for Fullmer."

"But that left. If he connects with that left."

"He won't," Heeley said. "He won't have a chance to get set."

"Well, you never can tell," Donofrio said. He lurched

173

against Corey as the car made a screeching turn, Heeley pulling hard at the wheel to evade a truck coming out of a side street. It was a one way street. The Squad car sliced through, going against traffic and narrowly missing a top down convertible filled with Saturday night teenagers. The convertible was forced to go onto the pavement. As the siren kept blasting and the Squad car came close to colliding with other cars, swerving frantically and going onto the pavement, Donofrio and Heeley went on chatting about the middleweight champion Gene Fullmer. They agreed that Fullmer was a very cagey operator and his style, which appeared to be clumsy and sloppy, was actually a series of tricky maneuvers that put the opponent at a disadvantage. They continued to talk about Fullmer as the Squad car pulled to a stop in the city hall courtyard. Going up in the elevator, they were still talking about Fullmer. In the corridor, heading toward room 529, they walked on either side of Corey, staying close to him but not looking at him. They were talking about Gene Fullmer. Coming closer to the door of 529, it occurred to Corey that something weird was taking place. He had the creepy feeling that shadows walked beside him, that other shadows were closing in on him.

They entered 529. The outer office was empty. From the inner office there was the hum of voices. The door of the inner office was opened. A squadman came out, looked Corey up and down, then stepped back into the inner office and closed the door.

"What's with him?" Corey asked. Heeley and Donofrio

didn't answer. They stood with Corey in the middle, their shoulders touching his shoulders.

"You're crowding me," he said, and started to move away. They pressed closer, holding him there. "This I don't get," he said, and made another try to pull away. They pushed in more tightly. It was as though they had him in a vise. For an instant he thought of arguing the point. Then he tossed the idea away, reminding himself that this was Night Squad and there was no arguing with Night Squad. Because they're screwballs, he told himself. Because they're the kind that oughta be in cages and if you get them upset, you're messing with homicidal maniacs.

The door of the inner office was opened again and three squadmen came out. Heeley and Donofrio stepped away from Corey and moved toward the three, then turned and faced Corey so that five squadmen stood in a row near the door of the inner office. The door remained open and Corey started toward it; but the five of them didn't move, they were blocking his path.

"Send him in," a voice from the inner office said. The five squadmen moved, giving Corey a path to the doorway. He walked in and saw McDermott standing at the side of the desk. In McDermott's hand there was a rolled newspaper. The detective-sergeant was watching a fly that circled the desk top. The fly made a landing and McDermott swatted, mashing it. McDermott stood looking at the squashed fly and said to Corey, "Close the door."

Corey closed the door, leaned back against it and watched the detective-sergeant who bent over the desk top, arms folded, eyes peering clinically at the tiny dead thing. For several moments McDermott studied the remains of the fly, then slowly turned his head, looked at Corey and said, "So how ya doin'?"

Don't answer him, Corey told himself. Don't give him nothing.

"Anything new?" McDermott asked, his voice mild.

There was no answer. There was only the sound of the distorted humming from the faulty electric fan.

McDermott smiled softly, pleasantly. He walked around the desk and sat down. He said, "Wanna buy a raffle ticket?" He opened a desk drawer and took out a book of tickets. "I got some tickets here, fifty cents a chance." He tossed the book to Corey. The raffle was sponsored by some fraternal organization and the first prize was a Plymouth. Corey glanced at the top ticket and tore it off. He moved to the desk, picked up a pencil and wrote his name on the slip attached to the book. Then he put a dollar bill on the desk top. The detective-sergeant reached into his trousers pocket, took out two quarters and handed them to Corey, who turned and walked toward the door.

"Where you going?" McDermott asked.

Corey stopped. He stood with his back to the desk. He waited a few moments, then said, "Second and Addison. I got a date."

"With who?"

"A double gin," Corey said. "Is that all right with you?"

"Sure," McDermott said. He drew a circle around the fly. He gazed at the fly as he said, "Got anything else to report?"

"No," Corey said without thinking. And then he thought about it and wanted to change his answer, but of course it was too late.

McDermott drew a second circle around the crushed corpse of the fly, inside the first circle. With the tip of the pencil he touched the two circles, then put down the pencil and took out a matchbook and struck a match. He applied the flame to the fly. In the blue-orange blaze the fly became a tiny heap of black debris. McDermott blew out the match, whisked the charred substance onto the floor and said to Corey, "I'm gonna letcha try it one more time."

"Try what?"

"Reporting in."

"Ain't nothing to report," Corey said.

McDermott got up from the desk chair. He walked past Corey and opened the door leading to the outer office. He beckoned to the men out there and then went back to the desk. The five squadmen came in, the door closing behind Donofrio who was the last to enter.

The five squadmen stood along the wall. Corey was standing near the middle of the room. Sitting at the desk, McDermott had his elbows on the desk top, his head leaning against the heels of his palms. Corey saw that McDermott's eyes were closed. For the better part of a minute the only noise in the room was the humming of the electric fan.

Then McDermott lowered his hands to the desk top, resting them flat. He leaned back in the chair, gazed up at the ceiling and said, "Look at them, Bradford."

Corey turned and looked at the squadmen.

"Count them," McDermott said.

You're gonna hafta do it, Corey told himself. You're just gonna hafta go along with it.

"How many?" McDermott asked.

"Five," Corey said.

"Five is correct." McDermott spoke softly. "There's five here and you're the sixth and there's one missing."

Corey breathed in slowly and held it. Something poked hard at his lungs and he grunted and let out the air. He breathed in again very slowly.

"One missing," McDermott said. He looked at Corey. "You know where he is?"

Corey shook his head.

"I'll tell you where he is," McDermott said. "He's in a casket."

"With bullets in him," Donofrio said.

"Four bullets," from another squadman.

"Four bullets," McDermott echoed. "One in the knee-cap, one in the pelvis and two in the belly. When they got him to the hospital, he was still alive. He lasted about forty-five minutes. When he checked out he looked worried."

"Now why would he be worried?" Heeley wanted to know. "That ain't no time to be worried. When that time comes, your worries are over."

"He was worried about his family," McDermott said. "He leaves a wife and nine children."

"And none of them old enough to go to work," Donofrio put in.

"I didn't know he had nine children," Heeley said. "I didn't know much about him. He never had much to say."

"I'll tell you about him," McDermott said, looking at the squadmen. And Corey thought, sure, he's looking at them but he's saying it to me. McDermott went on, "He was forty-four years old. His full name was Leonard Ward Ferguson. At seventeen he got into the navy. Got married when he was eighteen. In the Pacific he was in the thick of it and came out with dizzy spells from head wounds and also a peptic ulcer from anxiety. He was on three cruisers and they all got torpedoed. One time he was on a raft for eleven days. The war's over; he gets a job driving a truck and one night he goes through a guard rail on the turnpike. They had him in the hospital almost a year. The first six months they didn't think he'd make it. Both legs busted, compound, and he was knocked all outta joint inside. Comes outta the hospital and can't get a job, but he's got an uncle with pull, and the uncle gets him on the force. That was in 1947. In 1949 he was in the hospital again, two bullets in his chest. From some thugs knocking over a warehouse. He got the thugs. He got all four of them; with his gun he got three and with two slugs in the chest, he got the fourth using his hands around the man's throat. Again in the hospital they didn't think he'd make it. A couple months later he's outta the hospital, and then some time later, around 1952, he's in the hospital again. This time it's a bullet in the back and very close to the spine. But he got the people he was after. He was alone when it happened. He spotted thugs running out of a tap-room where they'd just finished shooting the bartender and two customers. Again it was three, and he went after them, shot it out and got them all. In 1954 he was kicked off the force. They kicked him off while he was in the hospital. He was in the hospital with a busted collar bone, his left arm busted, two bullets in his thigh and a bullet in his ribs and another bullet in his neck. Again it happened when he was alone. Seven hoodlums used blackjacks and brass knuckles on two old people who'd just closed up their candy store for the night. The woman was over seventy, the man was close to eighty. The hoodlums were beating them to a pulp, already had their money but kept on beating them. The couple begged for mercy and when Ferguson came running in, one of the hoodlums pulled a gun and shot him in the thigh. He stayed on his feet just long enough to get behind a parked car. They move in to finish him and he goes for his gun. He gets one of them. The others take off. Ferguson comes out from behind the car, but his leg won't hold up and he's on his knees. The hoodlums come back, they figure he's just about done, and they'll have some fun with him before he goes. So then it's another hoodlum dead and this time they really take off. A few minutes later the police cars arrive and Ferguson gets taken to the hospital, along with the old couple. Incidentally, that old couple, they're alive to this day, they still got that candy store.

"But here's why Ferguson was kicked off the force. In the hospital two suspects were brought in to be identified as members of that hoodlum group. The old couple weren't sure, or were afraid, so it's up to Ferguson. He looks at the two suspects and says yes. And the assistant D.A. says, 'You sure?' and Ferguson keeps saying yes. The assistant D.A. takes out a notebook and right there in front of the suspects, and with reporters there, mind you, he starts reading off a list of Ferguson's various injuries dating all the way back to the war. He says to Ferguson, 'Lemme ask you something. You still suffer from dizzy spells?' Ferguson makes a grab for the water pitcher on the table next to the bed and then he uses it like a hammer. The assistant D.A. gets a concussion. The two suspects were released and Ferguson was suspended, listed mentally unqualified. He's out of work for more than a year; then one day he comes in to see me. He wants to know if I can pull some strings and get him on the Night Squad."

"That was when?" from Heeley.

"That was late in 1955," McDermott said. Then he looked at Corey Bradford. "You getting all this?"

Corey didn't answer.

McDermott continued to look at him. "I wantcha to listen real careful now. In the five years Leonard Ward Ferguson was a member of this here Night Squad, he was carted to the hospital at least once each year. It was always injuries. It was stab wounds or bullet wounds or getting bopped on the head with a tire chain or something. Add that to all them other times he was in the hospital and you wonder how come he could take all that."

"He was made to take it," Donofrio said.

"That's one thing," McDermott agreed. "He was just made that way. The other thing is, he hadda take it. He was on assignment, and there's always that risk to be considered. But what he got tonight, he didn't hafta get. What he got tonight was my fault."

"It wasn't your fault," Heeley said.

"Now look, you shut the hell up," McDermott told Heeley. "I'm saying it was my fault. It was my fault because I made a serious error in judgement. I put trust where it didn't belong."

Corey winced.

McDermott got up from the desk chair. His eyes were wet. He said to Corey, "That's just about how it stacks. I trusted you and you did him in."

Corey mumbled, "I did what?"

"You did him in," McDermott said. Then something happened to his face, his mouth wide open, the corners stretched so that his teeth showed, his eyes glimmering, berserk. For an instant it seemed he would lunge at Corey. But then he turned away, leaning low over the desk with his hands gripping the edge of the desk top.

Corey looked at the five squadmen. They stood motionless, their faces expressionless.

McDermott leaned lower over the desk, then made a staggering move toward the desk chair. He sagged into the chair. He put his hands to his face, rubbed up and down, placed his hands on his chest and gazed up at the ceiling. He said, "All right, I'm ready now. I'm ready to hear it."

"Hear what?" Corey asked.

The detective-sergeant gazed at the ceiling.

Corey said, "There ain't nothing I can tell you. How can I tell you anything? I got no idea what this is all about."

It was quiet for some moments. Then Donofrio moved away from the other squadmen, came close to Corey and said, "Tell him what he wants to hear."

Corey remained quiet. Donofrio put his hand on the back of Corey's neck and applied a slight pressure.

"Take your hand off me," Corey said.

Donofrio increased the pressure. A current of pain caused Corey's mouth to tighten. "Tell him," Donofrio said. "You gonna tell him?"

There was more pressure, and considerably more pain. Donofrio's thumb pressed hard at a vein and Corey let out a slight groan. Then he smiled lazily. He didn't look at Donofrio. He brought up his elbow, it was a projectile coming up very fast and making contact with Donofrio's jaw. Donofrio's hand fell away from Corey's neck. The tall sad-faced Italian took three backward steps going toward the desk, his knees starting to give way. He reached back and held onto the desk to keep himself from going to the floor. His eyes were closed and he was shaking his head to get rid of the fog. While that was happening, nobody moved. Nobody made a sound. Donofrio opened his eyes and looked at Corey.

"You better not," Corey said softly through the lazy smile. Donofrio straightened to his full height of six feet one inch, mobilized all the power that amounted in weight to more than a hundred and ninety pounds, then walked toward Corey. "All right, then," Corey said, and slipped away from a right hand aimed at his head. Donofrio moved in rhythm with Corey's maneuver and was already hooking with the left as Corey started a counter to his head. Corey landed and Donofrio landed and they both fell back. Donofrio's hook had connected with Corey's side just under the ribs. Some blood came from Donofrio's mouth where

183

Corey's right hand had loosened a few front teeth. Now Donofrio walked in again. Corey was bent over with his right hand pressed to his side and his left out, jabbing. Donofrio chopped at the left, bringing it down, then hammered his right hand to Corey's head. Corey went to the floor.

Donofrio kicked Corey in the ribs, then aimed a kick at his head. Corey managed to roll away. Donofrio started another kick but McDermott got up from the desk and grabbed Donofrio who kept trying to kick at Corey's head. Donofrio got away from the detective-sergeant and took hold of a chair, raising it high with the intention of cracking Corey's skull. The other squadmen rushed in. Two of them hit Donofrio low, at the knees. The other two got him around the middle and at the shoulders. They were taking him to the floor, but he was maniacal at this moment and broke away from them. He still held the chair with one hand. Again he raised it as he ran for Corey, who was trying to get up from the floor. McDermott got between them, put a bear hug on the Italian and kept squeezing. Donofrio's head went back, his mouth opened wide, his arms limp and his knees buckling. McDermott kept squeezing. Donofrio's eyes rolled and he was losing consciousness. The detective-sergeant slackened his hold. Donofrio made a wheezing sound as he took in air. The chair was overturned on the floor and Donofrio gave it a sad look. Then McDermott let go of him and Donofrio collapsed on the floor beside the chair. He was semi-conscious, making wheezing noises, resting on his side with his knees close to his middle. His hands were clutching his middle.

Corey stood near the window. He was rubbing the side of his head. Then he put his hand against his ribs where he'd been kicked. He grunted and leaned back against the windowsill. McDermott went back to the desk and sat down. Donofrio remained on the floor. The other squadmen were grouped around him, ready to stop him in case he got up and made another try for Corey.

McDermott looked at Corey and said, "You hurt?"

"Sure I'm hurt. He damn near busted my ribs."

"Lemme get up," Donofrio said.

The four squadmen stepped closer to Donofrio as he tried to lift himself from the floor. He made it to his knees and Heeley put a hand on his shoulder, holding him down.

"Please lemme get up," Donofrio wheezed. "Lemme have him one more time. I'll get it out of him."

"No you won't," McDermott told the Italian. "You're gonna let me handle this. You interfere again, I'll take you apart. I mean that."

Donofrio lowered his head. He shut his eyes tightly and let out another wheeze. Then he was quiet.

Corey said to McDermott, "What is all this? I don't get none of this."

"You want it explained?" McDermott said mildly.

"I wanna know where I'm at," Corey said. "I'm beginning to think this is room number five in the Crazy House."

"This is room 529 in City Hall," McDermott said. "We got you here for interrogation."

"Concerning what?"

"You don't know? You really don't know?"

"There's nothing I can tell you, Sergeant. You're gonna hafta tell me."

"All right," McDermott said quietly. "What happened, we got a phone call. I'd say around eight-thirty. Or maybe closer to nine. I'm not sure. Anyway, it was nobody we knew. She wouldn't give her name."

"She?"

"Maybe a he-she, but I don't think so. Anyway, that don't matter. It's only what she said that matters. She said she wanted Night Squad. I tell her to go ahead and she says there's a member of the Night Squad getting shot at in the swamplands just off Sixth and Ingersoll. I tell her to go get her head examined and she says the squadman's name is Corey Bradford and he's outnumbered and if we don't hurry he ain't gonna come outta there alive."

"That's what she said?"

"That's exactly what she said. Then she hung up. We jump into a car and make it to Sixth and Ingersoll and then we're in the swamplands and we hear the shooting. We move in. We get in closer, we see them. But first they musta seen us, or heard us coming in. It's five of them and they don't wanna know from conversation. All they wanna do is get outta there. We gave them a warning shot and they kept moving. So then we really start shooting and they shoot back. We got two of them. They got Ferguson."

Corey was looking at the wall behind the desk. He told himself to look directly at the detective-sergeant. He tried, but couldn't do it.

He heard McDermott say, "Them others, they got away. The two that we bumped, one of them was still alive when we reached him. We put some questions to him and he wouldn't open up. Not at first, anyway. So then I hadda lit cigarette and used two fingers to open up his eye and keep it open. I bring the cigarette close to his eye and then closer and a little closer and he says he'll spill. I say to him, 'Who were you going after?' And he says, 'Corey Bradford.' Then I say to him, 'How come?' He says, 'This Bradford, he's been giving us grief. He's been finding out too much and we know it was him who knocked off Macy and Lattimore.' I say, 'You know that Bradford's a policeman? You know he's on the Night Squad?' And the man says, 'If he is, he's on two payrolls.' I say, 'Whaddya mean, two payrolls?' The man says, 'From the City and from Grogan. This Bradford, he works for Walter Grogan.' Then just as I start the next question, the man's eyes bulge and he's gone."

Corey moved very slowly toward a chair and sat down and gazed at the floor.

"Well?" McDermott smiled dimly.

"Nothing," Corey said. "All this tells me nothing."

"You weren't there tonight? You weren't in them swamplands?"

"Of course not."

"You don't work for Grogan?"

"Of course not," Corey said. He got up from the chair.

McDermott frowned down at the desk top. Then he looked at Corey and opened his mouth to say something. But Donofrio came up from the floor, pushing Heeley and the other squadmen from his path. On McDermott's desk there was a pair of scissors and Donofrio grabbed it and held it with the blades closed. He's gotta be kidding, Corey thought. But then Donofrio moved in.

"I'll get it out of you," Donofrio wheezed. "I'll carve it out of you," and the scissors came close, causing Corey's arm to function mechanically while he side-stepped. The motion of his arm was just a blur and almost in that same split second he displayed the gun.

The gun meant nothing to Donofrio. He kept coming, and Corey thought, you're just gonna hafta shoot him. There ain't no other way to stop him. At that moment McDermott lunged at the tall Italian, and with his left hand he grabbed Donofrio's wrist, stopping the forward thrust of the scissors. His other hand, clenched and functioning like a piston, banged Donofrio's jaw. He hit Donofrio six times on the jaw, but Donofrio wouldn't let go of the scissors. McDermott let out a despairing moan, set himself and hit Donofrio high on the jaw. The Italian went across the room and collided with the wall. Then he was face down on the floor, unconscious.

Corey stood with the gun in his hand. He was thinking that he ought to put the gun back under his shirt, but he wasn't sure about the other squadmen. Maybe one of them would snap as Donofrio had snapped. Or maybe all of them would snap. He told himself it was a matter of tactics, and he had to let them know he was ready to use the gun.

Then he saw that McDermott was looking intently at the gun.

"Gimme that," McDermott said.

Which is just what you're gonna hafta do, Corey told

himself. You either hand it over or use it, and you know you don't wanna use it.

He handed the gun to the detective-sergeant. The other squadmen moved in as McDermott examined the gun.

"This ain't no police pistol," McDermott said.

Corey didn't say anything.

"Where'd you get this pistol?" McDermott asked.

"Someone gave it to me."

"When?"

"A long time ago."

"Like how many hours?"

"Whaddya mean, hours?"

"Twenty-four hours? Less than twenty-four hours?"

"Look, Sergeant, I said—"

"Hold it," McDermott cut in softly. He smiled a trifle sheepishly. "I'm just guessing here." And then, the smile fading, "Now let's check to see if I'm guessing right."

McDermott went to a filing cabinet and opened one of the drawers. He took out some papers, studied them, put them back in, took out more papers. It appeared he couldn't find what he wanted. He pulled out another drawer and looked through the papers. Finally he had the paper he wanted. It was mimeographed. He studied something on the paper, then studied something on the gun. He put the paper back in the filing cabinet, closed the drawer and walked toward the prone form of Louis Donofrio. He gently patted Donofrio's head. The Italian stirred, opened his eyes, started to get up, then sighed heavily and went back to sleep. McDermott stood looking down at him with fondness, something close to tenderness.

The four squadmen moved closer to Corey. Then McDermott came toward them, coming very slowly, looking at the gun in his hand and saying, "There's a sales notation for this pistol. It was sold just a few months ago. It was sold to Walter Grogan."

Corey heard a low-pitched growl. It came from one of the squadmen. He wasn't sure which one.

McDermott said, "You've had this pistol less than twenty-four hours. Grogan gave it to you."

"Now look, I can explain—"

"No you can't. Not now you can't. This pistol does all the explaining. And proves it, too. Proves you're working for Grogan."

"Sergeant, if you let me—"

"I'm gonna letcha listen. Just stand there and listen. Last night them two masked hoods, they woulda got Grogan if it wasn't for you. That impresses Grogan. He puts you on his payroll. A few hours later you're in this office and I proposition you to join the Squad. All right, you sign in. And you don't say nothing about working for Grogan. That's why Ferguson ain't here now. That's why Leonard Ward Ferguson was only forty-four when they put him in the box."

There was another low-pitched growl. Corey glanced at the growler. It was Heeley. Now the same thing that had happened to Donofrio was happening to Heeley. Letting out another growl, Heeley started a move toward Corey. Moving faster, a squadman got behind Heeley and held him back.

McDermott said to Corey, "You better get outta here.

The next one that flips, we may not be able to hold him."

Corey started to turn away.

"Wait," McDermott said. "Here's your gun." Going toward the door, Corey tucked the gun inside his shirt and put it under his belt. Then he opened the door and walked out.

10

In the corridor, going toward the elevator, he felt a twinge very high on his thigh near his groin. As it hit him, the pain in his head went away. Then the twinge went away and the other pain came again, throbbing along the side of his head where Donofrio had clouted him, and also the searing pain in his ribs where Donofrio had kicked him. In the elevator he pushed the street-floor button. As the elevator went down he leaned back against the wall, shaking his head slowly. He had no specific thoughts, just a negative feeling, everything on the gloomy side.

The elevator came to a stop. Corey got out and walked slowly along the corridor. As he approached the doorway on the Banker Street side of city hall, he saw a framed poster on the wall. It showed a blue-uniformed policeman smiling cheerily and pointing to a large rubbish can. The caption read, "Let's Keep This City Clean." Underneath the caption there was a pencilled comment consisting of two words.

On Banker Street, walking toward a taxi stand, Corey took out a handkerchief and wiped sweat from his face. It was cold sweat. He told himself he needed a drink. In the taxi he said, "Second and Addison."

The driver said, "Right." There was no further talk. Corey leaned back, then leaned sideways, to lessen the pain in his ribs. He touched the side of his head, felt the bump and wished the throbbing would go away. Suddenly he sat up straight, forgetting the black and blue of his ribs and his bruised head. He reached for the back pocket of his trousers, took out his wallet and opened it. He looked at the police identification card that read, "Night Squad." Then he looked at the badge.

It's one for the puzzle fans, he thought. You've been clobbered by the Squad, you were damn close to getting torn to pieces by the Squad, and yet according to what you see here, you're still a member of the Squad.

But don't try to account for it. Don't try to account for anything that happens up there in Room 529. What happens in that room is something for the head doctors to figure out. And they couldn't do it in three weeks or even three months. You can believe that.

But look now, just look at this here card and this here badge. Whaddya make of this? Sure, you can tell yourself that McDermott took it for granted you were booted off the Squad; and he just forgot to mention it to make it official. You can say he just forgot to tell you to hand over the card and the badge. He was occupied with other matters, like dancing around with Donofrio. That would be a simple explanation. Except that ain't the explanation at all. You know it ain't.

You know there's gotta be another explanation why you

still got the card and badge. It's out there in the fog somewhere, maybe a little too far out for this explorer. But Jesus
Christ, what are you trying to explore? You think there's
any way to explore McDermott? To do that you gotta go
all the way down to hell, because that's where he lives. He
lives there with Mrs. McDermott who won't let him come
near her. Not because she don't care for him. It's a cinch
she cares for him plenty; you can bet she worships the
ground he walks on. You can also bet that she don't hardly
know what year it is. Or let's say it don't matter to her
what year it is, considering the fact that she went away
from everything some thirty-three years ago on that night
when they jumped her. Them nine. Them nine from the
Third Street Dragons.

Does that tell you anything? Does that give you any hint
at all or bring in any connection? The only connection is
Walter Grogan who these days is a respected member of
the Southeast Boat Club. Some thirty-three years ago this
same Walter Grogan was a member of the Third Street
Dragons. This Walter Grogan was the leader.

You know what that tells you? It tells you absolutely
nothing. The fog just gets thicker, that's all. And the fog
maker is Detective-Sergeant Henry McDermott, the man
with the mild eyes and the soft voice. The man who I swear
it's like he's with you right now and he's forcing you to
look at the badge.

Why? Why me? Of all people, why me?

And here's another silly question. The gun. How come
he pulled that ass-backwards caper and handed the gun
back to you and letcha walk out with it? But wait now,

that sorta ties in with the card and the badge. He letcha walk out with the card and the badge. But the gun, it ain't no police pistol. It's Grogan's gun, or to be more accurate it's the gun that Grogan gave you. So what it amounts to, you're sitting here with the badge that says you're a policeman, the card that says you're attached to the Night Squad, and the .38 that says you're working for Walter Grogan.

"Let's Keep This City Clean," it said on the poster. And somebody took out a pencil and scribbled two words. You go along with them two words, you save yourself a lotta worry, a lotta complications. Because it's them two words that simplify the issue, stating clearly and positively that we all come from the caves or the trees or maybe the bottom of the goddam ocean; and wherever we come from it's them two words that put us where we are today and give us what we got today, like for instance meat for the table.

Don't believe that, the badge said.

Corey grimaced, biting the corner of his mouth. He felt a twinge very high on his thigh near his groin. He closed the wallet and put it back in his pocket. Then he leaned back and his hand drifted toward the bulge where his polo shirt covered the .38. His hand touched the bulge and he smiled dimly. Some greed came into his eyes. He was thinking in terms of fifteen thousand dollars.

At Second and Addison the taxi pulled away and Corey walked into the Hangout. At the far end of the bar he found sufficient space to set his foot on the rail and get an elbow on the wood. The bartender looked at him. Corey nodded and the bartender served him a double gin. On either side of him some drinkers decided to call it a night; they moved off and he had that section all to himself. For some reason it was like being marooned.

And that's as it should be, a soundless heckler remarked.

Corey nodded slowly, in dismal agreement. He was thinking about Leonard Ward Ferguson.

But actually it wasn't your fault, he tried to veer away from the accusing finger. I mean, it wasn't your fault directly, it was just some circumstances—

And who set up them circumstances? the heckler came in again.

But what I mean—

Don't tell me nothing, the heckler cut in rudely. You ain't got nothing to tell. You're a wrong number from way back and the vote on that is unanimous.

Corey lowered his head and shut his eyes tightly.

A voice boomed above all other voices at the bar. It was Nellie, going over to aid the bartender who had his hands full with two youths wearing duck-tail haircuts and blue rayon club jackets. The youths claimed they were over twenty-one and therefore entitled to buy drinks. They looked about seventeen. Nellie told them to get away from the bar. They didn't move. They grinned at her. She asked them if they wanted stitches in their heads. The juveniles went on grinning and didn't move. Nellie gestured to the bartender. The bartender reached under the bar, came up with a foot long section of lead pipe and handed it to Nellie. The two youths looked at each other. Then they walked away from the bar.

"Out the door," Nellie said. They hesitated a moment,

one of them mumbling inaudibly. Nellie took a step toward them. They hurried to the side door, opened it and went out. Nellie returned the lead pipe to the bartender, grimacing with disappointment because she hadn't been given an excuse to use it. She moved along the bar, her eyes alert for any unruly behavior or anti-social chicanery. She came to a stop where Corey was bent low over the bar, gazing morosely at his double shot.

"Go on, drink it," Nellie said. "It don't do you no good just sittin' there."

He turned and looked at the big woman. "You pushin' sales?"

"Just nursing the trade, that's all. That's part of my job. I'm here to keep the customers happy."

"I'm happy," Corey said.

"Yeah. You look happy."

"Get off me," he mumbled. He gulped the gin. Nellie grinned at him and he said tightly, "Now what the hell's so comical?"

Nellie chuckled lightly. She said, "It always tickles me—"

"What tickles you?"

"When the slick ones get it. When the screwer gets screwed." She started away from him. Something zigzagged through his brain. He reached out and took hold of her huge arm. She stopped, looked at his hand on her arm.

"You messin' with me?"

"Just socializin'." Corey forced a smile. It was a weary smile, sad and lonely. "Lemme buy you a drink."

"It's rye. Beer chaser."

He ordered a double rye and a tall beer for Nellie, a double gin for himself. The big woman reached for the shot glass, brought it to her mouth, then frowned thoughtfully and set the glass on the bar. "How come?" she asked.

"What?"

"You never done this before. Buyin' me a drink."

"Don't make it a big deal."

"Jesus," she said. She stepped back and looked at him in wonder. Then her eyes narrowed and she peered at him as though studying a chart.

Corey Bradford squirmed and muttered, "Cut it out, Nellie. God damn it, cut it out." He snatched at his drink and tossed the gin down his throat. As he lowered the shot glass to the bar, he saw that his hand was quivering. He glanced quickly at Nellie. Her eyes aimed at his quivering hand.

"And now it ain't no joke," she said quietly, solemnly. "Whatever it is, you really been clobbered hard." She moved closer to him. "You wanna tell me, Bradford?"

He shook his head.

"Come on, tell me," Nellie said. "Lean it on me."

"It can't be handled that way," he mumbled. And wondered, now what does that mean? A voice burdened with sadness and choked with remorse called out to the bartender for another gin. It was his own voice and he said to himself, it can't be handled that way, neither. But as the double shot arrived, he went for it like an empty-bellied bird diving desperately for a breadcrumb in the snow. So you know what happens now? he asked the desperate drinker. It's them eleven faces you'll hafta live with, the face of Leonard Ward Ferguson and the face of his widowed wife and the nine faces of them fatherless children. Because you did it. Just like McDermott said, you done him in. And don't say it couldn't be helped. Don't even say you're sorry. If you were really sorry you'd go to Grogan and tell him the deal is off, and you don't need his fifteen grand. Can you picture yourself doing that? Can you picture a larceny expert running to the lost and found department with a five-dollar bill he found in the subway?

He heard Nellie say, "You know how long I've known you, Bradford? Since grammar school. Since fifth grade. And you still got that dent in your forehead."

"What dent?"

"Right there. Right above your left eye. Where I hit you that time in the school yard. With a brick. I threw a brick. You remember?"

"Too far back."

"You were calling me Ellie instead of Nellie. And I asked you why. And you said Ellie was short for elephant."

"You coulda picked up a stone. It didn't hafta be no brick."

"A stone wouldn't of left no mark," Nellie said. "Guess I wanted it to leave a mark. So you'd never forget."

"To call you Nellie instead of Ellie?"

"That's one thing."

"And the other thing?"

"We won't talk about that."

"But I don't know what it is."

"That's what I mean," Nellie said. She gulped the double rye and chased it with some beer. She started away from the bar. Again he reached out and took hold of her arm. She said tightly, "Now what?"

"Lemme buy you another."

"I don't want no more."

"The hell you don't," Corey said. He pulled the big woman toward the bar. He released her arm. She stood there and he ordered more drinks.

"Whatcha tryin' to do?" she muttered sullenly, almost bitterly. "You wanna get me drunk?"

"Let's both get drunk."

"And then what?"

"We'll be drunk. We'll be good and drunk, and what's better than that?"

"You asking me?"

"I'm asking anybody. What's better than getting really plastered? Absolutely looped?"

"Well now, let's see—"

"See what?" he cut in gruffly, almost angrily. Their shot glasses were empty and he called for refills. They drank the refills. He ordered more and said, "Ain't nothing to see. Ain't nothing better than when you're soused and I mean all the way soused, don't-give-a-good-goddam delirious, way out there where they got no clocks and there ain't no stipulations what you gotta do because of what you done. You're out there, you don't see no fingers pointing."

Nellie frowned thoughtfully, "Is that what they mean when they say blind drunk?"

"Who knows what they mean?" He lost track of the question. "Who cares what they say?" He turned and yelled to the bartender for more drinks. The refills came and then came again.

The refills kept coming.

At one of the tables there was a disturbance, two women were on their feet, going for each other's hair. Another woman moved in to stop it and got her face clawed for her good intentions. Someone yelled for Nellie as the female combatants went at it with more fury. Then others were yelling for Nellie and she turned toward them. She looked at the two women who were now on the floor, grappling, biting, scratching and screeching. A man shrieked at Nellie, "Come on, bouncer, don't stand there, do something."

"Go jump a giraffe," Nellie said.

The man turned away. He enlisted the aid of some other men and they managed to pacify the two women. Someone put a dime in the juke box and a blues singer lamented all the empty nights and wasted years. A bearded neurotic got up on a table and attempted to recite poetry that contradicted the singer's lyrics, and from the bar some unpoetic creature pegged a half-eaten, hot pork sandwich that hit the poet in the mouth.

"But I'm a vegetarian," the poet declared in a tone that was neither male nor female. To shut him up, someone handed him a fifteen-cent Tokay. He got down from the table and sat on the floor, murmuring phrases of endearment to the yellow wine in the glass.

The bartender brought another double rye for Nellie and another double gin for Corey Bradford.

From the juke box the blues singer was bewailing the moon and the stars and all the flowers of spring for having gone away. Nellie said to the juke box, "Don't tell me about it. I got my own grief."

"What grief?" Corey queried.

The big woman looked at him. Her hand came up. It seemed she was going to hit him in the face just because he happened to be there. But then her hand moved slowly and hesitantly, and finally her fingers came to rest on the dent in his forehead above his left eye. In the touch of her fingers there was something very tender.

And what's all this? His liquor-drenched brain groped for an answer. Then through the alcoholic haze he saw the yearning in Nellie's eyes.

So Carp was right, he said to himself, remembering last night when Carp had stated flatly, "She's hot for the man."

That's why she threw the brick when we were only nine years old. That's why in all these years the only words you got from her were cuss words and the only looks were mean looks. Last night when she broke your wagon down in front of all these Hangout people, her big hand tight on your arm, her thick fingers digging in to hurt you, to bruise you; it was just her way of saying, cantcha see, Corey? Cantcha see how it is? How it's always been?

But now Nellie's hand was away from his face, aiming at the shot glass on the bar. She lifted it, gulped the rye and said, "All right, I'll tell you what the grief is. I been told he's cheatin' on me."

"Who's cheatin'?"

"Rafer."

"You been going with Rafer?"

"You didn't know?"

"Nobody tells me nothin'," Corey said.

"How can they tell you? They never get close enough."

"Look, I live in this neighborhood."

"No you don't, Bradford. You live all alone on a cliff somewhere. Or maybe at the edge of a cliff."

"Well anyway, what's this with Rafer?"

"I gotta have somebody, don't I?"

"Let's have another drink," Corey said.

"This one I'll buy."

"No you won't," Corey said determinedly. Then he realized he was getting very drunk, evil drunk. Gotta have somebody, he gritted without sound. They all gotta have somebody. He turned and looked toward the far side of the taproom, focusing on the table near the door leading to the back room. There was no one at the table. Then he saw Lillian coming toward the table with a glass in one hand and a quart of beer in the other. He said to Nellie, "Order them drinks, I'll be back in a minute."

He made his way across the room, bumping into standing drinkers, shoving and getting shoved, finally arriving at the table where Lillian was pouring the beer. She looked up and saw him. Some beer spilled over the edge of the glass.

He said, "Look, I don't have no goddam dimes. So here's a quarter, and you owe me fifteen cents."

She stared at the coin on the table. "What's this for?"

"The phone call. The call you made to Night Squad."

She didn't look up. She didn't say anything.

Corey said, "Now listen, you. Listen good. Don't do me no more favors. I don't want no favors from you. I don't want nothing. You hear me?"

"I hear you." She sipped some beer. "I'm wondering what you're all worked up about."

"Don't gimme that," with his gin-glazed eyes seeing two blurred Lillians and then three blurred Lillians. "You know whatcha did," his gin-cracked voice was just above a whisper. "Looked out the kitchen window and saw me running from that alley. Saw them chasing me. Saw they had guns. Then later you heard the shooting. Next thing, you're scooting for a phone booth and putting in a call."

"So?"

"Whaddya mean, so? I wanna know why."

"Why I put in the call?" She shrugged. "You needed help."

"From you?"

"From anyone." She shrugged again. "Someone hadda call in. If that phone call wasn't made, you probably wouldn't be here now."

"You ran out in all that rain—"

"And spent a dime," she said. "So you owed me a dime and you gimme this quarter and I owe you fifteen cents." She opened a purse, put the quarter in and took out three nickels. "There's your fifteen cents."

He looked at the three nickels on the table. He reached for the coins and missed them. His hand hit the beer glass and knocked it over. Beer streamed over the edge of the table and dripped into Lillian's lap. Corey made another try for the three nickels. He missed again and his hand went sliding through the beer on the table as he lost his footing. His weight came against the side of the table, causing it to tilt. The bottle fell off, hit the floor and broke.

"Now look what I done," Corey said dismally. "Just look at what I done here."

Lillian had pushed back her chair and was on her feet, her fingers flicking futilely at her wet skirt.

"Gotta make it up to you," Corey said, reaching for his wallet. But his hand couldn't find the rear pocket of his trousers and he moved around in a gin-distorted circle. "Gotta pay for the beer," he mumbled. "Gotta pay for the skirt, to get it cleaned." He went around in another circle, still trying for the wallet. "Gotta settle all debts and meet all obligations." He tugged fretfully at his trousers that didn't seem to have a rear pocket. Then he found it, started to take out the wallet, but in that moment his legs got tangled and he fell to the floor. Sitting there, he saw Lillian headed toward the side door. "Hey you," he called to her. "Hey you—"

She didn't turn to look; she just kept moving toward the door. Then the door was open and she walked out.

Corey sat there for awhile, wondering if this was really a taproom floor. It seemed more like a slanting boat deck, the boat bouncing around in rough water. Corey tried to get up, couldn't make it, tried again and kept trying. Finally he was on his feet and staggered toward the bar. He saw Nellie reaching for a double rye, and called to her, "Hey wait—we're drinkin' together."

She waited while Corey lurched closer to the bar. She pointed to the double gin she'd ordered for him. In a solemn and slightly ceremonious way they lifted the glasses, clinked them together. Then instead of drinking, they stood holding the glasses.

Nellie said, "So what's the toast? Who do we drink to?"

"The precinct," Corey suggested. "The tried and true of the Thirty-seventh."

"Why drink to them?"

"They preserve law and order. They protect the citizens."

"From what?"

"From bingo games, that's what. Them wicked bingo games."

Nellie thought it over for a moment. She said, "Tell you what. Let's drink to Sally Sullivan."

"And who the hell is Sally Sullivan?"

"The captain's wife. The wife of the captain of the Thirty-seventh Precinct. And she's also vice president of the Women's Committee."

"Committee for what?"

"To wipe out filth. Prevent immoral influences. They've had her on one of them local TV programs, the city give her an award. And she goes around to them lunches, makes speeches. Gets her picture on the woman's page damn near every Sunday. Now I'll tell you something else, if you care to hear it."

"By all means," Corey said politely, patiently. But he wished she'd hurry up with it so they could drink the toast. He gazed thirstily at the gin in the shot glass.

Nellie said, "This Sally Sullivan, she's the one that Rafer's been seein'."

"The captain's wife? With Rafer?"

"Whenever she gets the chance. I won't tell you what they do. I mean, what she does. It would make you sick in your stomach."

"Who tipped you?"

"Rafer himself. So you know I got it on good authority."

"But Rafer's your man. Why would he tell you a thing like that?"

"He was high," Nellie said. "He was forty thousand feet up. On that mixture he drinks. Calls it California Clouds. Mixes it himself. A bottle of some cola drink, six aspirin tablets, two tablespoons of snuff. Puts it all together in a bowl and sips it from the spoon. In no time at all he's up there. California Clouds."

"Let's drink to that," Corey said. "Them clouds. And your man Rafer. Your cloud man Rafer."

They drank. Nellie called for refills. The bartender poured. Nellie reached for her glass, but a smaller hand was there first and by the time she looked around, the drink snatcher was halfway across the room snatching at another drink. Corey turned and saw Carp gliding past a table with his left hand getting rid of Nellie's empty glass while his right picked up someone's whiskey. Corey sighed and reached for his gin.

Then he and Nellie leaned against each other. His knees gave way and he started to go down. She held him up for a moment. Then they both leaned against the bar.

Nellie said, "Just answer me one thing. Do I hafta put up with it?"

"Absolutely not," he said, and wondered what she was talking about.

Her thick hand came down on the edge of the bar. "I'm gonna have a clear understanding with Mister Cloudman Rafer. He's just gonna hafta mend his ways, that's all. Wantsa climb up in them clouds, let him do it in a closet or someplace. Not sittin' there on the goddam bed where I'm tryin' to get some sleep."

"Absolutely," Corey mumbled.

"Sittin' there on the bed, dippin' that spoon and sippin' all that cloud soup. It hits him and he gets to talkin' all that talk. Just ain't no way to shut him up, and some nights it goes on all night long. Only thing I'll say for him, at least he never repeats himself. Except when he tells me the fairy tale—"

"What fairy tale?"

"Well, there's this palace he's gonna buy. A real palace, with everything in it only the best. With triple-size bathtubs so's we can take baths together. And all kindsa colognes and talcum powders on the shelves. With sterling silver toilet seats—"

"Say what?"

"I'm just tellin' it like Rafer tells it. This fairy tale. What sorta worries me, it's like he actually believes it. Keeps sayin' he's gonna buy that palace, and when I ask him where he's gonna get the money, he starts to giggle like a loon. Says he won't hafta work to get it. Says all he needs to do is make one fast grab because it's all in one package."

Corey shut his eyes tightly. A streak of bright light

stabbed his liquor-soggy brain. He heard himself saying, "It takes a lotta dimes to buy a palace."

"This ain't dimes, the way he tells it. This is paper money and it comes to a million five."

The streak of light stabbed deeper. He said, "Lemme hear that again."

"A million five." And then, through a hiccup, "He says it's hidden somewhere." She hiccuped again. "Just a fairy tale. It's gotta be a fairy tale."

"Sure," Corey said.

"Because—a million five, that's fairy tale money. And besides, a million five, you just don't go and hide it somewhere. You put it in the bank."

"Sure. Absolutely."

"But the way Rafer tells it, when he's up in them clouds, he says he promised Grogan that he'd never open his mouth. Because it's only the two of them who know where all that money is. And then he's bawlin' like a baby, sayin' how it hurts him in his heart because after all he's been with Grogan all these years. And he's in Grogan's corner all the way, but Jesus Christ it's a million five and where it is now it ain't doin' nobody no good. And bawlin' with real tears, sippin' more of that mixture from the bowl and then wavin' the spoon over his head like he's winding himself up. Like some mechanical toy, or like a talkin' doll that can cry and say Mama. And that's what he was sayin'. He was sayin' Mama it's a million five and it ain't doin' nothin' for nobody. It sure ain't doin' nothin' for the Chinaman—"

"The who?"

"The Chinaman. And don't ask me what Chinaman. Remember, it's just a fairy tale—" She hiccuped again. Then she let out a louder hiccup, followed with a grunt as the alcohol jolted her. Nellie finally closed her eyes, her knees giving way. She was going to the floor. Corey grabbed her, dragging her away from the bar. He managed to get her into a chair. She put her head on the table and fell asleep.

Corey Bradford leaned heavily against the table and wondered if he could make it to the street. He started toward the door, bumped into a seated drinker, went to the floor and got up, weaving, then swaying as he kept trying for the door. You're really soused, he told himself. You're just about ready to fall out.

Someone opened the door for him and he staggered through, trying to straighten up, telling himself he mustn't fade out. But that's what's gonna happen? he asked the ginhound who just couldn't straighten up, who'd had one too many double shots and nothing in his belly to soak it up. Because you didn't have no supper, he chided the goofy-eyed boozer. All you had today was a goddam cinnamon bun and coffee. But what's that she said about the China-man?

Well, we'll get to that later. That is, if we get the chance. If we live long enough. But according to percentages, it looks to be strictly up the creek and, jim, I mean a one way excursion. There's some hunters out to bag you and the condition you're in now, you can't move fast. You can hardly move at all. You're just an easy piece of cake for Kingsley and company.

Maybe what you oughta do is go back to the Hangout and put your head on a table and just drift off. At least you'd be safe at the Hangout. Until closing time, anyway. But that's just stalling the issue, and there ain't no dividends in that. The thing to do, or hope to do, is get back to your room and lock the door and get in bed with the gun.

So if you can just make it to your room, using these alleys—

He was lurching through an alley, holding onto fence posts for support. His hands slipped off the fence posts and he fell down. He got up very slowly, took a few steps and went down again. Come on, get up, don't pass out. And then, just in the moment before he passed out, he heard the footsteps coming.

11

His head was on a pillow. He opened his eyes and saw blackness. Sitting up in the bed, he reached instinctively for the gun, but there was no gun. He made a move to get out of the bed, but his limbs couldn't function. They got me tied with ropes, or something, he thought.

But it wasn't that. It was the alcohol. You got one of them real special hangovers, he told himself, really feeling it as it hammered his skull. He fell back on the pillow and let out a groan. Then he floated out again.

Later when he opened his eyes, the room was still dark. He sat up slowly, wondering where he was and what they planned to do with him. He couldn't understand why they'd brought him here instead of just getting rid of him. For awhile he sat there, trying to reason it out. Of course it didn't make sense that they'd neglected to put ropes on him and tie him to the bed. Or maybe they took it for granted he was helpless without the gun. But that's taking a hell of a lot for granted, he said to himself.

The hangover had lessened somewhat, although his head still ached and his belly burned. He got out of the bed, trying to peer through the darkness, hoping to see the outline of a table lamp or floor lamp. Something flicked against his face. At first he thought it was some winged insect just trying to be cute. It tagged him again and he took a swipe at it. Instead of insect it was string, dangling from the ceiling. He pulled the string and the room was lit.

It was a very small room and first he saw the single window, wide open. There was no rug on the loose-boarded floor and whoever had papered the walls, the job was fouled up something awful. Most of the paper was hanging loose. There was very little furniture in the room, just the bed, an unvarnished, homemade bookcase crammed with books, and a sagging armchair with its upholstery torn and the stuffing coming out. In the armchair a man was sound asleep. Corey blinked several times, shook his head slowly in bafflement. Then he moved toward the sleeper, shook the sleeper's shoulder and said, "Wake up. Come on, Carp."

The little man opened his eyes. He smiled placidly at Corey Bradford. "Good morning," he said.

"Piss on that," Corey said. "Where's my gun?"

"I have it." Carp sat up straighter in the armchair. Then he yawned and rubbed his eyes and yawned again. He got up from the armchair, stretched his arms, then reached under the chair pillow and took out the .38.

"What's the play?" Corey asked.

"Merely a precaution," the little man said. He handed the gun to Corey. "To put it mildly, you were rather intoxicated. It sometimes leads to the D.T.'s. In a state of delirium you might have used the weapon and caused considerable damage."

Corey tucked the gun under his belt. "How'd you get me here? You carried me?"

"Not exactly," the little man said. "In the alley I managed to lift you onto your feet. It was rather awkward. You kept trying to pull away as I dragged you along, and at times we both fell down. As you know, I imbibe rather freely myself; and I found it somewhat difficult to navigate. This alcohol, it's a tricky fuel. Sometimes it has you traveling backwards."

Corey was quiet for a few moments. Then, "How'd you know I was in the alley?"

"I followed you from the saloon."

"How come?"

"Well, you were totally inebriated, and I thought it best to keep you under surveillance. I mean, it appeared you were ready to collapse and I wanted to render assistance."

"It's appreciated," Corey said. He started toward the door. Then stopped and looked at the open window that showed the darkness outside.

"If I were you, I'd wait awhile," Carp said.

"Wait for what?"

"Until it gets light. The streets are much safer when the sun comes up."

Corey looked at the little man. "Whaddya mean, safer? You hinting at something?"

"Merely noting a fact," Carp said. In his palm there was an old-fashioned pocket watch and he glanced at it and murmured, "Seventeen minutes past three. It's meal time now for the creatures of the night, the eager claws that lurk in the shadows. I refer in particular to a certain venomous crew that craves to dine on you and you alone. And therefore I recommend utmost discretion—"

"Excuse me," Corey cut in quietly. He squinted at the little man. "What's all this noise from the trees? You flying around on some new kind of charge? You imagining things?"

"Not hardly," the little man said. "In the saloon this evening I heard some talk about a gun fight in the swamplands, in the vicinity of Sixth and Ingersoll."

"So?"

"So I recalled the errand I performed for you this afternoon. That is, I obtained the address you wanted, and I assume you went to that address. The address was sixseventeen Ingersoll."

Corey grinned wryly.

The little man glanced again at the old-fashioned pocket watch. "In less than two hours we'll have daylight. If you'll wait until then—"

"No," Corey said. He moved toward the door.

"As your friend, I urge you to wait," Carp said. "I'll make some coffee."

"Coffee." Corey lowered his hand from the doorknob. "I could use some coffee."

"I'll have it ready right away," Carp said, and got busy with a tiny one burner coal-oil stove that he pulled out from a corner of the room. On the floor near the bed was a glass jug half-filled with water. He poured some into a pot and set it on the stove. From behind the bookcase he gathered a couple of cups, saucers and spoons, a small sugar bowl and a jar of instant coffee. There was no label on the jar. Carp held it up for display and said, "It's my own blend. I use a hammer to mash the beans, borrowed here and there from various Turks and Syrians and so forth. Of course the preparation requires considerable time and effort. The hammer is an awkward implement and I'm thinking quite seriously of putting it aside and procuring a mortar and pestle. But on the other hand—"

"Excuse me," Corey interrupted. He was sitting on the edge of the bed, going through his pockets. "I'm outta cigarettes. You got any around?"

"A plentiful supply," Carp said, and went to the bookcase, reached in behind it, his hand coming out with a cardboard box containing some folders of cigarette paper and a paper bag bulging with tobacco. Carp's nimble fingers went to work.

Corey asked, "Where you get the tobacco?"

"From contributors." Carp's way of saying that he went around collecting stubs.

With fantastic speed and precision, the little man made two cigarettes. On the stove the water was boiling and he completed the preparation of the coffee. They sipped the coffee and smoked the cigarettes, and for several minutes there was no talk.

Finally Carp said, "There's something I've been wanting to tell you. That is, I feel it's your privilege to be informed—"

"Informed about what?"

"Me," the little man said.

Corey looked at him. There was a wistful expression on Carp's face, the slightest trace of a plaintive smile.

Carp said, "It's in regard to our agreement, our pledge of mutual trust and confidence. Which means that nothing should be held back, nothing at all. It also means that what's spoken in this room will stay in this room. Is that clearly understood?"

Corey nodded.

The little man sipped some coffee, took a slow pull at his cigarette, let the smoke out and said, "My name is not really Carp."

There was silence for awhile. Then the little man said, "It's essentially a matter of name reduction. That is, shortening my name to comply with certain adjustments that were necessary in order for me to exist outside a padded cell."

"Excuse me," Corey said. "You're talkin' way over my head."

"All right, we'll try it this way—" And then the little man was speaking just like any Swampdweller and Hangout lounger, saying, "The deal on Carp is that it used to be Henry C. Carpenter with a wife and four children and a hefty chunk of real estate out on the Main Line. From blue chips alone the income was somewhere around thirty thousand a year, inherited from the old man. He also left me the paper box factory that goes way back. It's been run by the family since the Battle of Yorktown, or thereabouts. So of course when I was born it was strictly velvet, right from the jump. All I hadda do was drift along with the tide. That is, you're a Carpenter. It's private school in Switzerland, and then it's Dartmouth, and then the eighteen months of traveling around the world. The boat tickets all first class, and the hotels only the best. And after that, in line with family tradition, they make me a member of that club downtown where in order to get in, you gotta have a pedigree. And of course that was all right with me. In them days everything that happened was all right with me. Especially what came later—the four little Carpenters and their mother."

For a long moment Carp was quiet. He gazed at the wall, seemed to be seeing something far beyond the wall, beyond the second floor front and the cobblestoned street below and all the streets and alleys of the Swamp, very far away from all that.

He said, "Only thing I can tell you about her, it was one of those unbelievable situations. Or call it a complete switch from the way these things usually pan out, because when you marry the girl that your family selects and it's more like a business merger than anything else, there ain't much likelihood that you'll get what you want in terms of companionship, and I don't mean only in the bedroom. But lemme tell you—the nine years I lived with that woman were nine years of absolute delight. That woman was what you see when you look at one of them pictures by Raphael. I tell you, she was something exceptional in this world. So one summer, and this goes back twenty-three years, she's got the children in the car, all four children. And they're driving to the seashore. They're on this road along the edge of an embankment high above a river—"

Carp closed his eyes for a moment. His face was placid as he went on. "There was only one witness. A farmer. And he said it was a hit-and-run situation. He couldn't describe the truck, except that it was big and it was moving very fast. So they never got the truck driver. But here's what the farmer saw—the truck came up behind the car, sideswiped the car and sent it crashing down the embankment into the river, into forty feet of water.

"All five of them," he said. "Down there in forty feet of water, and the car a chunk of twisted metal. A few days later the car was brought up and I saw what was in the car. They didn't want me to look; but I insisted on looking, and then they hadda give me a sedative with a needle."

Corey winced.

The little man said, "They wrote it off as an accident. But you know, I've always wondered about that. Of course, it could have been an accident, I mean there's no way to prove it wasn't. And also, at that time I was more or less out of my head and couldn't offer an opinion. Yet later, years later I'd sometimes get to thinking about it. I'd try not to think about it, telling myself it was no use, because I'd never know for sure whether or not it was an accident."

Corey grimaced puzzledly.

"So I didn't know then and I don't know now and I'll never know," Carp emphasized the uncertainty. "But this much I can tell you—if it wasn't an accident, it was a professional knock-off job."

"But why?"

"Some circumstances," Carp said. "My wife was a volunteer social worker. And not like you see them on the society page, sitting around at the luncheon table and smiling for the photographer. My wife was really a worker. She gave it all she had and then some. But calling her a worker is only part of it. Because mostly she was a soldier. She was a soldier for the poor and underprivileged, yelling her head off in City Hall, demanding action from the health inspectors and building inspectors and especially from the inspectors in the fire department. Telling them to go and see for themselves, to take a good close look at the neighborhood. And—"

"Hold it," Corey cut in. "What neighborhood?"

"This neighborhood," Carp said. "This neighborhood here. The Swamp."

The puzzled look gradually faded from Corey's face. His eyes narrowed as he looked off to the side. He murmured, "Someone shoulda told her—ain't no way to clean up the Swamp. Anyplace but the Swamp." And then, looking at the little man, he asked, "Wasn't she warned?"

"Just once. And it wasn't really a warning. It was more likely a friendly suggestion."

"Grogan?"

Carp nodded very slowly. He gazed past the wall, as though seeing the Swamp of twenty-three years ago when Walter Grogan had wiped out all competition and had the neighborhood in his pocket, controlling rent, the prices for plumbing improvements, for fire extinguishers which most tenants couldn't buy because they didn't have the money, controlling the interest rate on loans. And almost everyone borrowed at some time or other, inasmuch as money that would have been on hand to pay the grocer, the druggist and the doctor, was spent instead at the Hangout bar. All this was reflected in Carp's eyes as he nodded slowly.

He said, "It was all very friendly. She told me about it. She said that Grogan invited her to lunch and she refused and Grogan stood there and told her that he admired her for the work she was doing, but it wasn't really needed in this neighborhood. The people in this neighborhood didn't want any changes. And then he told her that many people resented her coming around knocking on doors, and he hoped she wouldn't get hurt. So what it all came to, he was telling her in a nice way that if she knew what was good for her, she'd stay away from the Swamp. But she kept coming back.

"And a few weeks later she was in the grave. And the children were in the grave. It was more than I could take. I kept trying to do away with myself, and finally I flipped all the way, and they put me in the booby hatch. 'Incurable,' they said."

"How long were you in?"

"Nineteen years."

Corey let out a low whistle. "How'd you get out?"

"Walked out. Walked across the lawn and climbed the gate and just kept walking, telling myself that with certain changes effected I could possibly go back to the world and live in it. But not as Henry C. Carpenter. It was simply the process of saying good-bye to Henry C. Carpenter and saying hello to Carp."

There was a stretch of silence.

Then the little man said, "You understand, I can't point the finger at Grogan. It's a matter of insufficient evidence; so in my own private courtroom, I've thrown the case out of court."

"But you know he hired that truck driver?"

"Yes, I'm quite sure he did," Carp said. "But there's nothing I can do about that. What I mean is, there's nothing I care to do."

"Then why'd you come to the Swamp?"

Carp smiled serenely. "To observe," he said. "To observe Walter Grogan from day to day, getting older, the teeth of Time nibbling away at him. There's some satisfaction in that, at least. Will you have more coffee?"

"No thanks," Corey said. "I gotta be shoving."

"But it's still dark outside," the little man said. He pointed to the window. "Look out there, see how dark it is."

"I'm not worried," Corey said. And then to himself, not much.

He smiled at the little man, quickly opened the door and walked out of the second floor front. He went down the hall and down the stairs, heading for the front door that led out to Marion Street. He stopped short and thought for a moment, telling himself that Marion Street was possibly a trap, and at any rate it was a risk, too much of a risk.

You never know, he cautioned himself. Because that Kingsley outfit, they coulda been moochin' around and puttin' out some casual questions to the local citizens, especially the street-corner loafers who got nothing better to do than broadcast current events. So maybe that Kingsley outfit is all set and ready to pounce. Maybe someone mouthed it to them, saying that you were seen with Carp, that you and Carp were last seen headed for Marion Street, where Carp's got a second floor front. What I think you better do is cancel out Marion and make it to the alley.

He went down the hall and knocked on the door of the first floor front. He knocked several times and finally the door opened. A woman stood there. She was tall and bony and most of her hair was white. She looked in her early sixties. There was some dried blood under her nose and she had a black eye. She muttered, "Whatcha want?"

Corey had the wallet out and he showed her the badge.

"Stick it," the woman said. She started to close the door, but he held it open. The woman said, "Now look, I didn't send for no police. Christ's sake, I don't know why it is, you lizards always come walkin' in when you ain't needed."

"Come on, move aside." He stepped forward, but she blocked the doorway.

She said, "I'm tellin' you, I don't need no police in here. I'm not gonna press charges, that's why. If I press charges, then he'll press charges. And you oughta see what I done to him."

"This don't concern you and him," Corey said. "It's just that I wanna get to the alley. We're lookin' for some-one."

He pushed past her and went through a dimly lit room where a very small, slim, youthful Filipino was sitting up

223

in bed, his face crisscrossed with shiny ribbons of clotted blood where fingernails had clawed. His mouth was out of line, as though his jaw was dislocated. His left eye was closed and puffed out and plum colored. He said something very fast in Spanish and continued chattering as Corey walked into the kitchen. In the kitchen Corey headed for the back door, opened it and crossed the backyard to the fence gate. He opened the fence gate very slowly, leaned his head out and scanned the alley.

It looks all right, he told himself. Except I wish there were some lampposts. It's awfully dark in this alley.

In the alley, he walked slowly, his arms loosely swinging at his sides, his right arm swinging in a smaller arc, ready to go for the gun. He was listening for the slightest sound other than his own footsteps. There was no other sound, and he kept moving along. He emerged from the alley where it intersected with Addison Avenue.

On Addison the street lamps showed some dogs partying and a boozed-up drifter stretched out, face down on a doorstep. A slight breeze was coming in from the river and there were no doorstep sitters. They're all in bed now, he thought. The breeze gave them a chance to get some sleep, which makes it nice and quiet. It's really very nice, this quiet, it's very good for the nerves.

You really nervous? Now come on, don't tell me you're nervous. You ain't the nervous type. If you were downright jittery, you'd be heading east for the river and thinking in terms of the piers, the docked freighters, one of them ready to sail in a few or so hours. You'd be thinking that's a sure enough way to preserve this meat; just put it aboard that freighter and get it hauled across the ocean, to someplace where there ain't no Kingsley and company.

Say, you know, that's an angle. You wanna consider that? You wanna stroll east to the river and have a look at them piers, them freighters? You actually wanna take a boat ride?

And you say you ain't nervous, he derided the slow moving target who sensed that eyes were watching, that every step he took going west on Addison brought him closer to calamity.

Come off it, he told himself. Get your mind on something else. On broads, for instance. Any broad. Now take Nellie—

Or take the riddle she handed you, when she was soused and told all about Rafer's fairy tale, the fairy tale that reads there's a million-five and it ain't doin' nothin' for the Chinaman.

And the riddle is—what Chinaman?

Behind him a horn honked softly. He turned and saw a car coming to a stop on the other side of Addison. It was an Oldsmobile, and through the glow of the street lamps and the glare of the headlights he could see who it was behind the windshield, he could see the platinum blonde hair.

It appeared she was alone in the car. She beckoned to him and he walked slowly across Addison, moving in a diagonal, going toward the car. He wondered if she was really alone, and considered the possibility that someone was crouched below the window level in the rear of the car.

Lita opened the car door. In the instant before he climbed in, he checked the floor below the rear seat. It was empty. Then he sat beside her, closing the door and said to himself, whatever's gonna happen, let it happen. Just go along with it.

He looked at her. She was wearing a pale green, low cut blouse and a flimsy skirt, striped green and yellow. Under that she wore nothing. She was facing the windshield; at first she seemed motionless, but then he noticed her hand moving, slowly raising the skirt up her thigh.

He leaned back in the seat and then, conversationally said, "How come you're out this time of night?"

"Driving around," she said. "Driving all around the neighborhood. Trying to find that Chink."

"Chink?"

"That little slant-eyed sneak."

"The girl? The house maid?"

"She sneaked out again."

"So?"

"So I won't put up with it," Lita said quietly. "I can't be bothered."

"Cut that."

She looked at him. "What did you say?"

"I said cut that. You ain't bothered about that."

Lita shifted in the seat, sitting sideways and facing him. Some moments passed and she didn't say anything.

Corey said, "You didn't come out to look for the girl. You been looking for me."

"Really?"

He nodded slowly.

She started to say something, tightened her mouth to hold it back, then said weakly, pleadingly, "Can't you sit closer to me?"

"Sure," he said. He moved across the seat. She took hold of his hand and put it on her naked thigh. She moaned and pressed herself against him. "I couldn't sleep," she said. "I just had to find you."

Then her hands gripped the sides of his face and she said, "I want it."

"Here?"

She shut her eyes tightly. She started to nod, then shook her head and said, "No, not here on Addison. All these street lamps—"

"Then drive. We'll find a place."

"And park?"

"Some little street where there ain't no lights."

"No," she said. "Not in the car."

"Where else?"

"Can we go to your room?" And then, before he could answer, "No, we can't do that."

"Why not?"

"If we're seen together—"

"You're right," he said. "We can't take that chance."

"Then where can we go?"

"Let me think—"

"Please think of something," she said. She moaned and tugged at his arm. "I can't wait."

"Don't get frantic. It ain't like you gotta go to the bathroom."

"You're awful. That's a messy thing to say."

"Well, it's a messy situation," he said. "Tell you what. We could drive outta town. Find a motel—"

"That takes time. And maybe they're all filled up."

"But maybe not. Let's give it a try."

"No," she said. "It's a long drive. And then we'd just be driving around looking for a vacancy. And I can't wait."

"So whaddya want me to do?"

"Take me somewhere. We've got to go somewhere. We just can't stay here. It's unbearable, just sitting here, and—" she broke it off and sat up straight, as though a sudden thought had come to her.

"Well?" he murmured.

"There's a house not far from here. It's one of Grogan's properties. The people moved out a few days ago. I mean, they were thrown out; they couldn't pay the rent. And Grogan wouldn't let them take the furniture. So there's a bed, and—"

"You got the key?"

"No. But let's try anyway. Sometimes they leave the door unlocked."

"All right," Corey said. "Let's go."

As the Oldsmobile pulled away from the curb, Corey Bradford thought, it's a gamble, and you're a goddam fool to take this kind of risk, but then on the other hand it's a calculated risk and there's fifteen thousand dollars riding on these dice. You see what I mean? Yes, I see what you mean.

The Oldsmobile made a u-turn and went east on Addison. A block away from the river the car turned left, going up a narrow street. Then it turned right onto a narrower street. There were no lights. A little more than halfway down the block she stopped the car. As they got out of the car, he expected that she'd pull some caper like pretending to accidentally honk the horn, but she didn't do that, and he wondered what the signal would be.

It's gonna hafta be some kind of signal, he thought. To let them know we're here. So they can get ready.

Lita pointed to the house. It was across the street. Then her hand clasped his arm and they walked across, went up three sagging wooden steps to the splintered unpainted door with a notice tacked on it: No trespassing. Lita put her hand on the doorknob and tried the door. It was locked. She kept trying it and the doorknob rattled loudly.

He stood behind her, smiling thinly.

The doorknob rattled very loudly.

He said, "Give it up. It's locked."

"Try the window," Lita said. She pointed to the grimy window adjacent to the doorway.

Corey went toward the window, stepped on one of the loose boards about eighteen inches above the pavement level and got a hold on the lower section of the window. He worked on it and it gave way. Then the window was open and she said, "Get hold of me. Lift me up." He got down onto the pavement and boosted her onto the loose board. She climbed through the open window. He followed. He lowered himself off the windowsill, onto the floor. It was very dark in the room and he couldn't see her; he couldn't see anything in the darkness. Then someone grabbed his legs and someone else got him around the middle in a very tight hold that shackled his arms. While they held him that way, someone's hands checked him for weapons, found the gun and took it. Now he began to see blurred faces through the darkness, but he didn't try to make them out. You'll see them soon enough, he thought.

His legs were released, but the hold that locked his arms was tightened and a man's voice, close to his ear said, "All right, let's walk."

Then the weight of the man pushed against him and they moved slowly going through the darkness. They went from the room into a hallway. Ahead of Corey some blurred shapes were ascending a narrow staircase. The voice close to Corey's ear said, "Now we're gonna go up them stairs. And you won't try no stunts, will you?"

"Of course not," Corey said.

"That's fine," the voice said. "Because one time I was takin' someone up to the second floor and he tried to throw us both down the steps. He ended up with a broken neck."

"He was just plain stupid," Corey said.

"He sure was," the voice said.

They went up the stairs and the man increased the pressure of his hold. Corey found it difficult to breathe; the thick arms wrapped around his middle were like bands of metal crushing his ribs. He said to the man, "You ever move pianos?"

"Not lately," the voice said.

"How much do you weigh?"

"Two-thirty. And it's all rock, sonny."

"That's a sure bet," Corey muttered. He grunted as the man applied more pressure. And then, with his eyes tightly shut, "Ease it, will you? You're breakin' me in half."

"I wouldn't do that," the man said. He slackened the pressure a little. "You're a high-priced item, sonny. This tag reads handle with care."

They came to the top of the stairway. The man retained his hold on Corey as they moved along the second floor hallway toward the back room where light showed through a crack in the door. Someone opened it and stood in the doorway. In the light flowing through from the bedroom, Corey recognized the man.

Corey said, "Hello, Creighton."

"I told you before," the colored man said, "my name ain't Creighton."

"You're kidding," Corey said.

"No," the colored man said. He was taking all this very seriously. He had a gun in his hand, and he raised it a little so that it pointed at Corey's abdomen. He said to the man who weighed two-thirty, "All right, let go of him."

The big man released his hold on Corey. The colored man gestured with the gun, and Corey walked into the bedroom. It was brightly lit, the glow coming from an unshaded, hundred-watt bulb dangling on a cord attached to the ceiling. There was a single window in the room and the shade was pulled down. The floor was very dusty, littered with cigarette butts and beer bottle caps. A row of empty quart bottles lined the wall near the door. Set close to another wall there was a cot, a brassière and panties on the cot; and on a shelf above the cot were some jars of face cream and deodorant, a large bottle of cologne and an expensive looking bottle of perfume. In the middle of the room there were a few uncushioned chairs. In the far corner, Lita was smoking a cigarette and talking in low tones with Delbert Kingsley.

Sit down," the colored man said to Corey.

Corey lowered himself into a chair. He focused on the pleasant, wholesome, rugged face of Delbert Kingsley. Then he focused on Lita's face. And then on Kingsley again. They didn't look at him. They were fully intent upon each other. Kingsley had his hands on her bare back below the halter, his hands pressing lightly, moving around familiarly, as though his fingers knew every inch of her body.

They talked in low tones. Corey couldn't make out what they were saying; it was just above a whisper. It went on like that for some moments; then Lita started toward the door. As she moved past Corey, she didn't look at him. It's like she don't even know I'm here, he thought as he watched her walking from the room. "Where's she goin'?" from the man who weighed two-thirty.

"The car," Kingsley said. "She's gonna move it."

"What for?"

"It's too close to the house," Kingsley said.

"Where's she gonna park it?"

"Next block." Kingsley was still standing in the far corner of the room. He hadn't looked at Corey Bradford yet. Now he squinted at the man who weighed two-thirty. "What's all the questions for? What bothers you, Ernie?"

"The car," Ernie said. He was five-seven and the excess poundage gave him the shape of a barrel. He was dripping sweat in the sticky heat of the room. Some of the sweat was from worry. He muttered, "The car oughta stay where it is. If something happens. I mean—I mean, if we gotta get to the car in a hurry—"

"You'll run," Kingsley smiled at him. "You got legs and you'll run."

"You kidding me?"

"It'll do you good to run," Kingsley said. "You'll lose some of that weight."

The colored man chuckled. Ernie looked at him with displeasure and the colored man chuckled louder. Ernie looked him up and down and then faced away saying, "Some people I'll clown with. Other people, no. Not under any conditions."

The chuckling stopped. The colored man said, "You signifyin'?"

"I'm telling it straight," Ernie said. "I'm allergic to chocolate."

The colored man stiffened. His eyes glittered. He started to say something, but Kingsley interrupted, "Forget it, Gene."

Gene was breathing hard. His mouth quivered.

Kingsley went to him and patted him on the shoulder, saying softly, "Come on, get hold of yourself."

"I'm all right," Gene mumbled. He looked away from Ernie. And then he was concentrating on Corey again, and he pointed the gun at Corey's head.

So now it's all professional again, Corey thought. But for a few seconds, it was just some sand lot monkeyshines, and maybe you coulda tried something.

Or maybe it's better you didn't, considering that you're sitting in a chair and it takes time to get up and make a jump for that gun. It's a long jump, it's at least nine feet, and that's suicide. And he ain't gonna come no closer, either. He knows what he's doing with that gun. He's a gunman, this Gene. You can tell from the way he holds it. Just from the way he holds it and covers you, the traffic signal is red—period.

Delbert Kingsley was lighting a cigarette. He took a few drags and then pulled up a chair and sat down facing Corey Bradford.

For some moments Kingsley just sat and studied Corey's face. Then he said, "You look sorta groggy."

"From liquor," Corey said.

"You soused?"

"Not now," Corey said. "I slept it off."

"You sure?" Kingsley prodded, frowning clinically. "You really look plastered. I can't let you fade out."

Corey grinned.

"What's that for?" Kingsley murmured.

"You can't let me fade out. That's a good one."

"But I mean it," Kingsley said. "You know I don't want you all chopped up. If I wanted that, you wouldn't be sitting there breathing."

"You wanted that in them swamps. In them swamps you weren't playing."

"Only because you cut loose. I couldn't afford to let you get away."

Corey grinned again. This time it was a tight grin. His eyes were saying, you still can't afford that.

It got across to Kingsley. He smiled pleasantly and said, "Let's keep it on the soft side. What the hell, I'm not a butcher. And it's a cinch I can't sell you for fertilizer. All I want from you is some talk. That is, if you know what I think you know."

Corey leaned back in the chair. His expression was passive, his arms hanging loosely at his sides. It looked as though he was very weary, just about worn out. That was how he wanted it to look.

Kingsley said, "If you know what I think you know, then it's just a matter of coming to terms and arranging a deal. The deal goes through, we both score."

"Score how?"

"You get a ticket outta here."

"On my feet?"

"Guaranteed."

"And you?" Corey spoke with his eyes half-closed. "What do you get?"

"The jackpot."

There was a long silence. Kingsley was waiting for Corey to say something, to show some reaction. Corey just sat there slumped, looking weary. Ernie moved closer, frowning anxiously. Gene stayed where he was, his dark face immobile, the gun braced in his hand as though locked in a vise, the muzzle aimed at Corey's skull.

Kingsley gestured impatiently to Corey, "Come on, feed it to me."

"I'm thinking."

"Whaddya mean, you're thinking? What's there to think about? All you gotta do is gimme the information. That is, if you got it to give."

"I got it all right," Corey said. And then he smiled lazily. "I got it to sell."

"Now look, you want that ticket, don't you?"

"It's gotta be more than just that ticket. A lot more."

Hard lines showed on Kingsley's face. He turned his head slowly, deliberately, his eyes aiming at the gun in the colored man's hand. His head turning again, he scanned the invisible path that stretched from the muzzle of the gun to the side of Corey's head.

He said to Corey, "You better wake up to what's happening here. You're in no position to quote prices."

"Don't bet on that," Corey murmured.

Kingsley blinked several times. Without moving he seemed to be squirming.

Corey spoke very softly. "You know what's in that jackpot?"

Kingsley shifted in the chair, wet his lips, rubbed his hand through his thick curly scalp. He muttered, "All right, tell me."

"It comes in around a million five."

"What?" Kingsley said. And then louder. "What? What?"

"I said a million five."

Kingsley's eyes were wide and his mouth was open. He looked at Ernie, then at Gene. They were gaping at Corey. Kingsley leaned toward Corey and said, "Let's have that music again. Let's have it nice and slow."

Corey said it very slowly. "One million five hundred thousand dollars."

Beads of perspiration gleamed on Kingsley's forehead. He didn't bother to wipe them off. He was rubbing his hands together and mumbling, "What a package, what a package—"

"We don't have it yet," Gene said.

"We'll have it," Kingsley said. Then he smiled fondly at Corey. "We'll have it soon, won't we?"

"If I'm included."

"For how much?"

"One third."

"Come again?"

"One third," Corey said. "Off the top."

"You're joking."

"Not hardly," Corey said.

Kingsley was quiet for a few moments. And then, "All right, we'll work something out. I'll talk it over with Lita. As soon as she comes back. You don't mind waiting, do you?"

Corey shrugged. He leaned further back in the chair. His tone was mildly curious as he said, "What's this with you and Lita?"

"We're tight."

"Since when?"

"Well, we been together a long time," Kingsley spoke matter-of-factly. "She was hooked to me long before she met Grogan. Then I'm doing a stretch, and she comes to visit me and says she's latched onto something and it looks like gravy. There's this certain moneybag, this Walter Grogan, and she's living with him and just playing for time until she can hit for dividends. I tell her no, I don't like it. Not because she was letting him get in. What the hell, I never cared who she slept with. For a cash return, that is. If you understand what I mean."

Corey nodded.

Kingsley went on, "But I didn't want her messing with Grogan. Because I'd heard about Grogan. You're in stir, you're always hearing about this one and that one, and I told her it's always a mistake to cruise a racketman. It's a good way to get some bones busted when he finds out he's getting cruised. She tells me not to worry, she knows what she's doing. And then gradually I'm getting to see it her way. Because it ain't like she's cruising him for a hundred here and a hundred there. It's more like she's putting a blindfold on him, selling him the idea that with her the money comes second. What comes first is reading the philosophers and looking at paintings and going to lectures and so forth.

"And meanwhile, of course, she's finding out more and more about his finances. Not that he ever tells her. And not that she sees it on paper. But there's times he's on the phone and there's another phone upstairs. Other times he's talking with syndicate people and they're sitting around in the parlor and she's upstairs in the hallway, listening.

"And what it all comes to, she says there's reason to believe he's got hot lettuce put away somewhere. She figures it's around a hundred grand."

Corey smiled thinly.

Kingsley went on, "Well, anyway, it got me thinking. I mean, what the hell. You don't walk away from a hundred grand. So the first thing I did when I got outta prison, I started a campaign to get released from parole. For a long time it was no go. I couldn't get to first base at the parole office. But then something happened. I found exactly what I needed. A front. The perfect front."

"Lillian?"

"Check," Kingsley said. "And we're married only three months when the parole office lets me off the leash. Because they don't keep a man on parole when he's living the good clean life with a decent respectable woman."

"And Lita? What about Lita?"

"We kept in touch. At first we couldn't get together like we wanted to. But later, when they took me off parole, we rented this crib. That is, Ernie pays the rent with the money we give him—"

"But what if the owner walks in?"

Kingsley appeared puzzled for a moment. Then he chuckled softly. "I see what you mean. She told you it was Grogan's property. She hadda tell you that. Fact is, it's one of the few houses in the neighborhood that don't belong to Grogan."

"And that notice on the front door? No Trespassing?"

"From a door across the street. I made the switch after I got the phone call from Gene. He spotted you on Addison. So then I give Lita some instructions—"

"Very neat," Corey murmured. "Except there's one thing I don't get. I mean, all this engineering with Lita, sending her out to put the flim-flam on me. What made you think it would pay off? Or lemme put it this way— what gave you the idea I had the information you wanted?"

"Lita tipped me," Kingsley said. "That is, she told me something that put some thoughts in my head. She told me what she saw today. Grogan sitting in his car, and then he opens the door for you. The car pulls away and an hour later it comes back and you're still in it with Grogan. Real chummy. So during that hour you weren't just talking about the weather. He musta been telling you what he didn't feel like telling you last night, when Lita was listening upstairs. Because last night he wasn't sure he could trust you. But today, for some reason, you're more than just another name on the payroll and it's buddy-buddy. He lets you get in that elegant Spanish car. I don't hafta tell you, he's very particular about who rides with him in that car. So I'm adding two and two and getting four, telling myself that Grogan rates you high enough to give you all the facts—to tell you what's in the jackpot and where the jackpot is stashed."

Corey pretended a look of wonder. He injected pure amazement in his slow-spoken words, "Kingsley, you're a wizard. I mean that very seriously."

Delbert Kingsley turned his head and looked at Gene and Ernie. "Didja hear that?" And then, louder, "Didja hear what he said?"

In the hallway there were footsteps and then the door opened and Lita came in. Kingsley got up from the chair. He took Lita to the far corner of the room. They stood talking in low tones, their backs to Corey. He couldn't hear what they were saying; he wasn't trying to hear. His thinking was running far ahead of that. He sat there smiling companionably at Gene and Ernie. They didn't smile back. Ernie was pacing around, restless. Gene stayed where he was, nine feet away from Corey with the gun still pointed rigidly at Corey's head. Then Kingsley and Lita faced about and came toward Corey, and he checked the way they were grinning at him. Very friendly, he told himself. Friendly like crocodiles.

Kingsley patted Corey on the shoulder. "You're in," Kingsley told him. "You got yourself a contract."

"What terms?"

"The price you quoted. One third off the top."

"Regardless of the take?"

"That's right. The take is what you say it is, you walk away with five hundred grand."

Ernie let out an anguished yelp. "That's way outta line."

"Close your head," Lita hissed at Ernie.

"But you can't let him have all that." Ernie was very agitated. "It don't make sense."

"Close it," Lita hissed.

"Don't you tell me nothin'," Ernie yapped back at her.

"I wanna holler, I'll holler. Christ's sake, I got a right to holler. I have stock in this corporation—"

"Me too," the colored man cut in quietly, and yet it sounded loud in the room.

Kingsley looked at the colored man. "What's the matter, Gene?"

"It's rotten eggs," the colored man said. "This time I go along with Ernie." And indicating Corey, "He's taking us. He gets that one third, he's cutting our throats."

"No he ain't." Kingsley spoke softly, soothingly. With his eyes he coded a message to Gene, and Gene's eyes relayed the message to Ernie.

Kingsley said to Corey, "Now here's what we do—first you spill. You gimme the location, the exact location where the loot is stashed. I go there with Lita and we pick it up and come back here—"

Corey was shaking his head.

"What's the objection?"

"Them," pointing to Gene and Ernie. "You leave me here with them, I won't be sitting in this chair when you come back. I'll be on the floor with a hole in my skull."

"Why do you say that?" Kingsley frowned.

"Because that's what'll happen if I let it happen. Because all it needs is one bullet. And that leaves me out and they get a bigger slice."

"Now look, I give you my word—"

"It's gotta be more than that."

"Such as what?"

"That's up to you," Corey shrugged. "You're the dealer

here." And in his brain he looked at the cards he was holding. He saw four cards, a ten, a jack, a queen and a king. He sat there waiting and hoping.

Come on, he spoke without sound to Delbert Kingsley. Come on, dealer, deal me that ace.

Kingsley was gazing thoughtfully at the floor. Some moments passed and then he said to Corey, "All right, let's try it this way—you make the trip with me and Lita. That is, you'll navigate. We pick up the loot, you get your split then and there. If it's cross-up, you get this," and from under his shirt he pulled out a .38.

Without sound Corey said, Thank you dealer man.

Ernie was saying, "What about me and Gene?"

"You and Gene stay here," Kingsley said.

"What for?"

"A caper like this, the less the better."

"How you mean?"

"Less chance of a foul-up," Kingsley said.

"That ain't how I see it," Ernie grumbled. "The way I see it, we oughta—"

"You starting again?" Lita frowned at Ernie.

"I'm only saying—"

"You're saying nothing," Kingsley cut him off. "You'll do what you're told and that's all. I'm getting tired of your goddam yapping. I'm trying to do some thinking here, and you stand there running your fat mouth. With noise coming out. Just noise."

"It's more than noise," Ernie stood his ground. "I'm makin' a point and you know it. You hit for that cash, me and Gene should be there when it happens. Ain't that right, Gene?"

The colored man looked at Ernie, looked at Kingsley, then at Ernie again. Kingsley and Lita exchanged a glance. Kingsley smiled pleasantly at Ernie and Gene and said to them, "Now look, you two wanna talk it over, that's all right with me."

They hesitated a moment. Then they moved off to one side and commenced a whispered conference. They had their backs to Kingsley. His pleasant smile remained pleasant as he aimed the .38 and pulled the trigger and almost in the same split second, aimed again and pulled the trigger.

On the floor the colored man was face down, motionless. Ernie was on his knees, coughing and bringing up blood. He crawled toward Delbert Kingsley. He was weeping and the tears dripped down, mixing with the blood that spilled out of his mouth. He said to Delbert Kingsley, "Why'd you do that? Did you hafta do that?"

Kingsley nodded slowly.

"No," Ernie wept. "No, you didn't hafta do that. Not that." He coughed again and fell over on his side. His mouth opened wide, making an effort to pull some air into his lungs. But before he could do that, his body became rigid.

"Check him," Kingsley said to Lita.

She went over to Ernie, examined him and said, "He's done."

"Check the jig."

Lita went to Gene and felt his pulse and told Kingsley

there was no pulse. She walked back to Kingsley and stood beside him. They both looked at Corey Bradford.

"Up," Kingsley said, motioning with the gun.

Corey got up from the chair. Kingsley and Lita moved behind him.

"Let's travel," Kingsley said.

The three of them walked out of the room.

13

There was no talk as they went through the hallway and down the stairs. Lita had switched on a light in the hallway, flicked another switch to illuminate the parlor. They moved slowly, going through the parlor, toward the front door. Corey was slightly in front with his hands at his sides. Kingsley prodded him with the gun and told him to clasp his hands behind his back. Then Kingsley told Lita to take a look outside. It was possible the shots had awakened some neighbors, and he didn't want heads sticking out of windows. Lita opened the front door, gave the street a long careful look, said there were no eyes out there. The gun nudged Corey's spine and he walked out of the house, Lita beside him, Kingsley close behind, letting him feel the gun as they moved along the narrow street. Corey said, "Why the pressure with the rod? We got a contract, ain't we?"

"Just wanna be sure you don't break it," Kingsley said.

Corey slackened his pace and glanced over his shoulder, giving Kingsley a look, and in the same moment aiming the look past Kingsley, checking the address of the house from which they'd emerged. The number was chalked on the splintered front door. It was four-thirty-one. He told himself to file that number, and went through the memory trick of adding one to three and getting four, then repeating the arithmetic until it was engraved in his brain.

There was a street sign posted at the intersection. In the darkness he could barely make it out. It read Harold Street. He'd turned his head only slightly to look at the street sign, but Kingsley noticed and said, "Whatcha lookin' at?"

"Nothing."

Kingsley prodded him with the gun. "Keep your eyes where they belong. In front."

Corey came to a stop.

"Move," Kingsley said. "Keep moving."

Corey stood still. Kingsley jabbed him with the gun, but he didn't budge. Kingsley and Lita frowned puzzledly at each other. Then Kingsley pushed the gun very hard against Corey's spine and gritted, "You feel this?"

"Get it off me," Corey said quietly.

The gun kept pushing against his spine. It was spreading pain through his back. He winced and squirmed. He heard Kingsley say, "You'll move or I'll split you in half."

"No you won't. You burn me, you're losing a million dollars."

Kingsley decreased the pressure of the gun, then gradually eased it away from Corey's spine.

"That's better," Corey said.

"Then move."

Corey started walking, Lita again at his side and Kingsley close behind him.

They were crossing the intersection. Lita was saying to

Corey, "What was all that about? That stubborn-mule routine?"

"Forget it," Corey muttered, making it sound as though he was bitterly resentful of the clobbering he'd taken from the gun.

Kingsley said to Lita, "Don't pay him no mind. He's just sensitive, that's all."

"Only at times." Corey accented his resentment. "Like when I'm gettin' pushed around. It didn't call for strong-arm and you know it."

"What a crybaby," Lita said.

"We'll hafta buy him a balloon," Kingsley said. "That's what you do with a crybaby."

"Screw that noise," Corey faked cold anger. He turned his head to let Kingsley see the ice in his eyes. "It ain't the black and blue marks that bother me. What bothers me, you clubbed me with the gun because you're jittery. And that makes it sloppy. Christ's sake, this ain't no small-time heist; it's strictly major league. We gotta handle it smooth and I mean smooth all the way."

"Listen to the man," Kingsley said to Lita. "The man talks big."

"And that's how it should be," Corey spoke firmly. "It needs big talk because the money is big. And I got every right to open my mouth—"

"With a gun at your back?"

"The hell with the gun," Corey said. "There's more important items on this schedule. We gotta make sure there ain't no slip-ups when we get where we're going. Because one mistake and we're all loused."

"He's right," Lita said. "He's absolutely—"

"Shut up," Kingsley barked at her. And then quietly, to Corey, "What gives here, exactly? Whatcha tryin' to prove?"

"Not a goddam thing. It's just that I wanna see gold instead of grief. I'm looking to get that percentage, that thirty-three-and-a-third."

Kingsley smiled. "You'll get it, partner. You'll get all you're entitled to, don't worry."

They were approaching the Oldsmobile. It was parked across the street. They crossed and Lita climbed in first, getting behind the wheel. Kingsley told Corey to get in the back seat, then followed and sat down beside him. Lita started the engine and said, "Where we going?"

"The house," Corey said. "Grogan's house."

The car moved off. Corey leaned back, his head resting against his folded hands. He didn't look at Kingsley or at the gun in Kingsley's hand. Kingsley sat half-facing him, the gun held low, somewhat loosely, not really aimed at Corey. But it's loaded, he reminded himself. It's a wall of fire and there's no hotter fire than a .38 slug.

Lita was driving slowly, carefully. The car turned a corner, made another turn and then another, and they were on Addison going toward Second. It was still very dark. There was no activity on Addison; the only sound was the engine's noise and Kingsley's breathing. Kingsley was breathing very heavily. So he's worried too, Corey thought. He's plenty worried and that breathing tells it, all right. It's a sure sign his blood pressure is way up. He's jumpy as a cat in an unfamiliar alley, because this party we're on, it's the kind that would scare any third-rate thug accustomed to third-rate jobs. He got jolted when you gave him the hint he was biting off more taffy than he could chew, when you told him this job was major league. And I'm betting if you put your hand on his chest right now you'd feel his pump banging away full blast.

The car made the turn onto Second Street.

Corey said to Lita, "Drive past the house."

"Why do that?" Kingsley asked. "Why not just park outside and go right in and—"

"Use your head," Corey cut in quietly. "Before we make a move, we check the layout. We take a good careful look at them windows. To see if there's any lights."

"There won't be any lights," Lita said. "When I left the house, he was sound asleep."

"He's a sound sleeper?" Corey asked.

"He sleeps like a stiff," Lita said.

"But it's best to be sure," Corey spoke with quiet urgency. "Just drive a little ways past the house—"

The Oldsmobile slackened speed. It was crawling at less than ten miles per hour as it passed Grogan's house. The windows were dark. On the other side of the street the Spanish automobile was parked. Lita braked the Oldsmobile, then put it in reverse, cut the engine and the Oldsmobile coasted back, coming to a stop directly in front of the Spanish automobile.

Lita opened the car door and started to get out. Corey said, "Hold it."

"What for?" Kingsley demanded.

"Instructions," Corey said.

"Not from you," Kingsley gritted through heavy breathing. "I'm running this show and I'll give the instructions."

"All right," Corey shrugged. "I'm listening."

Kingsley took a very deep breath, through his nose. Then he opened his mouth to talk but all that came out was air. He tried again and the same thing happened. When it happened a third time, Lita turned her head slowly and looked curiously at Delbert Kingsley. Her eyebrows lifted, her lips were tight at the corners. Without sound she was making a sarcastic comment. Then she said to Corey, "Go on, call the signals. Somebody's gotta call the signals."

"God damn it," Kingsley sputtered. "If you'll just gimme time to think."

"There's really nothing to think about," Corey said mildly. "It comes to instructions, there's just one thing we gotta remember. From here on in we move like cats. I mean absolutely quiet. We get in the house and we hafta talk, we'll talk in whispers. Another thing, we can't switch on any lamps. I'm gonna need a flashlight."

"Why no lamps?" Kingsley asked tightly, suspiciously.

Corey sighed patiently. "Police cars," he said. "They drive past the house and see a light, they might come knocking on the door. Just to ask Mr. Grogan if everything's all right. Because Mr. Grogan is a very important man and he's buddy-buddy with the precinct captain. And the police in this precinct, they give Mr. Grogan the best of protection."

"All right, all right," Kingsley muttered. "You don't hafta hammer it in."

Lita had opened the glove compartment. She took out

a three cell flashlight with a large lens and handed it to
Corey. As Corey tested the glow on the floor of the car,
Kingsley snatched the flashlight from him and handed it
back to Lita.

Corey gave Kingsley a mild questioning look.

Kingsley smiled thinly. "She'll hold the flashlight. That
is, if you don't mind."

"It makes no difference," Corey shrugged.

"It makes plenty of difference," Kingsley spoke slowly
to get the point across, mostly for Lita's benefit—to let her
know he was still in charge and that he knew what he was
doing. He kept smiling thinly at Corey. "If I let you hold
the flashlight, and you switched it off when we're in the
house, then I wouldn't be able to see you. Which means I
couldn't cover you with this," indicating the gun. "Because
it's this that binds you to the contract."

"I'm wise to that fact," Corey smiled lazily. He didn't
bother to look at the gun.

Kingsley said, "We ready?"

"Ready," Lita said.

"Ready," Corey said.

"Let's roll it," Kingsley gritted.

They got out of the car and walked slowly across the
street, then they quietly went up the steps. Lita took a key
case from her skirt pocket, Corey at her side and Kingsley
slightly behind Corey, the gun lightly touching Corey's
side. Lita delicately put the key in the lock, turning the key
noiselessly. Only a slight clicking sounded as the lock gave
way. She opened the door and they went in. Kingsley carefully closed the door as they stood close together in the

darkness of the vestibule. Then Lita switched on the flashlight and they went through the vestibule into the parlor. The glow from the flashlight was very bright and covered a wide area. The yellow-white brightness was reflected back at them from the shiny ebony and teakwood furniture, the jade and quartz lamp-bases and ornaments, the oriental brass fireplace and the glimmering bronze bulk of the placid-faced observer, the Buddha.

Lita half turned her head, whispering to Corey, "Where do you want the light?"

"On the fireplace," Corey whispered.

She aimed the flashlight at the fireplace. The light shone for an instant on the ornately designed brass andirons, then focused on the brass poker in its holder, and then back to the andirons.

"In closer," Corey whispered, and Lita moved forward going toward the fireplace. Corey followed close behind and Kingsley right behind Corey. The gun was pushing against Corey's ribs and there was a hissing noise as Kingsley breathed in hard through his teeth. The hissing noise became louder and Corey turned his head and whispered to Kingsley, "Quiet—quiet—"

Kingsley tried to calm his breathing; his mouth stretched tightly as he made the effort. He was staring past Corey, his eyes very wide and glittering, aiming at the fireplace. Like the eyes of an animal, Corey thought. A starving animal going stark raving crazy with knowing it's there. It's the feast and it's really there.

"Get it," Kingsley whispered, trembling. "Get it, get it."

Corey motioned to Lita, then pointed to the floor of the fireplace. She focused the flashlight in that direction, and Corey got down on his hands and knees, inching forward with Kingsley staying close to him, the gun now aiming at his head. He knew it was aiming at his head and he said to himself, well, here we go, and it's all or nothing, and come on dice be nice.

He was crouched at the side of the fireplace, reaching in behind the andirons, pretending to be very deliberate as his hands went sliding slowly across the brick floor of the fireplace.

"One of them bricks?" Kingsley whispered. "It comes loose?"

Corey nodded. Then he shifted slightly and bent lower and reached in deeper along the floor of the fireplace. Lita moved in from the side, the flashlight extended to provide more light. Kingsley stepped closer to Corey and hissed feverishly, "Which brick is it? Show me."

"Look there," Corey whispered, but didn't point to any particular brick. His pointing finger was waving vaguely. "Right there."

Kingsley leaned closer. He was peering over Corey's shoulder. Corey crouched lower, as though to give Kingsley a better view of the bricks along the back wall of the fireplace. As he did that, his shoulder was just a few inches away from the brass holder supporting the brass poker. And then, faking it, making it appear accidental, he swerved just a little to the side and his shoulder bumped against the brass holder and it was tipping over.

As the holder and the poker toppled toward the and-irons, Kingsley reacted instinctively to prevent the sound of brass crashing against brass. He made a grab for the falling holder, and in that fraction of a second he was an open target and Corey delivered a slashing blow with his hard clenched fist, the knuckles bashing Kingsley's jaw. Corey followed with another right hand to the jaw, then a sizzling left hook that hit Kingsley in the throat. Kingsley, now semi-conscious, was losing his grip on the gun but still tried to bring up the gun and aim it and squeeze the trigger. Lita stood there motionless, frozen, unable to believe what she was seeing. The flashlight was loose in her hand, her brain incapable of functioning technically. Without knowing it, she was aiming the flashlight at Kingsley, the glow showing Kingsley on his knees as he kept trying to bring up the gun. Corey hit him again on the jaw and he dropped the gun. Then he rolled over, flat on his back, his eyes closed.

Corey picked up the gun. He did it with his left hand, his right hand bent limply, the knuckles swollen and bleeding. He brought his right hand to his mouth and licked some of the blood from his knuckles. He had the gun pointed at Lita, smiling dimly, with pity. She didn't seem to know he was there. She remained motionless, the flashlight still focused on the prone senseless form of Delbert Kingsley. The sight of Kingsley stretched out cold was too much for her to take and her green eyes were wide and glazed, as though she was in a trance.

Corey started toward her, with the intention of taking the flashlight from her hand. He wanted to use the flashlight to find a wall switch and light up the parlor. As he reached for the flashlight, the ceiling lights were already glowing, switched on from the second floor hallway. The sleeper, awakened by the noise, was coming down the stairs. Corey turned and looked and saw a perplexed frown creasing the face of Walter Grogan.

14

Grogan was wearing yellow silk pajamas. There was a gun in his hand. At the foot of the stairway he came to a stop and just stood there looking at Corey, then at Lita, then at Corey again. There was no sound in the room. Grogan moved slowly across the room, with the gun he pointed to the man prone on the floor near the fireplace and said, "What's this?"

"The package," Corey said. "The one you wanted. The one who hired them two masked hoods."

Grogan kept moving forward to get a closer look at Delbert Kingsley. Lita was coming out of her daze, her face was milk-white with trapped-animal terror. She gestured pleadingly to Corey. He shook his head slowly, his eyes saying sadly, all I can do is feel sorry for you. I'm really very sorry for you.

She brought her hand to her mouth to stifle a whimper. Without sound she went on pleading, and Corey kept shaking his head.

Please, she said without sound. You know what he'll do to me. You know what happens to people who cross him.

But at least they get it fast. Without the suffering. They get off easy compared to what I'll get. And I'm begging you, I'm begging you—

Corey couldn't look at her. He said to himself, It's a filthy setup. Because you know what she's in for. You know it's gonna be slow, with screaming. And she don't rate all that hell. Sure, she's a wrong number but she's not that wrong. You come right down to it, she's just a small-time hustler. A year on a farm would maybe set her straight, if you wanna look at it that way. But you can't look at it that way. You want that fifteen grand. To pocket that fifteen grand you gotta prove some statements, and she's the proof, the only proof. But I'll tell you, jim, I wish it didn't hafta be this way. It's a scummy way to make money, and if it was a C-note or even five C-notes you'd possibly or probably cancel this transaction and walk away. But the point is, it ain't a C-note and it ain't five C-notes, it's fifteen thousand dollars, I said fifteen thousand dollars.

Just then Corey looked up and saw Lita backing slowly and furtively toward the front door. He made a warning gesture with the gun, telling her to stay where she was. She stood there and went on pleading without sound, her palms extended and quivering. And then, as though seeing it was no use, she lowered her head, her hands covering her eyes.

Grogan turned to Corey and indicating the man on the floor, said, "Gimme the score on this one."

"You don't know him?"

"Never seen him before."

"He's an ex-con."

"That means nothing."

"He lives in the neighborhood."

"And that means nothing," Grogan cut in again, his voice tightening. "He never had no dealings with me. So how would he know about my finances? Who tipped him?"

Corey pointed to Lita.

"No no no," she shrieked, making a frantic try for survival. "He's a liar, Walt. He's covering for himself," and with the flashlight pointing to the man on the floor, "I swear to you, Walt, I don't know that man. Got no idea who he is. And if you'll listen to me, if you'll only listen—"

"All right," Grogan said quietly, mildly. "I'm listening."

Lita's green eyes narrowed with cunning. And then, saying it matter-of-factly, "What happened was, I went out to look for Anna. She's been sneaking out late at night, and I'm thinking maybe she's out there turning tricks or climbing in windows and stealing. Who knows? Well anyway, I couldn't find her and I came back here and parked the car and just as I reached for the key to open the front door, I thought I saw something inside the house. Like a tiny light. I went back to the car and got the flashlight. Then when I walked into the house, there they were, the two of them, and they were using matches—"

"Matches?" Grogan murmured, his eyebrows raised just a trifle.

"So they could see what they were doing." Lita nodded emphatically. "They were looking for something in the fireplace."

Grogan turned and looked down at the fireplace. He

said softly, "There ain't no burnt matches on the floor."

"But that's what they were using."

"Convince me," Grogan said. "Show me some burnt matches."

Lita opened her mouth to say something. A gagging noise came out. Then she shut her eyes tightly and made another gagging noise.

Grogan pointed to the man on the floor and said to Corey, "Put a tag on him."

"Name's Kingsley."

"Connect him with her."

"They work together," Corey said. "They been together a long time."

"No no no," Lita wailed. She gagged on it. "Don't believe him, Walt. Please don't believe him."

Grogan motioned her to be quiet. He said to Corey, "Making a statement ain't enough. You'll hafta back it up. Can you back it up?"

Corey nodded slowly. He said, "It's a house number. It's 431 Harold Street. You go there, you'll see for yourself. Because it ain't no ordinary crib. It's mob headquarters, and you'll see two members of the mob. That is you'll see their bodies. Another thing you'll see, some personal items belonging to her."

Lita let out an anguished cry and then pivoted fast and made a frenzied attempt to flee. She lunged toward the front door, but as she neared the vestibule she stumbled and fell to her knees. Grogan went to her and helped her to her feet. She sagged in his arms, her legs dragging as he pulled her to the sofa. She collapsed on the sofa, her head far back, her arms limp, her face milk-white and her mouth quivering.

On the floor near the fireplace, Delbert Kingsley was coming to his senses. He groaned and sat up slowly, rubbing his swollen, discolored jaw. Seeing the gun in Corey's hand, he groaned again. Then he turned his head and saw Lita slumped in the sofa, kept turning his head and saw Walter Grogan. He groaned loudly, despairingly.

Grogan was lowering his gun into the side pocket of his pajama blouse. Through a long silence he stood looking at Lita, then at Kingsley, back and forth from one to the other. His hand was raised to his head and he was smoothing his silver hair.

Then his hand went into the side pocket of his pajama blouse and he took out the gun again. Kingsley stiffened, his mouth open and stretched tight at the corners. Grogan fired three times in quick succession and Kingsley sat there with two holes in his head and red-black rubble where his nose had been. His eyes remained open and he continued to sit there, propped against the brick wall of the fireplace. The valves of his heart had stopped pumping but his head was turning slowly, as though he was trying to get a final look at Lita.

Grogan pocketed the .38, turned away from the seated corpse and started walking out of the parlor. Corey said, "Where you going?" and Grogan murmured, "Just hold the gun on her. Be back in a minute."

Corey heard him going through the dining room, then heard a click as the light was switched on in the kitchen.

From the kitchen there was an assortment of metallic sounds, as though pots and pans were getting pushed aside in the kitchen cabinet. Then there was the rattling sound of other hardware and finally the slight popping sound of a vacuum sealed can as its lid was forced open.

Lita looked up. Her bulging eyes aimed past the gun in Corey's hand. She saw Grogan coming into the parlor, her mouth opened wide and she screamed without sound.

Grogan slowly moved toward her. In his right hand there was a metal can with the lid removed. Corey looked at the label on the can. The contents were stipulated in three large letters and Corey shuddered.

The can contained lye.

Grogan moved closer to Lita. For a moment she sat rigidly, then made an animal effort to get off the sofa, to veer to the side. Before she could, Grogan's free hand reached out and grabbed the platinum blonde hair, gripping hard and twisting and forcing her head back.

"Look at me," Grogan said quietly. "Look at me and take a good look. It's the last time you'll see me. It's the last time you'll see anything."

"No," Corey said.

Grogan didn't hear him.

"No," Corey said louder.

Grogan heard and ignored it. He was tilting the can so that the opened lid aimed directly at Lita's eyes.

"No," Corey shouted, and then knew that words wouldn't stop him, knew there was only one way to stop Grogan.

He aimed the gun and fired.

The can of lye fell out of Grogan's hand. It hit the floor and some of the contents spilled out, eating away at the carpet. Corey glanced at it for a moment, then looked up and focused on Grogan's arm, expecting to see a bullet hole in the wrist or in the forearm near the wrist. He was sure he'd aimed the gun at Grogan's wrist and he knew his aim was always precise, his gun hand was always steady. He was a sharpshooter and he was absolutely sure he'd hit the mark where he'd aimed.

There was no bullet hole in Grogan's wrist or anywhere near the wrist. Grogan turned slowly and faced Corey Bradford and Corey saw the bullet-scorched hole in the yellow pajama blouse. The hole was high up on the blouse, near the middle of Grogan's chest.

But it can't be, Corey said to himself. You aimed at his wrist. You know you aimed at his wrist.

Grogan stood there looking at Corey. Grogan's eyes looked puzzled giving way to something deeper, a kind of mystical wonder. Then Grogan faced away from Corey and moved steadily and very slowly toward the ebony armchair near the bronze Buddha.

On the sofa, Lita had fainted. Corey didn't look at her. He was staring in disbelief at Grogan, at the hole in Grogan's chest. It just can't be, he was thinking. Or maybe—

As Grogan sat sprawled in the ebony armchair, Corey stared past him at the dim all-knowing smile on the face of the bronze Buddha.

Without sound the bronze image said, no maybes. Because you didn't aim at his wrist. You hit him where you wanted to hit him. You wanted to put him away and that's what you did.

But why? Corey wondered. He focused on the bullet hole in Grogan's chest. He moved closer and saw that Grogan wasn't breathing. So he's finished. You finished him, all right. And why? What does it gain you?

If it does anything at all, it puts you in the loss column. Because what you've done, you've just thrown away fifteen grand.

And you, he said without sound to the Buddha. You sit there grinning, as if it's some kind of a joke. And if it is, the least you can do is let me in on it. Because I swear, I don't know why I bumped him, I don't know why I don't know why—

He kept staring at the Buddha. The slanted eyes gazed back at him, the unfathomable smile drifting toward him, causing him to quiver. What's happening to you? he asked himself. And then, to the Buddha, get off me, leave me alone. I mean it, I'm warning you, Chinaman.

Chinaman—

He said it aloud, "Chinaman—Chinaman—"

Putting the gun under his belt, he stepped close to the Buddha and used both hands to inspect the bronze head, the neck, the shoulders. The metal surface was smooth and remained smooth as his fingers covered every inch of the statue's chest. Then he examined the belly, and peering very close, he detected an extremely narrow line, thin as a hair, and then another hair-thin line, and a third and a fourth, all the lines connecting so that they formed a wide rectangle that covered most of the belly. Then he knew what that was, and he knew what he had to look for next, saying to himself, it's a panel arrangement. To slide the panel open, you gotta find the thingamajig that releases the lock.

On both sides of the slightly curved rectangle there were several rows of small spherical adornments, resembling carbuncle gems. There were twenty on each side. He began testing them, one by one, pushing and pulling, attempting to turn them as though they were knobs. His head rested against the bronze belly, like a safecracker leaning against a safe and listening for the slightest sound of mechanical reaction. The bronze protrusions on the left side offered nothing. He wiped his sweating hands on his trousers and then resumed the testing on the other side. There was no mechanical reaction, no sound at all until he came to the nineteenth sphere. He was pushing it with his thumb when he heard a tiny noise, a click. He pushed it again and there was a louder click. Then he was able to turn the sphere and he turned it slowly counter-clockwise and sensed that something was sliding into place. Then he heard the emphatic clanking noise that told him the lock was released.

His fingertips applied pressure to the panel, and it slid upward so that there was a rectangular opening in the belly of the Buddha. He looked in and saw the stacks of money.

For a long while he just stood there and looked. Then he reached in and took out one of the stacks. It was held together with rubber bands. It was very thick, mostly thousand-dollar bills. He counted it and it came to a little more than a hundred thousand dollars. He took out a few more stacks of bills and they were all a little over or a little under a hundred thousand dollars.

Salty beads streamed from his forehead and dripped into his eyes. He wiped them away with his forearm. They kept streaming down as he went on reaching into the belly of the Buddha and taking out the stacks of bills. In all, there were fifteen stacks. The total amount was one million five hundred and sixty-five thousand dollars.

15

It's real, he was thinking. It's genuine United States paper money, certified legal tender, endorsed officially with the signatures of the Treasurer and the Secretary of the Treasury. And that makes it gold. Pure gold.

All right, that's one thing. And the other thing is, it's yours. Did you hear what I said? I said it's yours.

That is, if you want it.

You kidding? Of course you want it. That's why you aimed the gun at his chest instead of his wrist. In that split second you didn't know what you were thinking, and even now you're wondering what was running through your mind; but it musta been you got the message from that certain fund-raising organization, The Friends of Corey Bradford.

With the message saying that fifteen grand was a nice fat round figure, and yet you didn't hafta settle for no measly fifteen grand. Not when you could add two zeros to that fifteen grand.

It musta been finance and nothing but finance that made

you aim the gun just a little higher, the line of fire slanting up above the wrist and above the ribs, your finger on the trigger getting the relay from your brain. Because it musta been you were checking again with Nellie, with Nellie saying it was just a fairy tale, saying that Rafer was up there in the clouds and his talk was all cloud talk, the coke aspirin stuff causing him to jabber way out of his head. For instance all that jabbering about the Chinaman—

So in that split second it musta been that your brain was revving like a jet engine, and you were telling yourself that Rafer's Chinaman was somewhere not very far away, and all you hadda do was find the Chinaman and hit him for the gold. But it's always first things first. And what you hadda do first was get assurance there'd be no interference, no complications later on. And you got that assurance, you damn sure did. You got it when you pulled the trigger, knowing exactly where the bullet would go, knowing it would put Grogan in the grave.

You know what you are? You know what you deserve?

The hell with that. You wanna preach, go take it someplace else. What we got here is a million five plus sixty-five. What we got here is the impossible and you still can't hardly believe it, but here it is. And it's yours. It's all yours.

He looked down at the stacks of money on the floor in front of the Buddha. And then something was happening to him and he wondered what it was. He had no idea what it was.

It hit him hard, and then harder. It was the twinge very high on his thigh near his groin.

Now it hit him very hard and he stood still not making a sound. Yet somehow he could hear the laughter; it was crazy laughter, aimed at himself.

His hand moved slowly, going toward the rear pocket of his trousers, sliding in and coming out with the wallet. He opened the wallet and looked at the badge pinned to the upper flap. For the better part of a minute he went on looking at the badge.

Then he focused on the lower flap of the wallet, seeing the card under the Celluloid. He was reading the two words that were rubber stamped across the card. It reads Night Squad, he told himself. It says here you're a member of the Night Squad.

It says you're a policeman, that's what it says.

On a teakwood table nearby there was a phone. He moved toward it, picked it up and dialed a number. A switchboard operator answered and he gave her an extension number.

While he waited for the connection to be made, he glanced toward the sofa where Lita was mumbling incoherently, gradually regaining her senses and slowly sitting up. She looked around dazedly, then sat up straighter as she saw the stacks of money on the floor in front of the Buddha.

Lita made a move to get up from the sofa. Corey told her to stay there. He said it quietly and there was no need to repeat it. The wallet was still in his hand and he was showing her the badge. Then he spoke into the phone. He was talking to Detective-Sergeant McDermott.

It was less than two hours later and the stacks of paper

money amounting to one million five hundred and sixty-five thousand dollars were in a vault in City Hall. Held without bail on charges of attempted extortion and criminal conspiracy, Lita was in a cell in County Prison. The bodies taken from the house on Second Street were in the morgue, along with the bodies found in the house on Harold Street. The coroner had turned in his report, confirming the report submitted by the Night Squad to the office of the district attorney. The district attorney applied his signature to both reports, then quickly returned to his home in the suburbs to resume his interrupted sleep. The reports were placed in a filing cabinet, the index card reading "Investigations Completed—Cases Closed."

Across the street from City Hall there was a small diner. The short order cook was alone in the place, seated at the counter, hunched over the sports section of the Sunday paper. He looked up as two men walked in. He recognized one of them and said, "Good morning, Sergeant."

"Good morning," McDermott said.

"Some iced tea?" the cook suggested.

"Black coffee," McDermott said, sliding onto a seat at the counter. At the cigarette machine Corey Bradford inserted a nickel and a quarter. Then he lit a cigarette as he went to the counter and sat down beside McDermott. The short order cook asked him what he wanted. Corey ordered creamed chipped beef on toast and a cup of coffee. He was telling himself that what he really needed was a double shot of gin.

The cook brought the platter and two coffees. Corey ate rapidly, mechanically, scarcely tasting the food. He didn't look at McDermott. He sensed that McDermott was watching him, like some diagnostician checking on the symptoms.

He pushed the empty platter aside and ordered another cup of coffee and lit another cigarette. He heard McDermott saying quietly, "You ready now?"

"Ready?" Through the tobacco smoke he squinted at the detective-sergeant. "Ready for what?"

"To spill. To put it in words. What you didn't tell in the written report."

Corey looked off to one side. He muttered, "The report was complete. If it wasn't, it wouldn't have been accepted."

"It was accepted officially," McDermott cut in softly. "But this here is something else. This is something just between you and me—" He leaned closer to Corey and his voice was almost a whisper. "Why'd you do away with Grogan?"

Corey kept looking off to one side. He sat stiffly, his lips clamped tightly.

"Why'd you do away with Grogan?" McDermott repeated.

You knew this was coming, Corey told himself. You knew it when you started outta the Hall. He's walking along with you and saying, "Let's go across the street and have some coffee—"

McDermott spoke in the same semi-whisper, "According to the written report, Grogan had a gun and he'd already used it to bump Kingsley. You weren't able to prevent that, and the only thing you could do was wait for an opening.

All right, that's logical. Fully acceptable. So then when he's got the can of lye and he's all set to commit mayhem, it becomes a tactical problem. To stop him you gotta drill him. You gotta hit him in a vital spot, because if the bullet merely creases him or gets him in the arm or the leg, it's a cinch he'll go for his gun, and you're not gonna risk getting shot. That's also logical—and fully acceptable. That is, your written report was acceptable to the coroner, and to the district attorney, and it'll be acceptable to the public when they read it in the papers. Only thing is, I can't go for it."

The detective-sergeant leaned back and gazed mildly at Corey Bradford.

There was a long silence. Corey put another cigarette in his mouth. He didn't light it. He let it stay there for a moment, then pulled it from his tightened lips and broke it in half, tossing the pieces onto the counter.

He heard McDermott saying, "Why'd you do away with Grogan?"

He heard himself mumbling, "It musta been the money. The million five. I wanted the million five."

"No you didn't," McDermott said. "If you really wanted it, you woulda made the grab. Instead, you functioned according to procedure. You picked up the phone and called city hall and got connected with room 529. And I'll tell you something—I had a feeling you'd make that call. I was waiting for that call."

Corey turned his head slowly. He looked wonderingly at the detective-sergeant.

"I'll tell you why you did away with Grogan," the detective-sergeant said. "You had the craving to destroy him."

"So what?"

"To settle with him. What they call retribution. In a strictly technical sense that's homicide, that's first degree because you took deliberate aim at his chest, and your intent was to take his life. You shot him in cold blood. I said cold blood. No other feelings involved. Just the message coming across. You were getting the message—"

"What message? From where?"

"From the grave," McDermott said. "From your father."

Corey shivered.

"Your father," McDermott said. "Your father who was my closest friend. Who was a real policeman. Who was absolutely pure in his heart and considered the badge something sacred."

Corey shivered again and he felt a twinge very high on his thigh near his groin.

He heard McDermott saying, "The mob that put your father in the grave was the Third Street Dragons. The leader of the Third Street Dragons was taken to the morgue tonight and that's where he shoulda been taken long ago."

Then McDermott said, "That's why I signed you in with the Squad. I was hoping you'd get the message. It couldn't come from me. It hadda come from someone closer to you. Inside you. Deep inside."

Corey nodded very slowly. He gazed past the detective-sergeant. His voice quivered just a trifle as he mumbled, "Will you do me a favor? A personal favor?"

"Depends."

"Lemme hold onto the badge. Lemme stay with the Squad."

"I'll think about it," the detective-sergeant said. He smiled dimly, put his hand on Corey's shoulder and pressed down hard. Then he placed some money on the counter and they walked out of the diner. They went across the street to the city hall courtyard and got into a squad car. About ten minutes later the car came to a stop at Fourth and Addison. Corey got out. The car made a u-turn and started back toward the bridge. Corey walked down Fourth toward the rooming house where he lived.

Approaching the rooming house, Corey saw someone sitting on the doorstep. It was Carp. His head was bent forward and he was dozing. Then he opened his eyes and saw Corey. He said solemnly, "A most welcome sight, indeed. I'm quite pleased to observe that you're still among the living." And then, getting up from the doorstep, Carp applied tender fingers to a slight bump on the side of his head.

"Who gave you that?" Corey asked.

"Nellie," the little man said. "I knocked on her door and asked for your address. She was somewhat annoyed at being awakened so early in the morning. After considerable discussion, she replied to my query and—" he broke it off as he saw the look on Corey's face. He murmured, "There is something you wish to tell me?"

Corey nodded slowly. He said, "Grogan's done. There ain't no Grogan no more. I put a bullet in him."

The little man closed his eyes for a moment. He didn't say anything. Corey stood still, waiting for a comment. Finally the little man looked at him and said slowly, very distinctly and with quiet formality, "It will benefit the neighborhood. It will be of considerable benefit. As a resident of this neighborhood I wish to express my deepest gratitude." Carp bowed ceremoniously. Then he turned and walked away.

Corey Bradford stood there for some moments; then he headed south on Fourth, going toward Ingersoll. Specifically, he was heading toward the first floor back of 617 Ingersoll.

At the door of the first floor back he knocked several times, and presently the door opened.

Lillian stood there in the doorway, wearing a tattered robe and blinking the sleep from her eyes. She muttered, "Whaddya want?"

"Can I come in?"

"What for?"

"Some things I gotta tell you."

Lillian started to close the door. Then she looked at him. It went on like that for awhile. Then she opened the door wider and said, "All right, come on in."

About the Author

David Goodis was born in Philadelphia in 1917. The publication of *Dark Passage* in 1946 established him as a leading author of crime fiction and after the success of the film, starring Humphrey Bogart and Lauren Bacall, he joined the Warner Brothers payroll as a screen writer. His collaboration with Hollywood was less than ideal and in 1950 he returned to Philadelphia and continued to write crime fiction until his death in 1967.

VINTAGE CRIME / **BLACK LIZARD**

— **The Killer Inside Me** $9.00   0-679-73397-3
    by Jim Thompson

— **Nothing More Than Murder** $9.00   0-679-73309-4
    by Jim Thompson

— **Pop. 1280** by Jim Thompson $8.95   0-679-73249-7

— **Recoil** by Jim Thompson $8.00   0-679-73308-6

— **Savage Night** $8.00   0-679-73310-8
    by Jim Thompson

— **A Swell-Looking Babe** $8.00   0-679-73311-6
    by Jim Thompson

— **The Burnt Orange Heresy** $7.95   0-679-73252-7
    by Charles Willeford

— **Cockfighter** $9.00   0-679-73471-6
    by Charles Willeford

— **Pick-Up** by Charles Willeford $7.95   0-679-73253-5

— **The Hot Spot** $8.95   0-679-73329-9
    by Charles Williams